WOKE UP THIS MORNING

WOKE UP THIS MORNING

Bill Stephens

FRANKLIN
SCRIBES™

PUBLISHERS

WOKE UP THIS MORNING

Published by Franklin Scribes Publishers. Franklin Scribes is a register trademark of Franklin Scribes Publishers.

Franklin Scribes books may be purchased in bulk for educational, business, fundraising, or sales promotion. For information please email: SpecialMarkets@ franklinscribes.com

Publisher's Note: *Woke Up This Morning* is a work of fiction. References to events, establishments, organizations, locals, and real people living or deceased are intended merely to equip the fiction with a sense of authenticity and shadings of local color. They are used fictitiously. All other names, characters, places, and all dialogue and incidents portrayed in this book are the product of my imagination.

First Edition

Shout Out to Author:
stephens.billy@att.net

Library of Congress Cataloging-in-Publication Data

Summary: Set against a backdrop of blues music, *Woke Up This Morning* is a humorous take on the conflicts caused in a small island community and in the island ecology by a wild growing field of marijuana.

ISBN 978-0-9886433-7-6

Printed in the United States of America

BILL STEPHEN'S OTHER BOOKS

NOVELS

Vámonos!
Horizons Past

SHORT FICTION

Life or Death

NONFICTION

Losing the Lard: Permanent Weight Loss

DEDICATED TO:

Donald Anderson, Ph.D.
Pastor, Mentor, and Friend

"WHAT DOES MATTER IS THAT WE COME TO RECOGNIZE THAT PLAYFULNESS (IN WRITING), AS A PHILOSOPHICAL STANCE, CAN BE VERY SERIOUS, INDEED . . ."

—Tom Robbins, *Wild Ducks Flying Backwards*

CHAPTER | 1

Harpoon Conroy stood in the bow of his shrimp boat, *Cordon Blues,* and stared into the blackness of the cloudy Gulf of Mexico night. Ol' Blues rocked easily on the anchor chain in calm water. He took off his "smiley face" bill cap and ran his forearm over his brow. *God, I wish I'd never gotten into this mess!* He heard the airplane's drone but saw no running lights. He cowered a little as its sound amplified into a roar. It blasted out of the darkness over the shrimp boat so low that all four men flattened on the deck in panic, while its prop wash rocked the boat. The plane waggled its wings as it faded into the night, gaining altitude.

"Jesus Christ." Harpoon leaped up shouting at his two passengers. "I didn't agree to haul you *hombres* out here to get sunk by an airplane." He looked at the two still prostrate on the deck. *What kind of a world forces a guy into a charter like this one?*

Gordo, the fat one, stood, pointed at the plane, and shouted in Spanish, *"They recognized us."* Bozo, his sidekick, busied himself by dusting off his Bermuda shorts and luminous Hawaiian shirt.

They couldn't be more conspicuous in the deck floodlights, Harpoon thought. He took off his ball cap and gestured at the two men with it, "How could they miss those shirts you're wearing, *amigos*?"

The plane's engine faded as it labored while gaining altitude. The second pass was higher, and the moon shining through a hole in the clouds illuminated three parachutes drifting toward the boat with what looked like a bale of hay below each. He pointed at the parachutes. "CARE packages, right?"

Gordo shouted, "Go get 'em."

"Easy, asshole, don't get your *pantalones* in a bunch." Harpoon walked into the wheelhouse, spotlighted the parachutes, and pressed the diesel engine's starter button. A sucking, wheezing noise that sounded nothing like the healthy engine that propelled them about sixty miles northeast of Port Aransas, Texas, issued from below.

"*¡Andele!* Get this piece of junk moving." Gordo gestured violently inside the wheelhouse.

Harpoon whirled and faced him. "Get outta here, *pendejo*. I've got a problem here, and you're in the way." He tried the engine again with no results.

Krank, the deckhand who claimed to be full-blood Karankawa Indian, even though that local tribe went extinct over a century ago, pulled Gordo out of the way and stood in the doorway. "The bitch need a little encouragin', Boss?"

"Go for it."

The deckhand disappeared below. An Indian chant accompanied by the clang of iron on iron drifted up from the engine room. Krank yelled up the hatch. "She feels better, Boss."

Harpoon pushed the starter again. The sucking noise became a growling roar. He engaged the prop, and *Cordon Blues* shuddered and moved toward her destiny.

A light breeze scudded broken clouds across the moon that rained sparks over the watery surface. Until now, the shrimp boat had smooth sailing as the wind lacked the vitality to kick up any waves. But it had shifted directly off the bow and now pushed up low swells that rocked the boat.

After they retrieved the parachute drops, Krank, Bozo, and

Gordo went immediately down into the crew quarters to sleep. *Cordon Blues* churned away on the six-hour trip back toward Port Aransas with Harpoon's tall, forty-year-old muscular frame slumped into the captain's chair. He pulled the "smiley face" bill cap low over his eyes and put his white rubber shrimpers' boots up on the wheelhouse firewall. *Now if I can stay awake.* He patted the thick envelope filled with hundred dollar bills in his blue jeans pocket and felt comforted.

The primordial diesel engine clattered away under him like a coffee grinder, a $12,000 plus sound. He wilted at the thought of the cost of dry-docking the boat, a new engine, and a new shrimp-net winch before the shrimp season opened again on July 4th. Suddenly he sat upright. The phosphorescent hands of his antiquated chronometer glowed through its scratched crystal in the darkness of a mid-May night. "Ten o'clock. Shrimp season doesn't close until midnight." He stood, tied off the wheel, went down the stairs into the crew quarters, and shook Krank. "We've got two hours left to shrimp, *amigo*. Let's hit it. We can make a few extra bucks that might help get us through the off season."

"Aren't they in a hurry to get back?" Krank rubbed his eyes and swung his legs over the side of the bunk.

Harpoon held his finger across his lips and pointed toward Gordo and Bozo. "Don't wake those two assholes. They'll never know."

After their second hour-long pull, Harpoon looked at the catch that poured onto the sorting table from the net bag. He checked his watch and smiled at Krank. "May 14, 2010 – Note to ship's log – nets up at 11:55 p.m. Shrimp season closed for six weeks."

Krank nodded his approval at the catch. "Not bad for two hours of pulling."

The Turtle Excluder Device had worked, and the net held no dead turtles. Harpoon especially hated killing Kemps Ridley turtles, the official Port Aransas High School mascot. "Go, you Ridleys!"

They heard someone run up the stairs from the crew quarters while they sorted the shrimp from the catch. Bozo broke onto the deck with both hands over his mouth, raced for the gunnel, and spewed over the side.

Harpoon watched Bozo heave. "I reckon it's a little choppy for ol' Bozo there."

Gordo's head popped up in the stairwell stretching his arms. "What's goin' on out here?" He scratched his privates as he climbed the stairs and saw Bozo hanging over the side. "He got a problem?"

Krank looked up from shrimp sorting. "He's feeding the fishes."

Gordo waddled toward the sorting table. "Hey, I paid you guys to take us out there and back, not to catch no shrimp. Why you catchin' fuckin' shrimp?"

"We'll look funny out here not shrimping," Harpoon lied.

"I don't give a damn how funny we look, man. You gotta get us back to town, man, and *pronto*!" Gordo walked around in circles, waved his arms, and screamed. He stopped short and looked at his watch. "*Madre de Dios*! We're supposed to be there in an hour. When we gettin' back to town?"

"Don't get your skivvies in a bunch, *amigo*. What's so important about getting there exactly on time, anyway?" Harpoon looked past Gordo and saw Bozo hanging over the side. "Maybe you better go make sure your friend doesn't fall overboard. Trying to pick him up before the sharks eat him would slow us down for sure."

"Sharks?" Gordo's eyes widened with fear. "Sharks! I hate sharks, man."

"I imagine there's a whole school of them following that chum line he's laying down." Harpoon's face contorted as he stifled a laugh.

Gordo turned and saw his buddy barfing over the gunnel. "Get back in the boat, asshole. You'll be shark shit if you fall overboard."

"Sharks?" Bozo recoiled so violently at the thought that he fell backwards, hit his head on the mast, and staggered about, dazed.

Gordo trotted over and checked out his friend. "Give me the radio, I gotta call Mako."

Bozo reached into his shirt pocket. "Aw, Christ, it musta fell overboard when I puked."

"You lost the radio Mako gave us. " Gordo's cell phone had no bars. He slammed it shut. *"¡Imbécil!"* He drew back his foot and kicked Bozo squarely in the ass and sent him headfirst into Harpoon.

Harpoon caught the man before he fell on his face. "Easy, Gordo. Cut the crap or Krank here will feed you to the sharks." Harpoon pointed at Krank who had tied his black, waist-length hair back with a leather thong, a practice of his forefathers (so he said).

Krank rippled his muscles under his "Go, You Ridleys" tank top and menaced the two men with his fiercest Indian look. "Say the word, Boss."

Gordo reached behind his back and like a snake striking, pulled out a black square-shaped pistol. "Keep your Indian to yourself, man. Now get back in there and get this tub moving at top speed. No more fuckin' shrimp. *¿comprende?"*

"What's this bullshit; you pulling a gun? You gonna shoot us, asshole?" Harpoon shook his head as he walked toward the wheelhouse. "You're one dumb bastard."

Harpoon slumped into the captain's chair as he checked the GPS. Incredible, we're still three hours out of port. He reached forward and tapped the GPS, the timeworn gesture of everyone hoping to alter reality. The boats' Magellan Global Positioning System's screen remained adamant; he cursed. That guy will be a psychopath by the time we reach port.

Gordo tried standing guard but eventually joined Krank and Bozo below when sleep overtook him. Harpoon finally sat alone at the wheel. With the wheelhouse and deck lights off, the boat's running lights did not interfere with the celestial chandelier that opened as the broken clouds dissipated. *So many stars; God help me, I do love it out here.* Harpoon raised the windshield. The salt air purged the wheelhouse but not all of his recriminations and rationalizations. As the diesel droned on for hours, they ricocheted around in his head: *I didn't know . . . .I needed the money . . . It was just another charter . . . They never said anything about . . . Marijuana should be legalized anyway, right? . . . Flat broke, shrimp season closed, a new engine and winch: bills piling up . . . Asian shrimp farms trashing shrimp prices. . . Fuel prices through the roof . . . Can't make enough for the fuel to pull the net.* He leaned forward, filled his lungs with the fresh salt air that rushed under the windshield, and shook his head while he tried to clear his thoughts. The symbolic gesture failed. From the get-go he'd known exactly what this trip entailed; Harpoon Conroy was a felon for the first time in his life.

An urge consumed him to rush out on deck, cut off the waterproof covers, and throw the contraband overboard. Maybe throw those two assholes with it. Rid the world of two drug dealing scumbags. To clear his thoughts of his felonious actions and their consequences, he pulled his harpoon (think harmonica) from his shirt pocket, primed it a little, and blew out an anguished wail followed by an arpeggio of bent notes landing on cross harp growls and clucking. His foot tapped out the rhythm of his shrimper's lament, and "The Red Tide Blues" drifted out over the Gulf of Mexico.

He caught first sight of the soaring lighted spire of the Crystal Epistle Church of Everlasting Enlightenment, about three a.m. The spire gleamed from its interior lights, but the beacon light atop this architectural wonder of glass and aluminum remained dark. He missed its welcome as the first sight of land. The beacon once gave a sense of dignity and purpose to the Island. The two high-rise condos, Port Aransas' skyline, came in clear view soon

after. The tiny fishing village sat on the north end of a barrier island called Mustang after the wild horses that once ranged there. Mustang Island was devoid of any natural features except a line of imposing sand dunes that stood guard for its entire length against the Gulf of Mexico. The small town had survived many hurricanes and economic downturns, always finding the will to rebuild.

Harpoon checked the time. They'd dock before four o'clock, a good time because the only shrimp boat birth large enough for *Cordon Blues* was abeam of Robert's Point Park in plain view of the whole Port Aransas harbor; a potential problem for their nefarious activities. Four o'clock's too late for the night's revelers, too early for most fishermen and shrimp buyers. Best of all, it's still dark, he thought as he tied the wheel down. He hollered down the stairs for Krank to get the other two up and ready for a quick evacuation once docked.

Harpoon pulled his binoculars from the peg above the wheel and checked the Crystal Epistle Church's Jumbotron. After a series of starbursts, the screen announced The Island Joynt's "All You Can Eat Breakfast Buffet, Only $4.99." Harpoon could not break his Island Joynt habit. Not so much the restaurant as the bar and its owner Lottie Langton – a fine-looking and indulgent woman. He could see himself chatting with Lottie at The Joynt (idling away the six weeks until shrimp season reopened) while much of his meager finances dissolved into beer mugs.

Krank, Bozo, and Gordo arrived on deck, yawned, stretched, and scratched, interrupting Harpoon's reverie. He had already aligned the Blues for entry through the piles of giant granite blocks that formed the jetties guarding both sides of the ship channel between Mustang and St. Joseph Islands. At the jetty entrance, he tied off the wheel and went out on deck. "Let's get something straight." He looked at Gordo. "You pull a gun on me again, you'd better shoot me; otherwise I'll shove it up your ass." He looked back and forth at the two criminals. "You're gonna unload that stuff yourselves. Krank and I won't touch it. I want it off the boat two minutes after we dock; then I want you guys out of my life. *¿Comprende, amigos?*"

The two glanced at each other with the look of men not used to being ordered around by anyone unarmed, but they let the disrespect pass. Gordo said, "I gotta get my truck, man. It's over in the parking lot, so forget your two-minute bullshit. If you're in a hurry, help unload while I get the truck."

They had cleared into the harbor, and Harpoon saw nothing stirring. "Yeah right, you two idiots in your Bermuda shorts and psychedelic shirts off-loading bales of ganja from a shrimp boat wouldn't look a little suspicious?"

"I've got a tarp in my truck. We'll cover them before we load." Gordo sat on the Port gunnel, waiting for Harpoon to tie *Cordon Blues* off at the dock. He leaped over the side. "Be ready when I get back."

Harpoon watched as the loaded red Ford pickup headed out of Roberts Point Park for the Corpus Christi Channel ferry landing. "Krank, I'm sorry, man, but looking at it from this side I'm afraid I've crapped in our nest here. Like the ads say, I should've 'just said no.'"

Krank, a sparse conversationalist, watched as the taillights faded into the darkness while he chanted softly and coiled the dock line on the deck. "Trickster Coyote always leaves a turd."

Inside the truck, Tito, the fat one, dialed his cell phone. "Mako, we just got in, man."

An agitated voice on the other end said, "Somethin's gone wrong. DPS has roadblocks on the causeways – everywhere. You can't get off the Island. Don't call on this cell again." The connection clicked off.

Pedro waited, then asked, "What's up, man? What's with Mako?"

Tito swerved left onto Cotter Avenue, then right on Cutoff Road. "We got a pickup full of ganja, and we can't get off the Island. Cops are everywhere. Roadblocks on the causeways – we're screwed."

Pedro's head swiveled in every direction looking for cops. "Somebody ratted us out. You know they'll look for us. No place to hide on this piece-of-shit island."

Tito slowed and stopped on Cutoff Road and pulled into a construction site. Someone had left a shovel leaning against the building "Go get that shovel. Hurry." He turned off the headlights.

"Man, we don't need no shovel, we need a helicopter." Pedro followed his orders and slunk through the darkness, retrieved the shovel, and threw it into the pickup.

Tito continued across Alister Street and followed Avenue G to the beach and turned south. Tents and camper pickup trucks dotted the beach, all dark. They passed only one person scurrying through the darkness toward the Port-O-Potty. "We're gonna bury this stuff and come back for it when the coast is clear."

"We better hurry, man, 'cause it's gonna be daylight."

Tito sped up and continued down the beach until he knew they had cleared the Port Aransas city limits and the hourly police beach patrols. The lights of Port Aransas and the beachfront condos faded in the rearview mirror. "It's gonna take a big hole to bury those bales. We'll break 'em up into smaller bundles. Spread 'em out."

"Pedro nodded his approval. "Yeah, and if somebody finds some, they won't get it all."

Tito pulled close to the dunes. "OK, we gotta bury the stuff over the dunes so they can't see we've been diggin'. Take the shovel and start digging. I'll break the bundles down."

"I've got a better idea: I break the bundles and you dig." Pedro saw the look in Tito's eyes. "Okay. Okay. I'll dig." Pedro struggled up the dunes, sliding back several times before he crested them and stopped short. "Hey, man, there's things crawlin' everywhere over here. It's dark, man; this really sucks."

"Just dig, we don't have all night." Tito's voice strained as he hefted a bundle to the pickup tailgate.

With the last bundle buried, Tito looked around: sunrise had not yet silhouetted the horizon. He looked at Pedro who breathed hard from digging six holes about a hundred feet apart. "We got 'em buried, *amigo.*"

"What do you mean, 'We'?" Pedro could feel the blisters when he rubbed his hands together. "You marked the locations, right?"

"Yeah, I put an 'X' mark on the beach for each. We'll come back tomorrow with a flashlight and dig 'em up."

"Where'll we sleep tonight? I'm tired."

"Tonight's already over, *amigo,*" Tito turned the truck around. "We'll go back toward town and park on the beach for a little shut eye in the truck."

A bullhorn broke the soothing sound of the breaking waves. Brilliant midmorning sunlight blazed through the pickup's windows. The two drug mules bolted upright and looked around frantically, blinking. Two DPS black and whites, a constable's car, and two Port Aransas Police cars surrounded them. They heard the bullhorn again, "Throw your weapons out the window and get out of the car with your hands in the air." The two looked at each other, then at the two Glock 9mm pistols in plain view on the seat between them. It had been hard to sleep with weapons in the small of their backs.

"How did you know they had guns?" The DPS officer asked a Port A policeman.

"They didn't have a beach parking permit, so I approached the truck to write a citation and saw the guns on the seat."

***

Diggs, the pocket gopher, had finished excavating an exceptional bachelor pad off the side of the main tunnel. His tunnel had plenty of headroom, and a lot of effort went into smoothing the floor. He had even added a pantry where food could be stored for a new mate. He stretched out in the nook and checked it again for comfort level. With a sigh of satisfaction, he nodded his affirmation. *If I can't get laid here – I can't get laid at all.*

Now he needed patience. He had to wait for a lovely young female to scurry down the main tunnel.

But Diggs wasn't into patience. In fact, his lifestyle remained unsatisfactory. For one thing, he had a little claustrophobia – actually a lot of claustrophobia. The darkness and dank air sucked the soul right out of him.

He knew that ancient wisdom said not too many surface shafts. They offered an open invitation for all manner of unwanted guests. Also a gopher stuck his head above ground at great risk: traps, rattlesnakes, coyotes, hawks, and guns lurked everywhere. And don't forget that people could unleash their Weapon of Mass Destruction down one of these shafts destroying a whole colony of friends and family.

When claustrophobic, ancient wisdom held no sway with Diggs. He only wanted fresh air. On his many trips up, after his eyes adjusted in the sunlight, he observed People. People lived infinitely more enjoyable lives; they didn't grub around in tunnels, and they didn't scratch ugly flea-bitten fur all the time. Instead, they had beautiful tanned skin covered only occasionally by something brightly colored. They all seemed to be drawn toward the huge sand piles that stretched into the distance. I've thrown up some sand in my time, but only a really badass gopher could dig that tunnel. Diggs nodded respectfully at the sand dunes.

While Diggs lay in his new bachelor pad, waiting to woo and win a fair damsel, he made a decision. There must be a better life on the other side of that big sand pile; otherwise why would people keep going there? He sat up. "That's it. I'm outta here. I'm tunneling to glory."

***

Sunrise promised another clear hot day by the time Harpoon and Krank finished cleaning and stowing *Cordon Blues*. Even though their nets filled with shrimp the previous night, the short pull time had netted them only a modest yield, small enough that they headed the shrimp to increase the value. They finished icing the headless shrimp when the first commercial buyer hailed them from down the wharf.

The buyer surveyed the catch. "You boys had hard luck last night. Ever' other boat's full to the gunnels."

Harpoon looked off toward the horizon. "Yeah, we had mechanical problems and didn't pull much."

The buyer motioned around the boat. "Maybe it's good the season's closing, so you can get the 'Old Blues' shaped up a bit."

Harpoon squinted at the man and kicked a piece of oyster shell that had evaded the deck clean up. "She needs a lot more work than I can afford with what you buyers pay for shrimp. Not to mention the price of diesel fuel these days."

The buyer squirmed a little. "Those slant-eyed bastards in Asia with their shrimp farms are running us all out of business."

"They've sure enough stuck a dagger in ol' *Cordon Blues'* heart." Harpoon moved his stoic gaze around his shrimp boat. Krank nodded agreement.

The shrimp buyer had offloaded *Cordon Blues.* Harpoon had paid Krank his cut and said, "The least I can do is treat you to 'All You Can Eat Breakfast Buffet Only $4.99.'"

"Sounds good, but I've got to check on Widow Robicheaux. I've not been by lately, and I have to cut her grass and a couple of other widows' also."

"You're a saint, bro."

Krank had earned his keep with yard work since his high school athletic days, while he lived in the home of the Port Aransas High School Fightin' Ridley Turtles (Go, You Ridleys!) football coach. He earned less money than he might have because he charged on the-ability-to-pay basis. Many took advantage of him, and Krank never charged any of the old original-island widows who subsisted on kindness. He liked working with the soil. Soil kept him in touch with Earth Spirit who lifted and sustained him when mortals crowded his world.

He found landscape planting particularly rewarding. The sandy soil of Mustang Island needed the rich mulch of composted vegetation available for free at the city dump. He first mixed it in with a shovel and spading fork, then massaged it with great care by hand. He felt Earth Spirit surge through his hands into the soil until he created a cradle for Life Force to purchase and prosper.

As a teenager, Krank's yard work had once saved a member of one of the Island's founding families, the old Widow Robicheaux. He had heard a faint cry while he hand-trimmed her hedge. He found her on the kitchen floor, apparently dying from a heart attack. He lifted her gently and sprinted almost one mile to the tiny town clinic. He still smiles each time he hears the urban legend exaggerated by the town folks. Currently the story holds that Krank got her there in half the time of an ambulance.

He hoped the yard work might wash his mind free of last night's activity.

CHAPTER | 2

The Island Joynt's crushed oyster shell parking lot crunched under Harpoon's pickup tires as he pulled into the space beside the lone handicap slot. At 6:00 a.m. his ancient Chevy pickup dieseled long enough after he turned off the ignition for him to check out the few other cars and trucks that dotted the parking lot. "All You Can Eat Breakfast Buffet Only $4.99" day brought out the regulars early, but today it appeared they had slept in. Harpoon felt ill at ease and needed companionship after his night's felonious adventure.

He wished Krank had joined him for breakfast. He knew the sun would be low before Krank finished the yard work for all the old Island widows, and then made the nine-mile trip out Hwy 361 where his tar-papered, makeshift "houseboat" floated on Wilson's Cut.

The aroma of bacon and sausage frying and biscuits baking overwhelmed the waterfront odors and interrupted Harpoon's reverie. The Island Joynt fronted the harbor with only a bulkhead and a wooden deck with a few fair-weather tables and chairs that separated it from the water. The front door opened off this deck, but only tourists used this door. Islanders always came and went from a side door that opened into the bar.

Only the perennial strings of Christmas lights lit the darkened bar when Harpoon stepped through the door. He stood for a moment and considered drawing himself a beer from the tap, but thought better of it – he'd wait for Lottie. As he strode through the bar and into the dining room, he recognized most of its few occupants, nodded an acknowledgement, and took a counter seat. The cook waved a greeting through the service window as Cindy, a big rawboned woman with a ready smile and raucous laugh, rounded the corner of the waitress station carrying a baker's sheet pan of biscuits.

"I see you beat the crowd this morning." Her laugh rattled the ice tea glasses.

"I can't stand bein' away."

Before she could respond, Right Reverend Hannibal Jones of the Crystal Epistle Church of Everlasting Enlightenment cleared out of the bar and into the dining room, smiling and waving at the mostly empty tables. Cindy lowered her voice. "We set our clocks around here by when the Reverend arrives on buffet day."

The reverend's rotund stature, shorter than most, came from years of parishioners' fried chicken, mashed potatoes, and gravy. For slimming he relied more on his tailor than on prudence at the dinner table. But ponderosity did not impede the reverend; his high energy translated into a catlike tread and mental quickness that outdistanced most – particularly in the pursuit of God's will and good food. His pulpit voice boomed. "Good Morning, all! It's a great day on the Island when a man sees a pan of hot biscuits held high above a beautiful woman's head. Purely a sign from heaven, I'd say, and amen!" He glanced at Harpoon. "Brother Conroy, you look lower than whale droppings. How about joining me at the Wisdom Table for a cheerful conversation?"

The Wisdom Table at The Island Joynt did not differ from those in any small town Texas cafe. It could seat about a dozen of the town's movers and shakers who ate there each day as they plotted the course of the community and the world at large. The mayor, constable, chief of police, football coach, successful businessmen, the intelligentsia (if any existed), and one man of God usually make up the denizens of any Wisdom Table. Substitute a couple of charter boat captains for a few of the businessmen, and set up a rotation through denominations for the man of God, and you have The Island Joynt's Wisdom Table membership. Reverend Hannibal Jones had lobbied successfully for Wednesday's "All You Can Eat Breakfast Buffet Only $4.99" day to represent the Crystal Epistle Church of Everlasting Enlightenment. Catholic, Lutheran, Methodist, and Presbyterian denominations had a loose rotation that often varied with fishing conditions. Amos McAlister, a retired Texas A&M Corpus Christi professor of oceanography, who represented the Island intelligentsia, seldom ate breakfast because of his morning survey of beach trash, but could be counted on at lunch.

Harpoon lifted his hat and scratched his head, stalling while he thought of a bogus excuse to avoid the reverend's invitation. He finished his coffee and thought, this morning, maybe even the company of a man of God might cheer me up. He set the coffee cup on the counter. "A kind invitation, Reverend. I'd be honored."

Cindy suffered a mishap while she dumped the biscuits into the warmer on the buffet line. A biscuit, desperately seeking freedom, caromed off the warmer, rolled down the buffet table, took a leap of faith, and thudded onto the floor. Cindy eyed the errant biscuit with the disgust of a golfer whose ball just rimmed out on a birdie putt. She kicked the biscuit soccer style into the waitress station. With her arms stretched skyward, she roared. "GOOOOAL!"

Harpoon chuckled and joined in the rustle of applause.

Following Reverend Hannibal Jones through the buffet line was like being stuck behind a street sweeping machine. The deftness with which the reverend handled two plates simultaneously – setting the one down while shoveling into the other, impressed Harpoon. The sight was so remarkable that he couldn't concentrate on his own provisions and ended the line with only a biscuit and three slices of crisp bacon.

"Brother Conroy, I fear you'll waste away with that meager fare." Both hands burdened with plates, the reverend nodded toward Harpoon's food.

"I guess I'm off my feed a little this morning." Harpoon stood for a moment and considered revisiting the buffet, but instead followed Reverend Jones toward the Wisdom Table where Cindy already had poured two cups of coffee.

"Cindy, my dear, no doubt Coach Bostich will want you to try out next fall for the Ridley's when word of your kicking prowess spreads over the Island." The reverend cackled at his joke.

Harpoon and Cindy shouted, "Go, You Ridleys"

Buffet regulars trickled in, and Harpoon saw several of the Wisdom Table's charter members cast suspicious looks at the table's interloper. "Maybe I better sit somewhere else since the regulars are arriving." He squirmed in his seat.

"Nonsense, brother Conroy. Keep your seat. You're welcome here. Like the Good Book says, 'If you snooze – you lose.' Thesocleastees: Chapter 10, verse 36, and amen." Harpoon settled back in his chair mentally recollecting the books of the Bible. "Besides," continued the reverend, "I have something I must talk to you about."

"Talk to me about?"

"A catastrophic incursion into God's divine plan by the Coast Guard's governmental bureaucracy extinguished our Beacon, God's Holy Light." Reverend's voice echoed at pulpit level. Heads turned all over the room.

Harpoon shifted in his seat, uncomfortable at the attention. "I'll admit I kinda miss the beacon. It was always a welcome sight coming into port."

"Well, brother Conroy, I mean to relight the Torch of God, and I need your help." With that the reverend pounded a fist on the Wisdom Table and bounced his empty plate toward Harpoon who fended it off with an elbow.

Harpoon, like everyone else on the Island, knew that the Coast Guard had declared the Crystal Epistle's beacon a menace to navigation after four Louisiana shrimp boats had run aground in front of the Crystal Epistle Church, when they mistook the light for the harbor channel beacon. The Guard overlooked the truth that everyone aboard the beached Coonass boats was so drunk they thought nothing of the incident until they sobered up the next morning to find about a hundred or so beach walkers, a constable's car, and Right Reverend Hannibal Jones, elbows akimbo, on the beach in front of the Crystal Epistle, all gawking at the shrimpers' predicament.

Before he learned that the Coast Guard intended to darken the Crystal Epistle beacon, Right Reverend Jones felt that, much like Jonah's whale beaching and belching him forth, this land-locked armada at the foot of the Crystal Epistle must be a message from God.

Reverend Jones had ruminated and prayed for days on how this transcendent liaison of the beached shrimp boats must be interpreted. He paced his office carpet and took long walks on the beach; for the correct elucidation of the divine message weighed heavily upon him. As he stood on the beach near sundown and looked at the Crystal Epistle's magnificent seaside façade, a lightning bolt of comprehension struck him. "Hallelujah! Praise the Lord." His basso profundo voice (that often shocked those who heard it for the first time) echoed down the beach.

Soon after, the Crystal Epistle installed a Jumbotron Screen and rock concert-class sound system facing the beach. Reverend Jones then announced from the pulpit and with a full page ad in The North Jetty that sunbathers, beach walkers, surf fishermen, and boats moored in the surf, all could worship in glorious Dolby Sound and Technicolor while soaking up rays and fishing. The Jumbotron project had difficulty with the church's deacons, who could not devise a method for collecting an offering from the surf and sand crowd. Then a deacon suggested advertisements for local and regional merchants be shown on the screen between church services. The Jumbotron (pulsing, winking, and blinking) then took its rightful place in the pantheon of modern religious expression on the prospect of a positive cash flow from paid ads.

Police Chief Farley Crump, Coach Bull Bostich, and fishing guide Wiley Coots arrived at the Wisdom Table, plates piled high. Reverend Jones raised his right hand heavenward. "I greet you men in the name of the Heavenly Father, and amen."

The three men nodded at Harpoon and said, " Mornin', Reverend."

"No need for a blessing as I have bestowed a permanent incantation for all those who break bread here today." Reverend Jones opened his arms as if spreading butter over the whole table.

"Sorry, I missed the blessing, Reverend, but I've had a busy morning." Chief Crump slid back his chair and sat down. "We locked up two illegal aliens this morning."

Harpoon glanced up from his plate. "What were they doing?"

"The stupid bastards were sleeping in their red Ford pickup down on the beach with two Glock 9 millimeters on the seat between them." The Chief laid his head back and loosed a belly laugh. "We'd never even known, except they didn't have a Beach Parking Permit."

Laughter ricocheted around the table except for Harpoon who felt color bloom in his face. He spoke without looking at the chief. "You know who they are?"

"I know they're drug mules. I mean, the sniffing dogs kept howlin' and pissin' themselves they got so excited. But we tore that pickup apart and couldn't find a thing."

Harpoon's head popped up. "I didn't know you had sniffin' dogs."

"Chief got 'em last week." Wiley Coots tore open a biscuit and slathered on butter. "They love goin' out in my boat."

"You take them out in boats?" The frantic pitch of Harpoon's question raised eyebrows.

Wiley's smile broadened. "Yeah, I'm trainin' 'em to sniff out trout and red fish." There was general round of mirth in which Harpoon laughed belatedly.

"And what's your plan for these illicit illegals." The reverend furrowed his brow with concern. "The Crystal Epistle could use a little yard work. Give them God's own Weed Eater redemption, so to speak, and amen."

"We got 'em on 'Possession of Unregistered Firearms' and 'Parking without a Beach Permit.'" Chief Crump nodded with satisfaction. "But INS and DEA both want a crack at them, so no yard work today, Reverend."

"Brother Conroy, you're lookin' a little peeked." Reverend motioned toward Harpoon's plate that still held his meager rations. "Could be the onset of malnutrition."

"No, like I said, I'm off my feed a little today." Harpoon took a bite of biscuit, forestalling further concerns about his caloric intake.

"In case you're wondering, gentlemen, Brother Conroy joined us here today so I might solicit his help in our efforts at relighting that bright beacon of hope, God's Holy Light."

Harpoon cast an embarrassed look around the table and stammered a bit. " How … how can I help?"

"I've prepared a petition that will circulate to all shrimp boats, charter boats, and private craft, demanding that the Beacon of God once again shine its protective beam over this blessed island." The Reverend Jones pounded the table and sent both his empty plates again bounding toward Harpoon. "If the heathen bureaucrats do not honor the will of the people, then I will call for a boat-in."

"A 'boat-in'?" Harpoon looked at the new Wisdom Table arrivals for clarification. They glanced up, shrugged, and stared back at their plates.

"That's right, brother Conroy, a boat-in. I will call for all God fearing sailors to form a flotilla of God's holy boats and block the entrance of the ship channel until the bureaucrats rescind the infamous order that darkened the Lamp of God."

Harpoon frantically saw the error of accepting the reverend's breakfast invitation. A felon had no business meddling in God's work or breaking bread with the dog sniffing law. He looked around for any reason why he might excuse himself, and saw Cindy walking toward the buffet with another baker's sheet pan of biscuits. One lone escapee biscuit; bruised, misshapen and recaptured, rode forlornly atop the other biscuits, all heading toward their certain doom on the buffet. Harpoon slumped back into his chair in resignation.

CHAPTER | 3

Some things bothered Krank about yard work and landscaping. Mowing grass seemed cruel. Why brutalize a living thing that tried desperately to survive and grow? Why replace plants that want to live where they are with other plants that can barely survive there? Why are some grass, plants, shrubs, and trees ugly and others beautiful? Why waste time, effort, and money destroying living things just because someone beyond memory once declared them ugly or worse, a weed. Why not reverse the decision and declare ugly plants beautiful and leave them alone, thriving and glorious in their beauty right where they grow? Unfortunately, mankind disagreed with Krank.

Dollar weed bothered him most. Left alone, dollar weed would paint a yard green in a few months with succulent green "silver dollars," which never grew higher than a couple of inches, required little watering, no fertilizer, and never needed mowing. Another plus, pocket gophers seldom surfaced through dollar weed. But the word "weed" was this plant's undoing. A weed, which he thought must be a plant that really likes growing where it is, must be uprooted and destroyed. So he found himself in a constant battle trying to eradicate dollar weed and replace it with St. Augustine carpet grass, yearning for return to Florida. St. Augustine carpet grass demanded constant watering, fertilizer, mowing, and took years before producing the same effect as dollar weed.

In high school he maintained a "C+" average in class work. His grades in the Humanities made up for those in math and science. History, especially about Texas, western literature, and geography of Native America, held his interest and reflected in his grades. Texas Gulf Coast Indian cultures carried special importance for him. The high school faculty seemed impressed by his ability to be a super hero on the athletic fields, while he maintained his schoolwork and his landscape business.

Girls in high school and later, women, posed a problem for Krank, the big time athlete with the muscular build, but their interest made him uneasy. Getting away from them was one of the reasons for shrimping. Anytime he made friends with females, they immediately wanted more attention and talked about the future. Krank knew his future, and he saw no women or children in it.

The Ridley coach, with whom Krank lived, insisted that he attend church each Sunday at the brand new Bible church outside of Port Aransas on a beachfront location. The young pastor's bass voice and belief in "a loving, rather than a vengeful God." enraptured the growing congregation of the Church of Everlasting Enlightenment. Krank never considered himself a Christian, as such, but he believed there was a Great Spirit with serious power over mortals. He also respected the sincerity of Reverend Hannibal Jones' beliefs.

From high school on, Krank had never charged for all the lawn work and landscaping he did for the Church of Everlasting Enlightenment. He thought the appearance of the Church grounds helped its membership grow and pleased the Great Spirit. He no longer attended services after graduating from high school, but continued with his religious lawn care.

Since he started shrimping with Harpoon, he still helped

out the widows and did yard work for the oil company that allowed his houseboat anchorage on Wilson's Cut. But he used the rest of his shore time caring for the church's lawn. Each year when shrimp season closed, he had six weeks of catch-up time getting the Crystal Epistle grounds picturesque and inviting for the summer tourists.

But this closed season was different because of last night's felonious activity. He hoped these six weeks would pass as quickly and quietly as in previous years.

CHAPTER | 4

arpoon squirmed through the remainder of the breakfast discussion. Visions of drug sniffing dogs swarming over the *Cordon Blues* popped a sweat under his smiley face ball cap.

"Boys, this may be the year of the Turtle." Bull Bostich, Port A High School football coach, spoke in his Game Day voice.

The table erupted, "Go, You Ridleys!"

Bostich was a bull of a man, but everyone at the table knew his nickname came from an incident when he played middle linebacker for the Texas Longhorns. No Texas youth crowned with a shock of blond hair could escape the nickname "Cotton," but after Cotton Bostich killed an attacking pit bulldog with his bare hands, he was always "Bull Bostich."

The Wisdom Table conversation roamed from Ridley football, to weather, to prognostications on this tourist season. The economics of the upcoming summer tourist season held their interest for an extended time, as it was generally agreed that the last few years had softened considerably and put a sizeable crimp in Port A's wallet.

God, Harpoon thought. These guys could talk green apples into red. But when Reverend Hannibal Jones swung the conversation back to "Relighting The Holy Lamp of God,"

Harpoon slid his chair back and stood so abruptly that heads at the table snapped toward him in anticipation. "Oh, sorry. I enjoyed breakfast, but I've got things to do before I run *Cordon Blues* over to Aransas Pass for repairs."

"Ol' Blues feelin' poorly?" Chief Crump asked.

"Nothing wrong with her a new engine and net winch wouldn't fix." Harpoon shrugged at the inevitability of the shrimp boat's future.

"Hope you've been savin' your pennies." Wiley Coots chuckled and shook his head at what those repairs might cost.

Harpoon nodded and moved toward the barroom exit. "Don't know any shrimper stashing money these days."

The shrimp buyer had completed his purchases, and passed *Cordon Blues* on his way to his refrigerated truck. "Harpoon, you're a man possessed. Scrubbin' down the Ol' Blues twice in one morning. Such fastidiousness is seldom seen in these parts."

"Cleanliness is next to Godliness. I expect rewards in heaven." Harpoon hoisted the scrub brush to port arms, acknowledging the buyer. "Takin' her in for repairs tomorrow, and I wouldn't want 'em thinkin' less of me for docking a skanky boat."

He'd soaped, scrubbed, and washed the deck without a letup since returning from The Island Joynt. Every nook and cranny that might conceal even the tiniest nug of marijuana had received his full attention. He leaned against the sorting table for a moment but continued reconnoitering hidden places that might still be exposed by the devil drug-sniffing dogs.

He looked starboard and saw a bay boat with a rotund, silver haired, khaki clad figure idling toward him with two dogs in the bow. It was Wiley Coots' fishing guide boat. Great God! Wiley's delivering those nosey beasts right to my doorstep. His imagination whirred with pictures of berserk dogs when they got within sniffing distance of *Cordon Blues.* He thought of jumping ship and running through Roberts Point Park, but held both his position and breath.

Wiley's Blue Wave 220 bumped the Blues, and he stood and reached for the shrimper's gunnel. The dogs waggled a greeting at a rigid Harpoon. The dogs looked up quizzically at the strange immobilized person and continued waggling.

"These Chief Crump's drug sniffing dogs, Wiley?"

"Nah, these old hounds couldn't sniff out a bitch in heat." Harpoon exhaled with a swoosh.

Wiley's chin was gunnel high on the shrimp boat, but he could see the deck. "By, God, Harpoon, you've got her ship shape."

'Takin' her in tomorrow for an overhaul, and I didn't want her lookin' gungy."

"Listen, I don't have a trip today, so I thought you might want to go out and get a few redfish for dinner tonight?"

"Wiley, that's very thoughtful, but I've got a lot to do today. You know, odds and ends before I take the Blues in. But I'll damn sure take a rain check."

"Yeah, I know. Things like seeing if an asshole banker will bankroll the Blues overhaul?"

"I guess you've been there before."

Wiley turned and pointed toward the Evinrude V-Tec 200 engine on the transom. "I only hope the bastard runs long enough to get it paid for." He shoved off and cranked the engine. "Think I'll go out for a while. Got a hankering for grilled redfish tonight." He reached for the throttle, then halted and turned toward Harpoon. "You know, I think Reverend Jones is dead serious about getting' us involved in his beacon project." He laid his head back and loosed a belly laugh.

Harpoon raised his hands over his head. "God, help us!"

***

It had not been an easy trip for Diggs, the pocket gopher. He was on a road less traveled when he launched into his great adventure and headed for the sand dunes. Gophers seldom visited the dunes. Dune oat roots didn't taste as good as carpet grass and those tasty roots growing around the beach houses. Old tunnels might make the job easier, but they didn't exist. It seemed he had dug forever and claustrophobia had overtaken him. "I gotta get some air!"

***

Harpoon had gone thirty-six hours without sleep, but anxiety still pervaded his thoughts. He might seek solace from beer and Lottie back at The Island Joynt, but she would not be there until 11:00 o'clock. He exited Roberts Point Park and continued across Cotter and turned his pickup abruptly past the railing marking the ferry entrance. A paved road now replaced the old sandy two-track that lead to Charlie's Pasture Pier. A short distance after the road ran parallel to the Corpus Christi Ship Channel stood Slidin' Will Picken's Bait Shop and Wine Bar.

Harpoon and Slidin' Will Pickens were buddies and played together in Will's jam sessions. Pickens, a legendary blues musician, had retired in Port Aransas and the relative obscurity of "Good Pickens Bait Shop, Wine Bar and Blues Emporium – Affordable Boat Rentals." Years of traveling as a blues musician, substance abuse, and too many women had reduced the formerly well-built, six-foot black man into a stooped shell of his former self. But enough fire still resided in Slidin' Will Pickens to light up the sky with his classic Dobro Guitar and the wine bottleneck-slide slipped over his fret little finger.

Chrome dinette tables and chairs crowded the wine bar – all full of blues music lovers every night, sniffing and swirling great wines. Since the wine bar was in the room beside the bait tanks, it was not uncommon for a wine snob with his nose in his glass to comment on the wine's unique piscatorial aroma with hints of seaweed.

Harpoon pulled into Will's parking lot, got his harmonica from the glove box and opened the pickup door. He could hear Muddy Waters on Will's boom box when he stepped down onto the crushed oyster shell.

Another mule's been kickin' in my stall.
Sho nuf another mule been kicking in my stall.
Harpoon felt a little thrill ripple through him as it always

did when he visited Will. Inside, Will looked up from pouring a glass of Henske's Hill of Grace Eden Valley Shiraz for a customer and broke into a broad smile. He came from behind the counter and hugged Harpoon. "I was wonderin' if I'd ever see you again."

"Yeah, I've had some bad stuff goin' on, and I was hopin' you had time for some blues. My head needs a little clearin'."

"You bring your harpoon?"

***

Claude the Coyote watched from behind a patch of Australian pepperbushes as the man entered the building from which issued sounds like a brother coyote in full yowl. Claude often visited the building a little before dawn for a bite to eat from the trash. It was daylight now, but he loosed a yipping howl in chorus with the strange sounds anyway. It was a howl of joy. Claude was in love.

Normally he lost interest pretty quickly after mating, but this time it was different. She not only was a looker, she even smelled good. And the sex, oh, my God, it was something to howl about.

He had already decided on sticking around for the inevitable pups. But first, he must help her with a den. No trees and little vegetation to burrow under existed on this side of the Island, so he headed across the Island toward the dunes.

God I hate crossing the black path. He thought as he hid in the grass next to the highway. It smelled bad and strange animals raced along it with no regard for others. One had attacked his friend, killed him, and never looked back. Why do evil creatures like this exist? It's not right, he thought.

Finally, summoning his courage, he bolted across the black path and into the weeds in the bar ditch on the other side. He spied a big overhanging clump of dune oats as he trotted alongside the dunes. "This will work," he thought and commenced digging their den. The den must be big enough for her and a litter of pups, protected from hawks, and not visible from the outside. Actually, Claude was quite proud of their new abode and felt sure she would be impressed.

Diggs was in a panic. He should have reached the surface by now. Claustrophobia tightened his throat and terror gripped his soul. Disoriented, he almost reversed and dug the opposite direction, when he broke through into a huge underground chamber much bigger than anything a gopher would dig. "My God, am I dead? This must be the "Great Burrow in the Sky' gophers always talk about." He crawled out onto the floor of the cave and immediately smelled something terrifying. "Coyote!" He looked out the mouth of the cave and saw movement. Something big blocked the mouth of the cave, and it was moving toward him. "Holy shit!" He leaped into the air, landed in the mouth of his burrow, and ran for his life down his tunnel. He didn't even look back at the furious digging behind him. Diggs kept thinking while he ran, It's wrong on so many levels if the Great Gopher in the Sky is actually a coyote.

CHAPTER | 5

The sounds from Will's boom box wafted into Harpoon's pickup truck as he pulled out of Good Pickens Bait Shop, Wine Bar and Blues Emporium – Affordable Boat Rentals' parking lot. A couple of glasses of good red and rocking out on several blues tunes with Will had mellowed him. Happy music did not cheer him up when he had the blues. Blues put him in tune with the certainty that however low he felt, others felt worse.

The salt breeze from the back bay increased his peaceful Port A feeling as he retraced his way through Charley's Pasture toward The Island Joynt. He smiled in anticipation of seeing Lottie. A beer with Lottie would make him right.

Last night's memory still lingered much like a pesky insect. He knew he wasn't a saint, or even religious, for that matter, but right was right, and wrong was wrong – no matter how differently he painted it or how desperately he needed money. He slammed on the brakes, ripped the gearshift into park, flung open the door, and jumped from the pickup. He lurched through the grass and weeds, his breath laden with emotion, until he topped a spoil bank thrown up when they dredged the Corpus Christ Ship Channel long ago.

From his vantage point he could see the Shrimp King

boats as they dutifully chugged up Aransas Pass Channel where they would sit, moribund, until shrimp season opened again. He could feel the life he so loved as a shrimper slip away, and a leaden sadness crept up his spine when he thought how little he could do to forestall its vanishing – short of remaining a criminal.

An oil tanker slid past, throwing up a bow wake where dolphin surfed and frolicked. Brown pelicans skimmed the surface of the water, anticipating a chance meeting with a mullet or two. Mullet, anticipating a chance meeting with a pelican, leaped and scattered in every direction like rocks skipping over the surface. The distant, fading thump of the ship's engine sucked life from the air. Harpoon gasped when he glimpsed his future – a life of crime and degradation that ended in his destruction.

***

Rodolfo Rattler had been coiled and camped out beside a gopher hole for eleven hours while he waited for one of the *cabroncitos* to show his head. No luck. Nothing! The sun beat down, and he needed somewhere shady for his siesta. Australian pepper tree bushes offered shade not far away, but his hunger made him linger in the hope of "Gopher Delight." He heard something coming. Near sightedness plagued his whole family, so he couldn't make out what approached.

Possibly a little lunch *momentito,* he thought, but as the sound increased he added, *Hijo! Es un big one. Muy gran almuerzo!* Rodolpho, was about to loose his signature "Cha Cha Cha" rattle before striking, when he recognized the creature. *"Ay carajo! Es un hombre."* Instead, he bolted down the gopher hole into safety. Why can't those *hombres* leave us alone? We're just tryin' to make a livin' out here, *comprende?*

***

Harpoon parked in The Island Joynt lot that faced Cotter Street, and waited impatiently for the engine to stop dieseling. I've got to get this piece of junk tuned up. The dashboard ignition light was dark, but the truck continued to chug on in fits and starts. Disgusted, he looked up at Cotter Street. Something had changed. Nothing moved on the vacant street. Trees, shrubs, grass: all stood like monuments. The same breathless sensation he experienced in Charley's Pasture crept into his lungs. He shook his head to clear it and heard the rumble of an eighteen-wheeler approach from the direction of the ferry. *Where are the other cars that must have offloaded with the truck?*

The truck, a huge cross-country rig, shimmered in iridescent, clear-coated black paint. Someone had crafted the rearview mirrors with great skill and effort into the pointy ears of a wolf, and the front grill into a cavernous, toothed, growling wolf's mouth extended by means of paint over the sides of the truck's hood. The headlights were fire-breathing nostrils. A translucent material appliquéd around the edges of the windshield delineated a mean-eyed predator's stare. The depth of the black paint on the semi-trailer seemed to suck at Harpoon's soul and invited him to plunge in. "Great God!" he said aloud.

The Wolf Wagon's transmission downshifted as the airbrakes hissed. The truck ground to a halt, and the engine growled like a malcontent canine. A dark film coated the cab's side windows and blocked Harpoon's vision. No traffic passed while the truck paused as if panting from exhaustion. After a short rest, Harpoon heard gears grind, and the engine roared and stirred the Wolf Wagon into motion. His head followed as the truck gained speed, but something caught his attention. He looked back and saw a figure standing in the street as the trees and shrubs again swayed in the breeze.

Slight of build, medium height, and clad entirely in black except for soft rumpled white leather boots, the figure wore a black woven poncho that covered his torso and thighs and exposed only the long sleeves of his black shirt. A black Zorro hat with big silver conchos on the band and silver mirrored aviator glasses added panache. On closer inspection, Harpoon made out the letters "SRV" embroidered on the poncho with silver metallic thread. A guitar, slung over his right shoulder, hung casually – neck down.

"Stevie Ray Vaughan?" Harpoon rubbed his eyes and gasped.

The figure neither flinched nor retreated as a Sysco Food Service truck lumbered between the two. The truck passed, and the street was empty. Harpoon hit his forehead in disbelief, looked in both directions, but saw only the normal complement of tourists, assaulting the souvenir shops. "I've got to get some sleep. I'm hallucinating."

He stood just inside the door of The Joynt's bar entrance and appreciated Lottie as she served a customer. A striking woman by any standard. Her fair complexion, untarnished by wind, salt, and sun, glowed in the dim bar lights. Blonde hair styled in a poodle cut crowned her shapely frame. Intense blue eyes that crinkled slightly at the corners with her ready smile seemed to see through a person's façade and focused instead on the person inside. A tinkling laugh and a friendly disposition rounded out what he thought must be pretty near the perfect woman.

Lottie looked up, screened her eyes from the overhead bar lights, and recognized Harpoon in the darkness. "Come on in, Pilgrim, and set a spell." By the time he reached the bar she had his Shiner Bock rolled in a napkin, opened, and resting on a coaster. She sensed something amiss, as Harpoon seemed distracted to the point he failed to smile. "Back from the wars?"

He replaced his beer on the coaster with exaggerated care after a long pull. "I guess you could call it that."

"You okay? You look like you've seen a ghost."

"I might have."

This was not the old Harpoon she knew. "You might have?"

He finally smiled at her and stretched across the bar to give her a peck on the cheek. "Naw . . . I'm okay. Just a little tired. It's been a long and very unusual day."

"I'll say unusual. Cindy said you got promoted to the

Wisdom Table this morning. Now that's what I call progress."

"That was just a mistake."

"A mistake?"

"Reverend Jones invited me to join him at the table, and I made the mistake of accepting his invitation."

"That's right. Today is 'All You Can Eat Breakfast Buffet Only $4.99' day. What did the Right Reverend Hannibal Jones want?" A smile flashed across her face at her jab at the porky pastor.

He slid his empty bottle across the bar toward Lottie before he answered. "He's launching a crusade against the Coast Guard to relight 'The Holy Lamp of God'."

"The beacon? How do you fit into that scene?"

"He wants all shrimpers, charter boat captains, and private boats to participate in a 'Boat In.'"

She shrugged. "Like I say. Where do you come in?"

"Somehow he thinks I can help organize the Boat In."

She laughed out loud. "You better be careful, or you'll be spending your Sundays at the Crystal Epistle."

"Fat Chance! By the way, didn't Stevie Ray Vaughan die?"

"Hello, Earth? Boy, where did that come from? Why do you ask that?"

"Just curious."

"Yeah, a long time ago. In a helicopter crash, I think." She picked up a bar towel, wiped down the bar, and wondered what on earth was wrong with her guy.

Harpoon stood, pulled an envelope from his pocket, and produced a one hundred dollar bill. "I've been up for almost 48 hours. I need to head home and get some shut-eye."

She stared at the packet of money and asked, "You rob a bank or something?"

He stuffed the money into his pocket. "Takin' ol' Blues in for repairs tomorrow. They don't take checks from shrimpers any more."

She slid the hundred back to him. "Beer's on the house today. You be back later tonight?"

"If I wake up." He turned to leave.

"Well, it's sure been nice visitin'," Lottie said sarcastically and stood, arms crossed, while she watched him retreat into the darkness, her face a mask of concern.

Harpoon shifted into neutral, turned off the ignition, and coasted into the driveway of his home, hoping to cut time from the engine's normal indecision about stopping. He sat for a minute and looked at the normally well-kept grass of his island bungalow. It's time for a good mowing and trimming. He enjoyed yard work. It kept him connected with the soil, something a seafarer can appreciate.

A commercial fisherman built the small 10th Street "Islander" to withstand hurricanes long before "tourists" threw up million-dollar villas like tract houses behind guarded gates. He had recently repainted the exterior, and a satisfied smile crossed his face as he viewed his earlier efforts. The glistening white walls trimmed in lemon yellow gave a Cape Cod look that separated it from others in the neighborhood that had not seen paint in recent decades.

There was an Island property boom and realtors scurried from house to house looking for owners who might sell for huge profits. He thought the realtor's valuation of his property completely ridiculous until his neighbor showed him a higher sales contract for his house in much worse repair.

As he sat in his truck now, Harpoon's brow clouded at the thought that current shrimping conditions rendered *Cordon Blues* unsalable, leaving his home his only asset. Sell my house or keep smuggling to get out of debt, he thought. God, what a choice.

Once inside his home, Harpoon went directly to the fridge and pulled out a Shiner Bock, popped the cap, and returned to the living room. He riffled through his collection of CDs and stopped at Stevie Ray Vaughan's "Texas Flood," and stared at the cover. A tingling sensation rippled through his stomach as he recognized the image as the man he'd seen on Cotter Street. The CD player sprang to life when he inserted the disk, and he moved back to relax in his stained, brown-leather BarkaLounger. The classic blues rhythm of "I'm Cryin'" filled the room with Stevie Ray's voice pleading, "I'm cryin'. What can I do?"

Harpoon sank further into the soft leather folds, pulled on the beer, and pressed his index finger and thumb into his tired eyes, temporarily relieving their sting. "What can I do? I'm cryin' whatcanIdocryinwhatcanIdowhatcan . . . I . . . can . . . do."

He awoke with a start when his beer bottle hit the floor and remained motionless, while he tried to reconstruct his condition. A vivid recollection of talking with Stevie Ray pervaded his mind – not actually conversing with Stevie Ray, but with his photo on the CD cover. His mind retreated from the idea that he had actually talked with a CD cover, but something stuck. Something wouldn't clear to allow his return to sanity. The vivid imprint of Stevie Ray's mantra, "If I just go with what's in my heart, and let it come out, then I'm okay."

CHAPTER | 6

arpoon had slept almost fourteen hours when he arose before daylight. Ground fog swirled around his legs as he strode toward his pickup. He paused for a moment, as if communing with the truck before he turned the ignition key. The motor caught on the first try, and he smiled in appreciation as he backed into the street. Port Aransas was just stirring, and occasionally the glare of headlights from the passing cars lit the interior of his pickup as he wended his way toward Roberts Point Park and the boat docks. The first day of the closed shrimp season saw a madhouse at the shipyards as all the captains crowded their boats in for repairs. He wanted to be at the front of the line.

When he arrived at the *Cordon Blues,* the sun just peeked over St Joseph Island. He threw a small waterproof bag over the stern and climbed aboard. He drew in a breath of salt air, yawned, and stretched. This was his favorite time of day on the harbor. The dock berths of the head boats that belched their exhaust as they hauled their loads of tourists offshore for fishing the snapper banks, all stood vacant. Only the most ambitious of the bay fishermen slid noiselessly by and talked in hushed tones as if the harbor's "No Wake" signs referred to noise, rather than speed.

Mean High Tide had just passed and the calm water in the ship channel between the jetties waffled – undecided on whether to ebb or flow. Scattered clouds blazed in the dawn; their reflection sparkled in the becalmed harbor. The musty smells of marine life and saltwater soothed Harpoon, both body and soul. He picked up the bag, unzipped it, and checked the packet of illicit currency. He shook his head with a resigned sigh, zipped up the bag, and threw it on the wheelhouse firewall deck. The third attempt at starting the cantankerous engine reminded him of what launched his current troubles. On the fourth try the engine issued a loud complaint, banged once, twice, and finally roared awake. Harpoon cast off the lines, returned to the wheelhouse, and patted the firewall deck affectionately. "Well, old girl, you'll feel better soon."

He engaged the prop and the Blues slid out of her berth for the short run up Aransas Pass Channel to Conn Brown Harbor and the shipyard where she would spend the next three weeks.

When ashore, Krank always awoke before sunrise, made coffee, sat in the old castoff lawn lounge chair on the deck of his "houseboat," and smoked his peace pipe. He sipped the muddy brew and puffed away on his pipe and enjoyed the sunrise over the dunes across the Island. The houseboat looked more like a barge made of old telephone poles that floated on two-dozen oil drums lashed together. He had decked over these and built a two-room tarpaper shack with a corrugated tin roof. He had no electricity, and his only nod toward modern conveniences consisted of a propane Coleman lantern, a propane hot plate, and an ancient, rebuilt Servel gas refrigerator. A wood-burning stove with a flue pipe through the roof provided winter heat. A Port-a-Potty handled that problem.

His primitive abode floated at the head of Wilson's Cut about nine miles south of Port Aransas. Although floating on the water was not trespassing on the adjacent land, anchoring the houseboat was. He occasionally cut the grass around the company's shops and offices at the mouth of Wilson's Cut to appease the oil company that owned the contiguous property. A few pounds of shrimp occasionally in the manager's fridge also helped his cause.

Krank had attended high school in Port Aransas twenty years before, and his Jim Thorpe type athletic skills made him a legend. The enigma that no one knew anything about his origin followed him his whole life.

Everyone on the Island knew Krank's legend: he just appeared as a high school student. No one ever met his parents or knew exactly where he lived or his name for that matter. Everyone knew about his athletic prowess before school officials questioned where he lived and with whom. At the Wisdom Table one morning in The Island Joynt, the then school superintendent voiced his fear that Krank might not be eligible for school in Port A. The other table denizens set up a clamor asking, "Why?" The superintendent said the school could not establish whether Krank actually lived in the Port A School District. So the football coach announced that Krank lived with him and his wife to quell the threatened uprising.

Krank reeled off four years of athletic accomplishments for the Port Aransas High School Fightn' Ridley Turtles that made them the envy of every small town in South Texas. College scholarship offers poured in, but Krank refused them all. He announced that, as a full blood Karankawa Indian reincarnation of the human-flesh-eating original inhabitants of the Island, he had more pressing matters. His friend and mentor, the football coach, tried to reason with him as Karankawa extinction was common knowledge – but to no avail.

Krank finished his cup of coffee and now wondered about his friend, Coyote. Coyote usually appeared on a spoil bank across the Cut each morning. He sat motionless among the spartina grass while he stared at Krank, and they empathized on a wide range of subjects. Since the coyotes had already chewed through most of the Island's rabbits, Coyote always wondered if Krank thought Island people would keep buying pets so the coyotes would have some food. Krank had a premonition that a big event would soon happen on the Island. He and Coyote spent much time communing over what might occur. They constantly sparred and joked about what shenanigans trickster Coyote had planned for the Island people.

But today — no Coyote.

The cell phone Harpoon had given him so they could stay in touch broke his reverie with an Indian war chant. "Hey, Boss."

"Hey, good buddy, we're in luck. I'll be through here in about an hour or so. If you'll pick me up at say, 12:30, I'll treat you to lunch and brewskis at the Joynt."

"There will be trouble at the Joynt today."

"God, I hate when you come up with your prophecies. I mean shrimp season's closed. We deserve a bunch of beer while we get quietly plastered – without any trouble." Harpoon's voice rose in pitch and angst.

"Sorry, Boss, but Coyote didn't come today. That means he's out causing trouble."

"Jesus, Coyote trouble? Will this be anything we can't handle?"

"I don't think even Coyote knows the answer."

The two old pickups pulled into The Island Joynt's parking lot in line astern and fanned out into available parking places. Harpoon waited for Krank, and the two entered through the bar's side door. They stood and waited as their eyes adjusted to the darkness.

Lottie looked out from behind the bar, shading her eyes. "Well, here's the amazing vanishing Shrimpman and his sidekick Krankster. Don't just stand there in the driving rain, go home!"

Harpoon looked at Krank. "Is this the trouble you talked about?"

"We haven't seen the trouble we're in."

"I don't know if I can handle double trouble." He turned and walked toward the bar with a broad smile. Krank took a seat at a table.

"You got a couple of beers for two guys who just handed over nine grand to save the old Blues?" Harpoon slid onto a bar stool across from Lottie.

"Nine grand?" Her eyebrows arched at the thought. "Your rich uncle died?"

"Would have been twelve except they had a rebuilt engine." He took the two beers and stood. "Listen, I'm sorry about last night, but I fell asleep about three yesterday afternoon and didn't wake up until this morning."

Lottie wiped the bar where the two beers had sat. "Well, you owe me one. Be sure you make it up to me tonight."

"That sounds ominous. Should I rig for heavy weather?" He chuckled and added, "Krank and I are having a celebratory meal in the dining room, but we shall surely return. You might check your Shiner Bock inventory in the meantime."

"Now that does sound ominous."

Harpoon handed a beer to Krank, and the two headed for the dining room door. Lottie called to them. She lifted the bar pass-through and came over and talked in a hushed voice. "Listen, I forgot, but three guys came in earlier asking if I knew somebody named Harpoon, the captain of a shrimp boat called *Cordon Blues*."

Harpoon's smile vanished. "Who were they?"

"I don't know, and I didn't ask. They looked Mexican. One wore an expensive silk shirt open at the neck, showing off a ton of gold necklaces. The other two looked like something out of a "B" gangster movie."

"Did they say what they wanted?"

"They weren't somebody I wanted to get chummy with, so I jest blew them off." Her brow knotted. "What the hell's goin' on, anyway?"

Krank tilted his head. "Coyote just howled."

***

Diggs, the pocket gopher, huddled in his tunnel and shook with fear while in the throes of his fifth claustrophobic attack. *I've gotta get out a here!* An eternity might have passed since his encounter with the Great Coyote in the Sky. He had never stayed below ground this long.

He lay there, a mound of indecision. *I need some fresh air, but if I dig a surface shaft, will Coyote be there again? Maybe I can find my way back to my bachelor pad in the Main Tunnel. Life wasn't all that bad there. Who knows, I might even lure a sweet little thing into the pad for a dalliance. Yeah, and shouldn't I share the news that the Great Gopher in the Sky is really a demon coyote? All those gophers that just disappeared didn't end up in the Great Burrow in the Sky. They ended up coyote crap. This whole idea of burrowing to the other side of the great sand pile wasn't such a hot idea anyway, was it? All this stuff just isn't right. I mean why does life have to be so hard? It's bad enough I spend my life groveling around underground. Why do creatures lurk everywhere trying to eat me? Who sends the poisonous dust to kill me? Why are there poisonous roots? And now there isn't even a Great Gopher in the Sky to help me, just Devil Coyote.*

Diggs worked himself into a rage. *This sucks! I'm outa here, Coyote or no Coyote.* He stood on his hind legs and dug straight up in double time. The roots proved tough digging. Occasionally he stopped for a nibble here and a nibble there. Just enough to keep up his strength. He could not imagine a shaft this long. "How far under ground must I be?" At regular intervals he backed down the shaft and moved the sand he had dug down the tunnel to make room for more. Back up he'd go for more digging. Then something happened. The sand fell away, and a strange substance blocked his progress.

Not sand or even dirt, the shiny material smelled different from anything before. It moved away when he mashed on it. He tried biting the stuff, but it slipped out of his mouth. He tried to burrow through it but could make no progress. He lunged forward, and the mystery substance sprung back. Finally, he was thrown back with such force that he fell to the bottom of the shaft. "Okay, that's it. You want to play rough – we'll play rough. YOU want some of THIS?" He pointed up the shaft and then at himself. "Well, here I come, Buster."

He shouted and ran up the shaft with all his strength, landing his best karate chop. "Take that!" His claws pierced the strange stuff, and he found himself dangling in the shaft. Before he could get his back feet stuck into the shaft wall, his claws ripped out, and he again tumbled down the shaft with something big chasing him this time. He thumped onto the tunnel floor, and before he could gather himself, really evil smelling stuff rained on him. Truly radical stuff buried him alive – something plant-like. He nibbled some and liked the taste. He nibbled a little more. He started digging his way out from under it. "Dig a little, chew a little, clap, clap, clap. Dig a little, chew a little, clap, clap. Dig a . . . chew a clap . . . clap. Chew . . .clap."

He had cleared from under the great tasting, evil smelling stuff and tried standing – with no success. "WHOOOAAH! Man, I'm feelin' right!"

Word about Diggs' discovery spread over the gopher "telegraph" with the speed of light. Gophers from everywhere made the pilgrimage to try Diggs' Stuff. Diggs told them all how he had discovered this amazing Stuff. He always started his story with, "I decided to tunnel to the other side of the great sand pile to see what made people go there." He ended, "And I discovered the Stuff that people wanted." In his heart he really didn't know if he had tunneled all the way to the other side, but that didn't seem important now.

He gave lots of Stuff away as there was an endless supply. In a short time, Diggs had all the gophers strung out on Stuff, and they always came back for more. He hardly had time to burrow for food. Then he realized the gophers could bring him pieces of root in exchange for Diggs' Stuff. The underground hummed like a Los Angeles freeway with gophers running back and forth with their roots for Diggs and returning with more Stuff.

As they moved their stash back to their gopher dens from Diggs' Emporium and Stuff Mine, merriment abounded and giggling echoed up and down the burrows. Bits of bloom and seeds fell along the tunnels, but the happy gophers could not be bothered with cleaning up their mess. The traditional gopher wisdom that the tunnels had to be kept clean of debris and scat didn't seem as important to most of the gophers these days.

Diggs didn't care much about such things any more, but some of the older gophers thought this lack of hygiene and orderliness wrong. They blamed the Stuff, and they periodically dug shafts and cleaned out the debris and seeds. The happiest of the gophers, including Diggs, felt great that they no longer had to dig shafts and clean. From time to time, a group would troop up a shaft, lay out, and soak up a few rays. This was paradise for a claustrophobic like Diggs – fresh air, sunshine, and blue sky – what could be better? None of his friends seemed worried much about rattlesnakes or coyotes any more either.

CHAPTER | 7

Harpoon and Krank entered the dining room and looked around for a table. The locals smiled as they recognized Krank, their football hero from the Ridley Turtles' glory years. Krank acknowledged their "Go, You Ridleys" greetings with a smile and a nod.

Harpoon turned to Krank. "They still remember you, good buddy, even after all these years."

"There's not much to remember on the Island."

Lunch was just winding down at the Wisdom Table, and several of its denizens waved to Harpoon and Krank. Wiley Coots lifted his glass of iced tea in a salute and laughed. "To *Cordon Blues* and the 'Great Beacon Boat-In'."

Harpoon glanced around the table to confirm Rev. Hannibal Jones' absence, and gave Wiley a thumbs up and a knowing smile.

"What's that all about?" Krank stared at Wiley.

"You don't want to know," said Harpoon

"It sounds like trouble."

"I'm hopin' it's trouble we never get involved in."

The dining room had its usual hum of customer conversation. The smell of chicken fried steak and fried shrimp wafted from the kitchen and made Harpoon's mouth water. They reached an empty table and pulled back their chairs. Once seated, Krank pointed toward the bar. "That guy in the bar gave me a chill."

"What guy?"

"The stranger at the back corner table."

"Was he one of those three Lottie talked about?" Harpoon squirmed a little in his seat.

"No. He looked different. He wore a flat brimmed hat and a poncho. A guitar leaned against the wall next to him. He made me shiver."

Harpoon leaped from his chair as if bitten by an insect; heads turned as he rushed back toward the bar. Krank watched with a stoic expression as Harpoon retreated.

Lottie looked up as Harpoon burst into the bar. He looked around at the corner tables as if he had lost something valuable. "What's the problem?"

"Who was the guy sittin' at that table?" He pointed.

"What guy?"

"The one in the flat brimmed hat and poncho with the guitar." He again pointed.

Lottie stared at him without speaking. "There was no one at that table today."

"Krank saw someone sittin' there."

"I think Krank sees things nobody else sees." Lottie's forehead furrowed with concern. "Are you okay? I mean, who did you think would be there?"

Harpoon thought for a moment, then relaxed, looking a little sheepish, and said, "Nobody . . . I guess."

The celebratory lunch passed quietly as only a meal with Krank could. Harpoon made several attempts to liven the party, but they all died with a grunt from Krank. Finally Harpoon asked, "You sure you saw a guy sittin' in the back corner of the bar?"

"He made me shiver."

Harpoon nodded. "Why would he make you shiver?"

"A spirit."

"A spirit?"

"I think he was a spirit." Krank stared out the window as if looking into next week.

"You saw a spirit?"

"I see many things others don't see."

"There's an echo in here" Harpoon gestured around the room.

"Echo?"

"Just a joke. Lottie said the same thing about you earlier."

"Smart woman." Krank returned to gazing into the future.

Experience told Harpoon that the conversation had ended, so he waved to Cindy for the check. She approached the table with a raucous laugh. "Well, if you two aren't just the gabbiest wild and crazy fellows – yammering on and on. I mean if you two had a conversation contest, there wouldn't be a winner."

Krank looked at her with a questioning expression. Harpoon laughed and pointed at Krank. "We commune on many levels. Right , Krank?"

"Ugh."

Harpoon stood. "That's Indian for yes, and now we're going to commune on the Shiner Bock level."

Two tables of shrimpers and a couple of singles were idling away their time when Harpoon and Krank entered the bar. Harpoon stopped at one of the shrimper tables. "I see you men made your table reservations for the closed season."

A rustle of agreement went around the table. "It's important to beat the rush," one shrimper answered as they all laughed.

Harpoon and Krank took a seat at the bar where Lottie had two beers rolled in napkins, resting on coasters. "So you two need a little Shiner Bock therapy, right?"

"A shrimper without his boat is a pathetic creature." Harpoon lifted his beer in a toast to Lottie.

Lottie shook her blonde poodle cut. "A few brewsters and a blonde can cure that."

Krank raised his bottle. "Smart lady."

***

Claude the coyote collapsed outside the den in which his mate had birthed their pups when he returned from his nocturnal search of the big boxes in town behind the places with the singing. He stayed vigilant because something had burrowed into the den even before he got her situated. The five pups would not open their eyes for many days, and he knew she would not allow him in the den until they were older. For some reason she got really testy when he tried to come inside for a cuddle. It doesn't seem right. I dug the den and now I can't even get in. She doesn't have any trouble taking my food, though. She almost ate the whole dead possum I found before I got any. Females! They're hard to figure. He knew he had to feed his mate so she could take care of the pups. With few rabbits left, food was harder to find. Before these pups, he would go into town and pick up a cat or dog. He preferred cats. He could catch them easier, and they tasted like chicken. The cute little pocket gophers are now in season. I don't know why gophers are so easy to catch now. I mean they just lie around on the sand, giggling. Like they don't even care I'm there. Best of all – eat a couple of gophers, and I'm singing and laughing my head off. They used to be hard to catch and not really tasty – a little too earthy – but now, wow! I'll do a little gopher hunting when it's daylight.

***

The afternoon had passed quietly as Harpoon and Krank paced themselves on the Shiners while visiting with Lottie. Patrons came and went as Lottie kept up a lively exchange of running jokes with the table customers. Her forays from behind the bar to serve the tables allowed Harpoon a break in the conversation to enjoy the blues and soul music CDs Lottie played in the bar. He had helped her compile the music from his collection. The music ranged from Robert Johnson to Robert Cray. From Sweet Erma Thompson to Ruthie Foster. There was a liberal sprinkling of Slidin' Will Pickens' tracks from his performing days. The CDs contrasted the gut-string grumbles of John Lee Hooker to the electric angst of Stevie Ray Vaughan.

A Stevie Rae Vaughn track, "Wall of Denial," cranked up on the sound system, and Harpoon swiveled the bar stool around to look at the back corner table. "Is the guy in the flat brimmed hat and the poncho back there at the corner table?"

"No."

"How do you know? You didn't even look."

"I don't have to look."

"That's right. You see things other people don't see." Harpoon chuckled.

"No. I can see the table in the back-bar mirror."

"I thought ghosts can't be seen in mirrors."

Krank thought for a moment. "There's something about this spirit you haven't told me."

"I used to think there's a lot of bullshit in all your hocus pocus, but yesterday I saw the same 'spirit' you saw today."

"Where?"

"The whole world stood still yesterday while he crawled down out of a big black truck out there on Cotter Street. Then he vanished." Harpoon added. "I haven't told anyone about what I saw. Lottie thinks I've gone bonkers."

"Do you know him?"

"He looked like Stevie Ray Vaughan."

"Was Stevie Ray Vaughan a good man?"

"I don't know about that, but he was an amazing blues musician."

Krank took his usual good time to comment. "The Powers are converging on the Island. Something big will happen."

Lottie carried a tray of beer bottles and glasses through the trapdoor in the bar. "Those three guys I told you about came back!" she whispered.

Krank stared at the mirror images of three men standing in the bar. Without changing expression, he said, "There will be trouble.

CHAPTER | 8

The reflection of the three *hombres* Harpoon saw in the bar mirror loomed large. They stood in the middle of the barroom obviously looking for someone. Finally, the gold-chain guy asked something of a shrimper who pointed in the direction of Harpoon and Krank.

"Oh, shit!" Harpoon said under his breath. "I don't know who these guys are, but they look like the trouble you keep talking about."

"Trouble's very close." Krank's gaze locked on the three in the mirror like a heat-seeking missile. "Do you feel physical?"

"Physical? Actually, I feel more like another Shiner."

"Good! You might need a beer bottle in both hands."

The gold chain guy moved toward an empty table in the corner of the room and motioned one of his goons toward the bar. Harpoon watched as he made his way toward him. He stopped behind Harpoon and Krank, and rested his hands on the backs of their bar stools. His eyes honed into Harpoon's in the mirror. "You gotta boat named *Cordon Blues?*"

Harpoon took a long pull on his beer and set it down squarely on a coaster without answering.

The guy shook Harpoon's chair. "Hey, asshole, I asked you a question. You have a boat named *Cordon Blues?*"

Harpoon swiveled slowly and met his eyes. "Don't shake my chair. You might spill my beer."

"I'm asking you, man. You the guy named Harpoon who's gotta boat named *Cordon Blues?*"

"Who wants to know?"

"My boss, Mako, wants to know 'cause he wants to talk to you." The guy pointed in the direction of his two friends. "And he don't like waitin'."

Harpoon looked at the table. "I never saw your boss in my life. Why would I want to talk with him?"

Lottie watched from the other end of the bar and moved in front of Harpoon. "What do you and your friends want to drink?"

The guy glanced at her and paused. "Give us three of these." He pointed at Harpoon's beer.

"I'll serve them at your table."

The guy looked at Harpoon. "You comin'?"

"Tell your boss, if he wants to talk to me, I'm right here." Harpoon turned back facing the bar.

Lottie followed the guy with three Shiners. Mako, the gold chain guy, looked at her. "You said you didn't know the one with the *Cordon Blues* boat."

"What makes you think I do?" She set his beer in front of him.

"You seem friendly with the guy at the bar."

"I'm friendly with everyone who comes in here." She turned and walked away.

Mako looked at the other two. "So why isn't he coming over here?"

"He said if you want to talk with him then come over there."

Mako lifted his beer and took a long draft, slid back his chair, and rose with a purpose. He straightened his silk shirt and arrayed his gold to its best advantage. He hitched up his pants and ran his hands over his black, greased-back haircut. The other two looked at each other, then finally stood, mimicked their boss, and fell in behind him as he walked across the room. Mako looked thirtyish, short, trim, and slightly muscular. His two goons stood taller, but their beltlines suffered from taco overload. The contrast turned the heads of other patrons, and provoked a few chuckles that did not escape Mako.

Mako stopped about three feet behind Harpoon. "I think you have something that belongs to me."

Harpoon toked his beer before turning around. "I never saw you before in my life. Why would I have something of yours?"

Mako glanced at Krank whose unblinking stare menaced. "What you lookin' at, Cochise?"

"I'm lookin' at pretty nearly a perfect asshole."

Mako grimaced at the insult, but he stopped the two goons starting in Krank's direction. "What's this guy's story?"

Harpoon grinned. "He sees things other don't, and he can't tell a lie."

"Listen, Homie, I think you know what I'm talkin' 'bout."

"I don't have an idea what you're talkin' about, and I'm not your Homie."

Lottie walked up. "Is there a problem here? I don't want any trouble."

Mako looked at her, then Krank, then Harpoon. "Ok, *ese,* we'll talk again." He turned on his heel and ricocheted off his goons who still stood sentry. "Outta the way, *pendejos!*" He shoved them aside and headed for the door.

Lottie waited while Harpoon turned toward her. "What the hell's that all about? I mean, who are those guys?"

"I have no idea!" He shrugged, arms in the air. "Krank said there would be trouble, and sure enough."

"That was talkin', not trouble." Krank stared through the bar mirror at something no one else saw.

***

Rodolfo Rattler could not remember a better time. He'd crawled through the gopher hole maze for what seemed an eternity. Finally he had emerged into a new life somewhere near the great sand pile. Gophers scurried around everywhere, laughing and singing,

"Dig a little, chew a little, clap, clap, clap."

I have *mucha hambre*, man. Starvin', *hombre!* Ain't had nothing for days. No wonder I couldn't find no gophers. They're all over here havin' a fiesta. He coiled, ready to strike the closest gopher. Look at that *pendejo estúpido.* He's dancing around like a loco right here in front of me. There's something wrong with this, man. This is way too easy. *Comprende?*

He looked around making sure there wasn't a trap or a human nearby. Okay, I'm gonna give him the old rattle, just in case there's something wrong here. His signature Cha, Cha, Cha! rattle began its staccato buzz.

The endangered pocket gopher stood for a minute before picking up Rodolfo's beat. When he danced again, he moved in a somewhat more interpretive style than a classic Cha, Cha, Cha. More like a conga line.

"Cha cha cha cha cha - ugh!

Cha cha cha cha cha - ugh!"

Other gophers joined in behind the first, laughing and kicking. The line circled Rudolfo.

This is some crazy stuff, man! Rudolfo couldn't believe the scene before him. *I got gophers into the next century, and they're dancing around me like I'm their closest buddy. I can't stand it. Man. I gotta eat.* He struck the last gopher in the conga line. Rudolfo's rattle stopped, but the conga line continued on through the dune oats toward one of the many gopher holes where they all disappeared.

"Cha cha cha cha cha - ugh!"

Rudolfo had a full, contented feeling after the gopher settled into the sweet spot in his stomach. Actually, very contented. He was feelin' right and felt like swaying. Maybe even dancing, except snakes don't dance. *Man, I'm feeling good. I can't get the gopher song outa my head. I feel like smiling, 'cept snakes don't smile.* He started his rattle again but instead of his famous Cha, Cha, Cha, he rattled the gopher dance.

"Cha cha cha cha cha - ugh!"

He swayed back and forth in time to his rattle and shook his booty. *Hey, man, life's really good. Know what I mean?*

***

The rest of the afternoon had passed pleasantly for Harpoon and Krank at The Island Joynt. The beers came at regular enough intervals, sustaining a sense of well-being but not inducing euphoria. Krank joined in the conversation at one point and showed an uncommon level of wisdom not normally associated with jocks, shrimp boat deckhands, or drunks. He even tried verbalizing his sense of foreboding about the Powers coming together on the Island: that something big would change the Island. "Spirits are collecting. Much Power's coming to the Island. Big conflict. Good and evil struggling. Maybe dangerous."

"Sounds like a Port A city council meeting," Harpoon quipped.

Lottie screwed her face into a question mark. "Spirits? What spirits?"

"Actually, you had one in here earlier." Harpoon cringed at his slip.

"A spirit in here? Today?"

"It gave me a chill." Krank shivered, remembering.

"Ok, guys. That's it. No more beer. Bar's closed for you two." Lottie picked up their beer bottles.

Harpoon's resigned expression showed nothing more to lose. "Actually it was Stevie Ray Vaughan."

"Stevie Ray Vaughan? Here today? Right!" She looked disgusted. "You two really gotta go home and sleep this one off."

"But . . ."

Lottie was adamant, They must go home and sober up. Harpoon had argued their way out of the disgrace of being chauffeured home in a cab. She did agree, except for the crazy talk, they really didn't seem particularly drunk. The two exited the Joynt and stood hugging up as only two inebriates can, then separated toward their pickups.

The afternoon sky had clouded up and now hung dark and foreboding. There were still a couple of hours before sundown, but already getting dark. Thunder rumbled in the distance. The wind gusted and a few whitecaps glistened in the harbor.

The heady smell of saltwater mingled with negative ions, heightening awareness and sending tingles racing up Harpoon's backbone. Very refreshing, he thought, as he looked skyward. The oyster shell gravel crunched behind him while he fumbled for his keys. He turned and saw Mako's two associates standing closer than he wished.

"Like I said, Mako wants to talk to you." Goon One motioned Harpoon in the direction of their empty waiting car.

"I've got a better idea. Why don't you two assholes get in your car and get out of town?"

The Goon Two said, "You dissin' us, man?"

"'Dissin' you? What does that mean?" Harpoon asked.

"Are you dis-re-spectin' us?"

Harpoon laughed. "I've never respected you. How can I dis-re-spect you?"

"Maybe you can respect this." The first goon pulled a square shaped pistol from behind his back in a blur of movement.

Harpoon studied the gun. "Whatever happened to pistols with round barrels?"

"Cut the crap, Homie. Get in the car." He motioned with the gun.

Before anyone could move, a lighting bolt and ear-splitting thunderclap ripped through the heavens. A reflex sent the goons' hands to cover their ears. Harpoon stood transfixed. *I swear that sounded like the Stevie Ray Vaugn's intro to "Wham."* Krank appeared from nowhere. Harpoon had never seen anyone's foot move as fast. In addition to his other football feats, Krank was the punter. He landed a kick on the point of the gun-toting goon's chin that would have cleared the end zone. The goon folded like dirty laundry while his gun rattled across the gravel. Goon Two considered his options for an instant before Krank's kick landed on the side of his left knee. He crumpled with a howl.

"I don't think you've lost a single step since high school, Good Buddy." Harpoon picked up the gun, ejected the shell, released the clip, and threw all the pieces into the harbor. They dragged the two to their car and propped the cripple behind the wheel. "Now get off the Island and tell your *amigo,* Mako, to stay away from us.

CHAPTER | 9

The events of the last couple of days troubled Lottie. Her ongoing relationship with Harpoon Conroy had provided a year of emotional tranquility – something she treasured. She could rely on Harpoon, even though he was often away shrimping. An independent, self-reliant woman, she knew his absences let some air into their romance, which otherwise might die of asphyxiation. Besides, these hiatuses heightened the pleasure of their time together. But something was different. She didn't understand Harpoon since he'd returned from his last outing.

He had been worried about his finances for some time and had on occasion, after a few beers, complained he didn't see a way out if things didn't change. She knew he didn't fear financial ruin. He had other options if he found himself without his beloved *Cordon Blues.* He feared the loss of a lifestyle, which he loved. A lifestyle of a family farmer eking out an existence from the soil when he and his family would be better served by his working in a factory somewhere.

Now Harpoon saw ghosts – Stevie Ray Vaughan, for crying out loud! Only a blues musician like Harpoon would see a blues musician's ghost. Then, these cliché criminal types showed up wanting something from Harpoon he could not or would not provide. She could see clouds forming on her life's horizon and stormy weather ahead.

Her life had never sailed on tranquil seas. As she went about her bartending duties with less than enthusiasm, her uneasiness recalled a life that had really begun only when she had rolled into Port Aransas, sixteen years earlier.

She was born thirty-five years ago in the tiny township of Wallkill, New York, on her family's dining room table. Her mother's labor set in suddenly, so a neighbor helped with the birthing, since the Catskill Regional Hospital in Ferndale was out of the question. Her dad got the traditional "plenty of hot water." None of this proved distinctive in itself, but the events taking place across town in the Wallkill Town Hall at that exact time provided the historical significance. The town council busied itself by passing an ordinance (applauded by the one-hundred fifty or so hippie-hating townsfolk packed into the tiny hall) prohibiting the Woodstock music festival from occurring in the town's industrial park that had contracted for the event. This shortsighted hippie exclusionary decree thus propelled the now iconic Woodstock Festival onto Max Yasgur's dairy farm pasture near Bethel.

The Wallkill hubris at flouting this undesirable hippie invasion soon faded as the event bourgeoned into more than four hundred thousand attendees, producing the largest traffic jam in New York State history. The lost commercial opportunity for the town's merchants proved debilitating, but as "Woodstock" entered our lexicon as defining an event that changed the culture of a nation, Wallkillers realized the festival would have put their town on the map for all eternity. For decades the sense of loss pervaded the small town like a pall and left the folks reminiscing endlessly about what might have been.

Lottie's childhood in this vacuous mental environment resulted in a bothersome itch about learning exactly what was missing from her life. Her adolescent beauty fueled the problem, as, at an early age, she had to fight off the advances of any male not already gelded. Before puberty she knew she had something men desperately wanted.

As the ink dried on her high school diploma, she headed south for The Big Apple. She found New York not easily conquered, and legions of pretty girls just like her were in the fight. Big Apple life became an exercise in survival not soon forgotten. A nice conventioneer from Ohio rescued her from a topless bar and took her home to wed.

Three years of small town married life mirrored Wallkill enough to resurrect her itch. She had been careful about not getting pregnant, so when she discovered her husband's affair with his high school sweetheart, she decided to scratch the itch. A note left for her philandering husband said she would send him a forwarding address for the divorce papers.

She departed in January during a snowstorm after she taped a thermometer onto her 1962 Chevrolet's radio aerial. She would drive south until the thermometer registered seventy degrees.

Fortunately, her thermometer hit seventy-two degrees on the Mustang Island Causeway; otherwise, the Gulf of Mexico provided a problem for driving further. Cotton-candy clouds dotted the eye-glistening blue of the sky. A light breeze blew landward and pushed up low swells that smoothed out on the beach with filigree foam. She fell in love with the saltwater and the beach. The healing balm of salt air and the rustle of the surf cleansed away her itch as she wiggled her toes in the sand

The Island Joynt in Port Aransas hired her as a waitress. "Lifers" staffed the venerable old café, a fixture in Island culture for as long as anyone could remember. They kept their fingers on the Island pulse while they dispensed flapjacks, biscuits, chicken fried steaks, fried seafood, gossip, and wisdom. The owner, overcome by the bright eyed, blonde beauty, went against custom and hired a newcomer. The old guard, both staff and customers, felt cool toward the interloper at first, but her enthusiasm, charm, and natural beauty won them over. She settled into a lifestyle she never dreamed possible back in Wallkill. After five years, the owner, now quite old, made Lottie restaurant manager. His decision to sell the restaurant came after a bout of illness. Lottie finessed a loan and bought the Joynt with the help of her then boyfriend and town banker.

Over the years, she improved the facility, added a bar, enhanced the menu, and a restaurant critic from Texas Monthly wrote that she produced food worthy of a Port Aransas trip.

She morphed into island life like a native and even developed a skill at fishing. She spent all her free time in the bays chasing trout and redfish rather than on beach time and bar hopping. At first she went fishing with suitors who all dreamed of getting a little outdoor loving. When she could afford a fifteen-foot scooter with a forty-horse outboard, she fished alone much of the time. Like Helen of Troy, the sight of Lottie wade-fishing in a bikini knee deep in the shallows, could draw a flotilla of fishing boats.

A lifetime of dealing with unwanted advances from the opposite sex served her well in her deep-seated feeling that marriage didn't suit her. Her one serious relationship with Park Ranger Jeffrey Randall after the hurricane several years back finally crumpled under the weight of the memory of a friend they both loved, the reclusive poet, the only fatality of the hurricane. The responsibility they felt for his death pushed Lottie and Jeffrey into a platonic friendship.

She could recount a litany of wannabee suitors who provided entertainment, but little else, until this handsome shrimper showed up in her bar a few years back. At first they had a sparring friendship with the usual chucking and jiving between bartender and bar stool sitters. She could not understand why in the years they were friends, he never made a pass.

A year ago, she changed her tack. "So, Harpoon, tell me again what you do when you're not wearing your little white rubber booties on your boat?"

"I always wear my little rubber booties."

"Even in bed?"

"Especially in bed." Harpoon's face split into a randy grin.

"Why, Harpoon Conroy, you're hittin' on me."

"No, but I think you're comin' on to me."

"If I was comin' on to you, I would invite you over for a simple peasant broth I fixed this morning."

"I take simple peasant broth well. Actually, the simpler, the better."

"Well, now. Let me get Cindy to sub in here, and we're off to see the wizard, so to speak."

One of her best decisions ever, she knew. Forget that sex with him had an unaccustomed tenderness, the urgency of a man just returned from two weeks at sea, and the stamina of a beautiful, fine-tuned body. The warmth of his giving soul convinced her she'd found what had been missing for so many years. Her life was complete – at least until two days ago.

"So where's your true love tonight? I know he's not shrimping." Wiley Coots lowered his ponderosity onto a barstool.

"He and Krank had an extended bout with Shiner Bock today and lost. I sent them home for R & R." Lottie rolled a longneck in a napkin, popped the top and set it in front of Wiley.

"A guy in the parking lot said he thought he saw a scuffle between Harpoon, Krank, and a couple of other guys. Said Krank was a draggin' a guy back to his car by the hair."

"My God, what will happen next!" She threw open the bar pass-through and ran into the parking lot. She stood in the pelting rain with her hand shielding her eyes and searched for Harpoon or Krank. Back inside, she dialed Harpoon's cell phone.

"Hey there . . ."

"Harpoon, what the hell's goin' . . . "

"Harpoon here, leave me a message and I'll get back to you."

"Jesus Christ, he's not answering his phone." She

slammed the phone into the cradle with such force the customers all turned to look.

"Well, now, aren't we getting' a little too excited over our boy?" Wiley asked. "He's a big strong man. He can take care of himself, right?"

"Harpoon's not who I'm worried about. It's those thugs that came in here lookin' for him today."

After they disposed of the two malfeasants, Harpoon and Krank high-fived and hugged again.

"This first class beer buzz should not be wasted on sleep, *amigo*," Harpoon said.

"What you thinkin'?"

"It's Jam Session Night at Good Pickens Bait Shop, Wine Bar and Blues Emporium. Maybe we should celebrate our victory and lay down some blues."

"Sounds like a plan. I'll go home and get my tom toms."

Harpoon nodded agreement. He knew Krank could beat out some crazy blues backup on his ancestral instruments.

Close to Krank's houseboat, a blaze of lightning illuminated a car parked at the double-track leading off the highway into Wilson's Cut. It looked like the car driven by the two guys he had roughed up in the Joynt's parking lot. The car sat there for several minutes before roaring off in the direction of Corpus Christi.

He looked across the cut before going inside for his drums, and saw Coyote sitting in the Spartina and smiled at him. *You're gettin' wet.*

Coyote kept up his silly grin. *That happens to us coyotes.*

You have caused much mischief today, Coyote.

Actually, I was chowin' down on gophers. Forget dogs and cats, these little buggers are everywhere—laughing and singing. The Island's a veritable buffet. Life is good. I feel like singin'.

You conjured up spirits and bad people today. Krank grimaced.

Coyote let out a howl not unlike Sweet Irma Thomas. *No man! No time for that.* He howled again. *Lord, I feel right. So what's happnin, Bro.*

Goin' down to Slidin' Will's and beat out some blues.

Maybe I'll see you there. Another howl – reminiscent of Stevie Ray Vaughan's "She's My Pride and Joy."

CHAPTER | 10

The inclement weather had cleared the beach and the tourists scurried for alternate forms of entertainment. Good Pickens Bait Shop, Wine Bar, and Blues Emporium filled up rapidly with condo commandos, Island Trash, and tourists, since Slidin' Will didn't charge a cover at the door on Jam Session Night. Slidin' Will and his bartenders popping wine corks and long necks sounded like the Fourth of July, while the revelers settled in and adjusted their attitudes. The familiar smell of the bait tanks drifted into the dusky room and made the regulars feel right at home.

Harpoon nursed a Shiner Bock at the bar and waited for the jam session to crank up.

"You still look like shit, bro." Will slid a fresh beer in front of Harpoon. "Thought you might be in a better mood than the other day."

"These are different times, Will. Lots of things don't make sense."

"Well, you're in the right place. Some blues can straighten things out. Looks like we're gonna have some guys with real chops blowin' tonight, and a good crowd to boot." Will looked around the almost full barroom, and at the Fightin' Ridley High

School Band director as he set up his tenor sax on the bandstand.

"I don't suppose Stevie Ray Vaughan will sit in tonight."

"OK, that's your last one!" Will grabbed up the beer he had just served Harpoon.

"I'm tellin' you, man, I see and hear Stevie's ghost everywhere. It's makin' me crazy."

"If you see him in here tonight, give me a head start, 'cause I don't want to run over nobody."

"I don't know about Stevie, but Krank's bringin' his toms."

Will grinned and shook his head. "We might be the only blues place ever with a Indian on tom toms."

Krank came through the door with three drums slung with leather thongs over his shoulder. A couple of tourists sat in Krank's accustomed place next to the bandstand, but they reconsidered when he stared at them – close range. After they fled, Krank set up his drums and moved on to the barstool beside Harpoon. "I saw Coyote out at the Cut."

"Oh, Jesus, not more trouble."

"Says he didn't cause all the mischief today."

"Not even the spirits."

"No mention of spirits."

"What else did he say?" Harpoon toked his beer in anticipation of bad news.

"Not much. Mostly he just grinned and howled. He was stoned."

"Stoned?"

"Says he gettin' right eatin' gophers these days."

"Can anything good come from a gopher-stoned coyote?"

"He sings pretty good. Sounds kinda like Stevie Ray Vaughan."

"Jesus! Not again." Harpoon slumped on the bar.

A tall, skinny, disheveled man in dirty jeans and a "Go, You Ridleys" tank top that showed his hairy armpits shuffled in. His gray beard hung below his waist as he made his way through the crowd. He climbed onto the bandstand and sat at the Hammond B3 and nervously flexed his fingers. He switched on the organ and reverberator and noodled aimlessly on the keyboard, quietly at first, barely heard above the din of conversations. But as he gathered himself and pounded out a truckin' rhythm that built in volume, the crowd shifted their attention. Finally, Big Momma Thornton's original version of "Hound Dog" rocked out of the B3 and caused a quiver on the bait tank water.

Slidin' Will, with his Gibson slung over his shoulder and his green bottleneck slide on his little finger, approached Harpoon and Krank. "It sounds like Fuck-'Em-All-Ted came to play tonight. How about we jump in?"

The three moved to the bandstand where Ted wailed on the organ and the high school band director backed him on sax. Krank's tom tom beat filled in the cracks, while Will's guitar riff and Harpoon's cross harp growls rounded out a stompin' "Hound Dog." Will took the first vocal:

> *You ain't nothing but a hound dog*
>
> *Been snoopin' round my door*
>
> *You ain't nothing but a hound dog*
>
> *Been snoopin' round my door*
>
> *You can wag your tail*
>
> *But I ain't gonna feed you no more.*

Pent up frustration over recent events overtook Harpoon as he stepped to the mike. His passion growled through the harp, and the melody threaded through glissandos melding into bent notes and arpeggios that cascaded over the audience like summer rain. When he eased into the vocal, the audience erupted in standing applause.

Will swung into a slidin' guitar solo and everybody in the room rocked and swayed when he took the last verse. Fuck-'Em-All-Ted moved in behind with a howling organ solo, leaving no question what an asshole Hound Dog is. Ted modulated up one key and amped up the volume and sax, harmonica, guitar and tom toms swung in behind. The whole place jumped up screaming. Then, from somewhere, a guitar roared in with a technique, electric angst, and power never heard on the Island before. People stood like statues and looked for the source. The band missed a beat but recovered and kicked back in and riffed a background for the guitar solo while they looked at each other in disbelief. After thirty-six bars, the guitar faded out as quickly as it had materialized. The band finished the chorus and ended abruptly.

Shaken, Will mumbled, "Well, there you have it, "Hound Dog" like it's never been done before."

Ted squirmed on the organ seat and looked around the room dazed and showed his closest approximation of a smile. "Hey, hey! Fuck 'em all!"

Will covered the mike and asked Harpoon, "Tell me one more time about Stevie Ray."

"Man, I don't know where that came from."

Will pointed to the sound system. "It came out of there, but the Lord only knows how it got in."

Harpoon's load lifted a little as the night progressed. Everybody seemed inspired by the mystery guitar solo, and each played like they were gonna blow Good Pickens Bait Shop, Wine Bar, and Blues Emporium down, while the crowd roared with pleasure.

After "last call," the musicians had divvyed up the tip jar over one last beer, and Harpoon and Krank stood in the empty parking lot. Two crew boats chugged up the ship channel, their outlines silhouetted in the full moon. The musty smell of wetlands and diesel smoke permeated the air and Harpoon drew in a big breath and slowly exhaled. "She's been in dry dock only two days, and I miss ol' *Cordon Blues* already."

Krank adjusted the leather thongs that hung over his shoulder. "Those assholes will be back. You know that."

"Did Coyote tell you that?'

"Don't need Coyote to know this. Bad guys aren't used to gettin' their ass kicked."

"They'll be lookin' for payback?"

"They'll be lookin' for a ton of ganja that's gone missin'."

"My God, what a mistake this whole thing's turned out to be. . . ."

Before Harpoon could continue, he heard singing and turned and saw four coyotes sitting together on a dune, silhouetted by the moon, all in full throat belting out Hound Dog in close harmony like the Back Street Boys. After a long minute, the two focused properly and assessed what they saw. They looked at each other, then back at the apparition.

Harpoon spoke first, "Okay, you think this is not the sixteen continuous hours of beer drinking, and we're actually hearing four coyotes sitting on a sand dune singing in harmony?"

"It's possible."

"Ok, let's say we're actually hearing them sing, then who's backing them up on guitar?"

"Don't know, but it sounds like . . . ."

Harpoon held up his hand. "I don't want to hear it!"

CHAPTER | 11

Something about Dick Walzem, minister of music at Crystal Epistle Church Of Everlasting Enlightenment, bothered The Right Reverend Hannibal Jones. Short and bespectacled, Walzem might have appeared the consummate religious professional except for the coiffed hairstyle, shifty eyes, and God-awful cologne. These negative vibes made Rev. Jones wish he had chased down Walzem's references with greater enthusiasm. Walzem had responded a year ago to an ad placed in the Texas Bible Church Herald. God, it seems, had called the previous Crystal Epistle Minister of Music to a televangelist show with international outreach that offered a much bigger paycheck.

Rev. Jones had felt time-pressed to fill the position since the congregation and television audience felt the Crystal Epistle's music a major part of its services. He knew many in the radio audience listened just for the music. Now, a year later, after he had rushed hiring Walzem, Rev. Jones had issues needing attention. Walzem's penchant for Praise music particularly bothered him. Rev. Jones squirmed in his leather executive's chair as he read the A.C. Nielson audience ratings for the previous month's TV and radio broadcasts. The numbers had drifted south month to month like an ebb tide until this past month – when they plummeted. "This frigging Praise music's gonna bury us!" The reverend slammed his meaty fist on the massive desk

Uncomfortable from overindulgence at the Wednesday breakfast buffet at the Island Joynt, he pulled open the middle right desk drawer, removed a plastic bottle of chewable antacid pills and crammed two of them into his mouth. He was busily crunching the tablets when Dick Walzem arrived for the ten o'clock meeting requested by the reverend.

"Mornin,' Reverend, and a beautiful day today. Maybe we should adjourn out to Mud Island and round up a few redfish." Dick slouched into a chair across the desk from the Reverend.

"Redfish, my ass! Take a look at the radio and TV ratings for last month. A few more months of your Praise music and we'll be sellin' fish roadside." Rev. Jones leaned forward so forcefully when he stuffed the reports into Dick's hands, he found himself standing. Not wanting to lose poise, he walked around the desk and hung his left butt-cheek on the groaning desk. "Gospel music's what got us here and Gospel's what'll get us back. The Good Book says, 'Make a joyful noise unto the Lord.' First Serbians Chapter 6, Verse 8, and amen. Now I'm here to tell you Praise music is anything but joyful."

"But, Reverend, it's what's happening. I mean, watch those other televangelists, and you see those folks with their arms over their heads swayin' back and forth like they're hypnotized." Dick stood demonstrating.

"Hypnotized? They're asleep! We need to see them wavin' their wallets and checkbooks back and forth. My God, man, Praise music is seven words and seven notes sung seven times. They might as well be stoned after that. We need the old hymns. We need Gospel. I'd even take blues music over that Praise stuff. By that I mean blues with Godly lyrics of course, and amen. You gettin' my drift? I want people to rejoice in the Lord and to fork it over by the bushel, and amen."

Dick sat for a minute and studied the reports, then stood.

"Reverend, if it's Gospel and blues you want, Gospel and blues you'll get."

The Right Reverend Hannibal Jones raised his arms in exultation. "Halleluiah! Praise God, and amen!"

The fishermen arrived before dawn; all needed bait, fishing tackle, and rental boats after Will had only about an hour of sleep. The wine bar was a wreck from all the revelers the night before and had to be cleaned as time allowed. The rush of serious fishermen had slowed, and during the time before the more casual anglers arrived around nine o'clock, after their lattés and scones, Will had set the chairs on the tables in preparation for mopping up all the fun that had spilled over the previous night.

Will heard the cowbell on the screen door, but could not see the entrant through the forest of chairs on the tables. His nose twitched when assaulted by truly industrial strength men's cologne overpowering even the bait tank odor. Moving among the tables and chairs was a small bespectacled man in a pompadour hairdo.

He approached Will with his hand outstretched. "Brother Pickens, I'm Dick Walzem, minister of music over at the Crystal Epistle Church of Everlasting Enlightenment."

Will held his hands up to indicate they were dirty from cleaning and therefore unshakable. "I've seen you here before. You need some bait?"

"Actually, not this time. I need your help." Walzem pulled out an ironed handkerchief and patted his brow.

Will waited in anticipation of a request for a church fundraiser donation. When none came, he asked, "So . . . how can I help you?"

"I know you're a well respected blues musician, and I've heard some of your early recordings. I know local musicians perform with you here. Actually, I wanted to come for your jam session last night, but we had a special prayer meeting over at the Epistle."

"Should'a come. Made a believer out'a me."

"A believer?"

"Yeah, but I don't know in what. I've never been religious, but now I believe there's some strange stuff out there."

"Well, you see, Brother Pickens, that's what I need to talk to you about." Walzem took off his glasses and cleaned them on his ironed handkerchief.

"I don't quite understand."

"We need you and some of your musician friends to play for the Crystal Epistle services."

"Play what?"

"Why, blues, of course."

Will stood, mouth agape. He did not understand what he had just heard or how to respond. Fortunately, the screen door cowbell clanged again. He held his hand toward Walzem and signaled a pause. "'scuse me a minute."

Walzem took a chair from a table and with his handkerchief, carefully cleaned it before he sat down. After several minutes Will returned, and Walzem popped up with an expectant smile. "So, Brother Pickens, what do you think?"

"Let me get this straight. You want a blues band to play for the Crystal Epistle Church services?" Will took another chair down and slowly lowered onto it.

Walzem followed suit and sat again. "Actually just for the broadcast services on Sundays."

"Broadcast? You mean television and radio?"

"That's right, Reverend Jones wants to broaden our appeal to our electronic audience with Gospel and blues music."

"Gospel too?"

"Yes, I'm headin' over to Corpus Christi from here and talk to Sweet Bessie Thompson about bringin' a Gospel quartet to the Epistle.'

"We'd be playin' with Sweet Bessie?"

"Certainly some of the time." Walzem's face took on the radiance of progress.

"Sunday's our busiest day here at the bait shop. There's no way I could get away even if I could get anybody to play on Sunday. Most musicians sleep it off Sunday mornings."

"Of course, we will pay for your services. Enough for someone to watch your bait house with profit left over."

"You pay musicians?"

"Oh, yes. It's very common. Larger churches pay for organists, soloists, and even orchestras." Walzem's smile gained confidence.

"It's crazy, man. We don't know no religious songs. We mostly sing 'bout folks tryin' to get laid, or folks miserable 'cause they baby done done 'em wrong."

"Think about it, though. Twelve bar blues is one four-bar phrase repeated, followed by a four bar resolution. So that's sixteen beats, sixteen beats, and another sixteen. That's not a lot different than Praise music except we just keep on singin' the same Praise until everybody gets sick of it."

"You're losin' me."

"Let's just pick up some Praise lyrics and drop them in a blues format. As far as Bessie's concerned, Gospel uses the same format, so you can just fill in behind her quartet. Simple, right?" Walzem beamed with the light of revelation.

"I got a bad head today." Will lowered his head into the crotch of his thumbs and rubbed the throbbing place between his eyes. "I gotta to think on it. Just don't seem right to me, blowin' blues one night here in the wine bar and in church the next day."

"Never forget, Brother Pickens, Jesus turned water into wine."

"Yeah, there's a juke joint 'cross town still doin' that same thing. Besides, the players I know got no church-goin' clothes."

"No worry there. We will provide choir robes for the musicians."

A huge guffaw rolled out of Will. "A blues band in choir robes? You gotta be kiddin'."

Walzem sensed he might be losing ground and said,

"Maybe we should pray about it, Brother Pickens."

"There's probably prayin' to be done, okay, but it's you prayin' 'bout whether you gone plumb crazy."

Dawn broke much sooner than Krank expected or wanted. He rubbed his throbbing head and bloodshot eyes then struggled up and shuffled to the hot plate and made his coffee. He considered his peace pipe, but instead, steadied his coffee mug and moved out to the chaise on the houseboat deck.

He downed his third swig before he focused on Coyote sitting in the spartina across Wilson's Cut. *Maybe you had too much fun last night.*

When you feel this bad, you just know you had too much fun. Krank gestured toward Coyote with his mug. *Besides, you were whooping up it pretty good yourself – howling Back Street Boys harmony with three of your buddies. You better ease up eatin' those gophers, or you might get a buckshot butt massage.*

We were kickin' it though, right?

Oh, you were on it big time, but who backed you on guitar?

Strange things are in the air. Coyote loosed a howl and trotted off, stopped, and turned. *Diablos are descending – be diligent!* Another howl, and he bounded away.

CHAPTER | 12

His head still ached from yesterday's beer-a-thon, but Krank knew the Epistle grounds needed lots of work. The local nursery always helped him on prices for plants he needed. The hybiscus bed was already prepared for a colorful display in front of a wall of three-year-old oleanders. Hibiscus and oleander topped his list of favorite interloper species because their root system tapped the ground water, and they grew rapidly without additional watering.

He stopped first at the Family Center Store for groceries and to exchange two empty twenty-pound propane tanks from his houseboat, and bumped into Lottie in the produce department.

"I'm pickin' up fruit for the bar and some other items needed at the Joynt. You look like you could use a little pick-me-up yourself." Lottie's smile showed surprise. "I didn't expect you'd be up so bright and early after your big day."

"Yesterday was big, alright."

"You and Harpoon had a little adventure with the hoodlums, I understand."

"Nothing we couldn't handle."

"You guys make me crazy. They're obviously bad guys. They look like they kill people just to stay in practice." Fire flashed from her eyes.

"They need more practice."

"Christ Almighty, you two have just gone plain goofy on me." She wheeled down the aisle without a backward glance.

The landscape nursery owner helped load the two-dozen hibiscus plants in and around the lawnmower and other equipment in Krank's pickup. "You've got yourself a big project there, Krank."

"Good weather for it." Krank closed the tailgate and walked around the truck to the driver's door. "Thanks for the help on the price."

"We need to thank you for all the good things you do around town, good buddy."

Krank wanted the plants in the ground and watered before the heat of the day. He immediately unloaded the gallon cans and spaced them for planting. He had them rowed up like grave markers by eleven o'clock and then unloaded his mower and grass edging equipment. He cherished his John Deere riding mower, although he had a gasoline push mower for the smaller widow's yards. The John Deere fired up immediately, and he started mowing at the front of the property and worked toward the beach.

About one-third through the mowing, he noticed the missing gopher holes. Instead of the usual five or six mounds normally needing repair, only one stood like a small sand volcano. As he mowed closer he saw three gophers lying out on the sunny side of the gopher mound sunning themselves. Usually, the slightest movement in the area and gophers scurried down their holes.

He mowed within feet of the mound before the three rodents stood, stretched, and moseyed toward their hole. Krank knew he was still hung over, but he would swear each of the rodents held up a high-five as it disappeared down the hole.

He sat and stared at the hole. "Strange things are in the air." He got off the mower with his small gopher-shovel, filled the hole, spread the rest of the sand, and continued mowing toward the beach dunes.

The Epistle practiced perfect dune-maintenance according to the laws governing them. Islanders considered messing with the dunes one notch below child molestation. About a twenty-foot-wide patch of grass occupied the space between the dunes and the end wall of the sanctuary that supported the Jumbotron overlooking the dunes and beach below. Krank turned the corner of the church and launched into this last bit of grass butchery but stopped dead and turned off the mower. What a sight. The water stayed blue to the beach with only low swells. The beach was clean, and sea oats topped the dunes beautifully spread with the brilliance of yellow sea daisies entwined by purple morning glory flowers and railroad vine. How could anyone wish for anything more than time for enjoying this sight. . . Wait a minute!

"What's happening?" He involuntarily pointed at three vehicles about one hundred yards down the beach parked beside the dunes. Three men dug in the dunes with shovels while another wandered around with what looked like a metal detector. A fifth man stood down on the beach and directed their efforts. One of the men limped badly, another's face looked like a mummy, and the man on the beach sparkled like King Tut from all the gold around his neck. What are these assholes doing here? They can't be digging in the dunes. That's against the law.

Harpoon answered his phone sleepily on the third ring. "I'm seriously compromised this morning, good buddy."

"You won't believe this."

"What?"

"The bad guys are down the beach from the Epistle diggin' in the dunes."

"It's against the law to dig in the dunes."

"I don't think that bothers criminals."

"You think they're lookin' for their ganja?"

"Coyote says, 'Diablos are descending'."

"Sounds like they're already here."

"Be diligent." Krank closed the cell phone.

He stood by his mower, wondering what to do, when an

argument broke out between the four in the dunes and the guy on the beach. Too far away to hear them shout, he read their disagreement from their gestures.

"We know those two fuckin' *pendejos* buried the pot in the sand dunes, right?" Mako shouted at the four guys up in the dunes. "So start digging, assholes."

"When he called from Guadalajara, did Gordo say where they buried it?" The metal detector man held up the device, "This thing's as useless as Gordo."

"Yeah, man, the Islands got twenty miles of sand dunes. You want us to dig them all up?" Goon One had a hard time being understood when he talked through all the bandages holding his chin together.

"He said they were pretty close to town and that they scratched 'X's' in the sand to mark the spots." Mako made an "X" with his arms.

"He scratched in the sand?" Goon Two shifted his weight to his good leg. "Those X's didn't last until they got back in their truck. This is ridiculous. I'm outa here." He heaved the shovel skyward, and unfortunately, it landed very near Mako.

"If that shovel had hit me, you'd be diggin' yourself a hole, *sabe*? You need to be more careful, especially with your mouth." Mako watched all four of the men climb down the dunes and circle around him. He knew when to fold 'em. "Okay, okay! I got another idea. I still think the Harpoon guy and Tonto know where they buried the weed. For all we know they helped those two idiots bury the stuff."

A general mumbling of agreement followed.

"They would remember the place even without Gordo's *pinche* X's." Mako laughed at Gordo's stupidity. "The Gringos only gotta wait awhile, and then come back and dig it up, right?"

Goon Two nodded at Goon One. "We know where Cochise lives."

Goon One chimed in, "And we have a big score to settle with him. Maybe we come back out here tonight for a little show-and-tell session with the Indian?"

CHAPTER | 13

Krank watched Mako's gang stand around arguing and gesturing, until finally they piled back into their cars, driving away from Port Aransas. He continued watching them drive down the beach until they turned onto the access road and headed out toward Corpus Christi. He finished his mowing, edged, loaded his equipment, watered the hibiscus again, and picked up the empty plant containers for recycling.

Back on Wilson's Cut, he opened a bottle of Shiner Bock and stowed his groceries. Then he secured his yard work equipment in the shed. He stood on the deck and felt the onset of an epic sunset. A gentle Gulf breeze during the day had made his landscaping and yard work more pleasant. The musty smell of nature's cradle of life now wafted on the breeze, and tiny wavelets scudded down the Cut – spreading out to nestle among the spartina grass lining the channel. The wind had hatched a striped mackerel sky with bands of high, thin cirrus clouds. The edge of the glowing, blood-orange ball dipped slightly below the horizon and each cloud band caught fire in succession and raced toward Krank. The sun's reflection exploded in the back bay, and the panorama bloomed into a painting impossible to capture on canvas. Through this vision floated a flock of pink spoonbill roseates flying toward the bird sanctuary on Shamrock Island.

Krank stood transfixed, arms outstretched until the sun dropped from sight – then nodded an appreciative smile. Great Spirit Show good. Movement down the Cut caught his eye. Baitfish rustled around in the spartina and small mullet leaped frantically. An underwater force moved toward Krank. He quickly grabbed his bait-casting rig, bent down to his live well, and dipped up a mud minnow. He baited his bottom-rigged hook and cast down the Cut toward what must be a school of red fish headed his direction.

When the underwater movement reached the spot of his cast, he felt something hit the bait. He set the hook and tussled with a recalcitrant red fish. Within minutes he landed a nice seven-pounder. The ill-fated fish turned into two skin-on "half-shell" filets in less time than catching it.

Harpoon checked Caller ID and answered his cell phone. "So what happened with the bad guys?"

Krank said, "Redfish on the half-shell."

"When?"

"Three beers away."

"I'll bring a twelve pack." Harpoon clicked off.

Harpoon looked at Lottie across the bar almost apologetically. "Urgent business."

She cocked her head, a question mark on her brow. "With the bad guys?"

"That was Krank."

"Urgent business with Krank?"

"You know Krank. He doesn't call unless he wants to powwow."

"A twelve-pack powwow?" Lottie leaned over the bar almost nose-to-nose. "I think it's about time we had a little powpow, Buster!"

"I'll be back before midnight, I promise. So get powdered up, okay?" He smiled over his shoulder as he walked out.

"I'll be waitin' at home."

Krank took a handful of the small diameter mesquite limbs piled next to his grill. He broke them to length and placed them carefully on the fire grate over smoldering kindling. Satisfied the mesquite would catch fire, he took the filets into his rudimentary kitchen. He pulled out his culinary treasures from a small medicine cabinet and made a basic mixture of two parts sesame oil to one part rice wine vinegar. Into this he stirred teriyaki sauce, asian fish sauce, and a tablespoon of classic hoisin sauce. He spread the sauce over the two filets and put them in the refrigerator for marinating. He hand-smeared butter over two ears of corn while he held them with the shucks pulled back. Then he put the shucks back in place and tied the ends with a strip of shuck.

Out on the deck, coals gathered under the fire as they should. Good sign. He opened a fresh beer and stretched on the lounge chair and waited for Harpoon. He fell asleep minutes after he set his beer on the umbrella table:

Wilson's Cut looked like quicksilver under the immense full moon. Silence. Stillness. No surface ripple.

Coyote howled in the distance. The quicksilver quivered. "A good night for a midnight swim."

"Water's still a little cold."

"The grave is colder."

Krank awoke when Harpoon stepped onto the houseboat deck. "Good timing, partner. I was about to let the coals burn out."

Harpoon looked into the grill. "I'd say it's time for some cookin'." He held up the twelve-pack, "And of course a brewski or so wouldn't hurt either."

Krank took the beer into the fridge and brought out the fish filets and corn. "How 'bout dunkin' the corn in the Cut to soak the husks?"

Krank placed the half-shells on the grill, its scale/skin side down, and took the wet ears of corn from Harpoon and nestled them in the coals. Both men seemed satisfied with their efforts, so Krank added the grill lid, and rivulets of steam, smoke, and remarkable aromas wafted upward into the night.

"Won't be many folks eatin' better than us tonight." Harpoon opened his first brew.

Krank toked his beer and looked about to speak before lapsing into silence. The silence extended into awkwardness. The breeze had died, and the viscous stillness coated the scene and created the sense of life in slow motion. The grill smoke danced and slithered toward the full moon in ghostly apparitions. Occasionally, the plop of a leaping mullet and the far off whine of vehicle tires on the highway broke the stillness.

Harpoon had settled into a chair and finally interrupted the stillness. "I reckon you had more than red fish on your mind when you called."

Krank spoke after another uncomfortable pause, "Big problem comin' with bad guys."

"That's hard to argue, pardoner. We can't call in the cops, what with bein' co-conspirators, and all."

"They must think the pot's buried in the dunes."

"Sounds like somethin' those two idiots, Gordo and Bozo, would do, alright. Sorta accounts for the drug sniffing dogs goin' crazy, and Chief Crump not findin' any marijuana in their truck."

"The bad guys didn't know where to look." Krank lifted the grill lid to check progress.

"It won't be long before they decide we helped them bury the ganja, or worse, that we dug the stuff up and moved it, right?"

"Big problem then." Krank went back inside and left Harpoon to contemplate the magnitude of their dilemma. He returned with two platters, a spatula, and tongs. Harpoon got up and went for paper towels, forks, butter, and beer.

The spatula slid like a scalpel between the white of the meat and the crisp skin, and he lifted the filets onto the two platters and added an ear of corn with the tongs. The two embarked on a meal few people ever experience.

Krank's marinade did not mask the red fish flavor, but rather elevated the fish to a different sensory level. The fire-roasted corn turned life into a true wonder dancing on the two men's palates.

The conversation sagged again – the only sound was their chowing down with great pleasure. Finally, Krank looked up, leaned back, and finished his beer. "Coyote has us boxed in."

"How's that?"

"If we do nothing, bad guys surprise us one day – we lose. If we fight back and win, the police wonder what bad guys were after – we lose."

Harpoon leaned forward with a serious face. "I don't suppose there's any chance you could talk Coyote over to our side?"

"Trickster Coyote always leaves a turd."

"Yeah, you already told me that. I really wish he'd pinch one off on somebody else's doorstep every now and then."

Krank laughed for first time in awhile. "Might get lucky."

The meal passed pleasantly, and on their second beer after dinner, Harpoon's face lit up as he remembered his conversation with Will Pickens earlier in the day. "Will called me today. He said the minister of music from the Crystal Epistle visited the Wine Bar this morning."

"Early thirst?"

"He wanted Will to put together a blues band for their Sunday services at the Epistle." Harpoon laughed at the thought. "Will said they'd pay good money."

"Strange things are in the air."

"Actually strange music's in the air. Any music'd be better than the stuff I heard on their radio show last Sunday."

"Will wants a drummer?"

"An idea like this needs tom toms, don't you think?"

"Something different on TV. Indian beating tom toms in the Epistle."

"Will says they're tryin' to broaden their radio and TV audience with music."

"Tom toms need to raise the dead to get many new Indian listeners."

The subject of the dead sobered the two somewhat. Harpoon said, "What about our current problem; any ideas?"

"Wait."

"I guess the ball is in their court."

"Maybe they make a mistake."

"You out here alone bothers me if they decide to come after us with a whole gang. Why not move in with me until this blows over?"

"Coyote will keep me safe."

"He'll probably lay another chunk for me." Harpoon sat up and looked straight at Krank. "You know this whole idea was mine. If the law gives us trouble, they will only know you came along as crew and had no idea about the drugs. It's turned out to be a really shitty idea, and I wish I could undo the whole mess."

"Things always work out."

"Did Coyote tell you this?"

"No, I liked the sound of it."

Harpoon stood to leave at about eleven o'clock after they ran out of beer. "Thanks, good buddy. Best meal I've had in recent memory, but I told Lottie I'd be back before midnight. So I better hook 'em up and head out." The two hugged and Harpoon strode off the deck, down the gangplank and left in his truck.

Krank doused the coals in the grill and carried all the cooking equipment and dishes back inside. He scrubbed and stored the utensils in minutes. The butane lantern lit the room and chair where he read, but last night's late jam session and all the days work ruled out anything but bed. He fell asleep within minutes. A coyote howl awakened him. Cursing, he turned over still half asleep. His eyes popped open when he remembered his afternoon dream. He swung his legs off the bed and sat up.

Headlights turned off the highway and headed down the two-track toward him as he stood in the dark on the houseboat deck. The lights went out. He slung a coil of stainless wire fishing leader over his arm and slid off the deck into the Cut. *I'm not sure the grave is this cold.*

He swam across the channel underwater and lay in the spartina in Coyote's usual place. The moon silhouetted the car coasting within thirty yards of the houseboat. The car doors opened and Goons One and Two slid stealthily out into the night. They crouched and skulked toward the houseboat. Actually, the skulking went poorly. Goon Two with the bad limp could hardly skulk at all, and made an audible grunt each time he put weight on the bad leg. Goon One's mummy-head bandages glowed in the full moon like the Jack-o-Lantern from hell.

About halfway to the houseboat, Goon Two's bad leg hung on a snag that sent him crashing on the ground. "Oh, great Jesus, that hurts. Why in the hell are we skulking around out here in the dark? Why don't we walk up there and blow the fuckin' Indian away?"

"You idiot, I think we've lost the element of surprise here. Why not go back and honk the horn. Maybe he'll come out and invite us in?"

"A few well placed shots would stir him up."

"Idiot, what good's a dead Indian? We're here to find out where they buried the ganja, right?"

"Yeah . . . well."

They continued their substandard skulking trying to catch Krank asleep. At the gangplank, Goon One held his finger up to his bandages indicating quiet. Unfortunately, they went up the gangplank together, and the boards sagged and emitted a groan approximating the death rattle of a bull moose.

Goon Two caught his balance before almost falling into the water. "What the fuck was that? This Indian got some living dead around here?"

Goon One, figuring Krank must be dead himself if he

wasn't awake by now, seized the night and ran up the gangplank, across the deck and burst into the houseboat cabin, pistol at the ready. Nothing. Goon Two limped up behind Goon One in the darkness and tumbled them both into the bedroom. No Indian. "We did that really well, don't you think?"

When the two Goons entered the house, Krank sprinted across the sand at the end of the Cut and slithered into the Goon's car back seat through an open window. He crouched on the floorboard between the seats and peeked out the window. The Goons limped and glowed their way back to the car.

Goon Two slid into the passenger seat with some difficulty. "This Indian's really pissin' me off. If I ever lay eyes on him again, I'm gonna cap him right there."

Goon One sat behind the steering wheel while he dug in his pockets for his car keys. "I'm with you on that one."

Using both hands, Krank slipped the wire garrotes over their heads unnoticed. He jerked their heads back against their headrests and drew a little blood without cutting their jugulars. Both men froze and ran damage control. Krank gave another light jerk, insuring full attention. "Use two fingers on your pistol handles, slowly remove, and drop them out the window." Goon Two made a fast movement and Krank brought him up short. "One good yank on the wires, and I will deliver your heads on Mako's front porch."

He heard the two pistols hit the ground outside the car. "This is number two for you. Number three, and your game is over. Seek out other employment, as you're not very good bad guys. You're lookin' for your marijuana, right?"

A burble of agreement sounded but no head movement. "If I told you, my friend and I have no idea where your marijuana is, would you believe me?" Another burble of agreement with no head movement. "Since Harpoon and I have no idea where your marijuana is, can you think of any reason Mako and you assholes need to bother us again?" A much louder burble and a dismal attempt at head shaking.

It took several minutes before they figured out Krank had tied the garrotes to the headrests and was gone. With each other's help, and with great difficulty, they extracted themselves from the devilish devices. The doors flew open as they lunged for their pistols – gone. The two leaned on each side of the car and tended the cuts on their throats. Neither spoke. Back in the car, they said in unison, "That fucker's gotta die."

CHAPTER | 14

ottie had worked at the Joynt until eleven o'clock, when she turned over the reins to the night manager. She hurried home, ran a hot bath with fragrant crystals, and soaked herself for half an hour. She had dressed again in shorts and blouse because she loved when Harpoon undressed her. Ripping off a nightgown over her head wasn't as romantic. As promised, he arrived before midnight, and went straight to the fridge, grabbed a beer, and plopped down in an easy chair.

"Why don't you make yourself at home, Friend?" Her sarcasm was not lost on Harpoon.

He leaped up, crossed the room, and enveloped her in a big hug. "I'm sorry. I've got a lot on my mind."

"I'd venture a lot of beer in your belly also."

"Krank and I knocked off a little over a twelve pack."

"How little?"

"I'd say I'm over the legal drivin' limit, but certainly not over the legal lovin' limit." He scooped her up and headed for the bedroom.

The sex was adequate if only perfunctory. They had achieved all the usual goals, and now Harpoon lay next to Lottie breathing heavily with his eyes shuttered in what seemed reflection – not of their lovemaking but of some interloping consideration.

After their year-long relationship, Lottie had no questions about Harpoon's talent on the connubial couch. Attentive, creative, and enthusiastic would best describe his approach to sex. He constantly amazed Lottie with his magical ability to transform his rough, calloused shrimper hands into velvet as the tips of his fingers explored her body – not just all the usual places, but her whole body. The backs of her shoulders, the undersides of her arms, her temples, the sides of her face, her neck and the area above her breasts felt like he had brushed her with feathers. She would shudder all over when he kissed the depression in her clavicle with his tongue. Once, on her birthday, he had drunk champagne from her clavicle. She smiled and thought back. Now that's creative lovemaking!

She sighed. Tonight's tryst was the Reader's Digest version. Maybe it was all the beer. She studied him in his close-eyed lassitude. Most of our lovemaking comes at two week intervals when he returns to port, horny as a New York traffic jam. It's really only been a couple of days, so maybe he's getting' caught up. She elbowed him. "So, should I be worried?"

He didn't open his eyes. "About what?"

"The other woman."

His eyes popped open, and he semi-sat up on one elbow with eyebrows furrowed. "What other woman?"

"The one you're savin' your good lovin' for."

"First off, I don't have to save up my lovin' – I'm spring loaded. Second, why would I want to be with another woman when I can be with you?" He now sat upright with a question mark for a face.

"You wouldn't be the first man to screw up a good thing."

"Cleverly said, but way off the mark. You're about the only thing I'm proud of right now."

"You must admit for the last three days you've weirded out to the point you could be Fuck-'Em-All-Ted's roommate."

"Trust me. It's nothing to do with you."

"Well, here we are, sittin' together buck naked, so out with it. The naked truth." She crossed her arms under her breasts, accenting her seriousness.

He closed his eyes again and lay quietly and hoped this too might pass. The elbow almost cracked a rib this time. When he opened his eyes, she was sitting cross-legged, arms akimbo with a fierceness in her eyes he had never seen before.

"I made a stupid mistake, that's all."

After a long pause she replied, "You made a stupid mistake? Nothing else?"

"It's a long story and one you shouldn't get involved in."

"Oh, well then, maybe there're other things I shouldn't get involved in. Like making half-assed love to a weirdo who obviously needs electric shock therapy."

"You aren't gonna let this go, are you?" He faced her while his eyes darted around avoiding eye contact."

"Right, good buddy. You're getting' close to losin' the most exciting thing in your life. Not to mention a pretty damn good friend. . . . So fess up, big boy."

"I committed a crime." His head hung, hiding his eyes.

"So you're a criminal. I'm sittin' here naked in front of a felonious violator of the laws of this great land. What law did you violate?"

"It's a long story."

"You've already told me that. You just haven't told me this story." She put her finger under his chin and raised his head. "So start from the beginning."

"A couple of weeks ago two guys came down the wharf while Krank and I washed down the Blues after we unloaded the shrimp. Their dress and accents made them out to be Mexican nationals. They asked if we would take them out on the *Cordon Blues*. They said stuff about always wantin' to see how a shrimp boat works. I told them we didn't give people rides on the Blues. They persisted and asked if I would meet them at Shorty's in about an hour."

"So you met them?

"Yeah, I thought maybe I could make a few bucks off them. You know I didn't have the Blues repair money. They sat at a back table, each with a beer, and greeted me like compadres. We talked for a few minutes while I figured what they wanted and why they wanted my boat in particular. They said the Blues was the biggest shrimp boat in the harbor. Then one pulled out a slip of paper with GPS coordinates and asked what I would charge to take them to this spot and back on the night of May 14th. They specifically said we had to be there by 9:00 p.m."

"It was obviously a smugglin' operation, right?"

"Sure seemed like it, so I got up tellin' them they had the wrong boy. Then the English speaking fat one grabbed my arm and pulled me down again. 'You ain't heard the whole deal, *amigo*,' he told me. He laid an envelope half an inch thick on the table and said, 'There's ten thousand dollars in there. It's yours for the job and nobody knows about it'"

"Good God! Ten thousand dollars?" Lottie held the back of her hand against her forehead in disbelief.

"Exactly what I said. This could cover the new engine and net winch for the Blues. We sat there starin' at each other across the table for quite a while."

"But you took the deal?"

"I'm ashamed to say I did. We picked up three bales of marijuana, brought them back, and put them on their pickup. We've' not seen them since, but it's all really turned to shit."

"What do you mean?"

"Chief Crump told the story the next morning at the Wisdom Table about arresting the two yo-yos we had on our boat the next morning for no Beach Parking Permits."

"No parking permits?"

"They also had unregistered pistols and no identification except Mexican. Even with their new drug sniffing dogs they couldn't find the marijuana."

"What happened with the two guys?"

"Chief Crump turned them over to INS and DEA agents after they paid their parking permit fine, and I guess they're either in the poky somewhere, or deported."

"That explains the hotshot golden boy and his two goons, then. They're lookin' for their weed."

"You got it! And they think Krank and I know where the stuff is. They think it's buried in the dunes, and before long they'll come for us to show them the location."

"And you don't know where." She thought for a minute. "Talking to Chief Crump will implicate you and Krank?"

"You catch on fast." Harpoon, silent, sat fiddling with the sheets. "Add bumpin' into Stevie Ray Vaughan's ghost everywhere I turn, and you have a very disturbed boyfriend."

"The Stevie Ray thing bothers me as much as the felony."

"Bothers you? How about me? And it's not only me. Krank and Slidin' Will have had some SRV close encounters also."

Lottie sat silent for a long time and grew angrier by the minute. "You know this makes you dumber than a wharf piling. God, Harpoon, we could have put the Joynt up as collateral to get a loan for fixing the Blues. Sell the Blues, and work here at the Joynt. You could have mortgaged your house. Anything but this! God, I can't stand this!"

She saw the hurt darken his face at her suggestions. "I'm sorry, this makes me furious that you wouldn't talk to me about this before you got involved. We could have worked something out." She sat shaking her head. "I'm very angry . . .very angry! I should throw your dumb ass out right now. God, I'm in love with a felon."

The felon leaned forward and kissed her clavicle with the slightest touch of his tongue. Well, she thought, the Good Book does say a lot about forgiveness.

CHAPTER | 15

Amos McAlister stared at a small mattress half buried in the beach by the ebbing tide. He kicked it, and then bent and grabbed the tag, which read in Spanish "Hecho en Honduras." He studied his clipboard for a few seconds then wrote in the "Miscellaneous Column" – "Honduran baby bed mattress."

Morning showers had plagued beach lovers throughout the month of June, but today was glorious for taking his "Daily Beach Trash Inventory." A light landward breeze cooled the air under a cloudless sky, and the sun, just passing the horizon, had not yet warmed the sand from the tide. The heavy moisture in the salt-laden air smelled clean and not befouled by the decay of expired marine life. This was the first year in many that Sargasso seaweed had not smothered the beach.

Amos was a retired professor from the Texas A&M University at Corpus Christi. Since returning to Port Aransas after his retirement, he'd become a fixture on the beach. Every day he walked two miles south from Caldwell Pier, clipboard in hand, and took his inventory. The tall, tan, shirtless (except in winter) figure, wearing only shorts and hiking boots, stood out, especially once his bushy grey beard and hair came into view. He theorized the Gulf of Mexico currents contributed as much toward beach trash as beach goers.

He had liked teaching the "Currents" chapter in his oceanography classes. He spent most of this section on Gulf of Mexico currents, because of their proximity. His beach trash study gave him his theory.

The Loop Current that passes between the Yucatan Peninsula and Cuba feeds the Gulf of Mexico. At the tip of the Yucatan, the current shears off into two currents as the Florida Current passes between Florida and Cuba and into the Gulf Stream. The Mexico Current circulates northward along the Mexican coast and then east along Texas. The Florida Current again shears into two at the tip of Florida and sends a portion northward along the West Coast of Florida and from there west along the coast of the Southern States.

These two currents collide off the Coast of Mustang Island, and entrained sand and detritus falls to the bottom of the Gulf. This creates a continental shelf extending sixty miles out from Mustang Island before reaching only fifty fathoms. He always pointed out that this phenomenon made Mustang Island one of very few accreting beaches in the Continental USA. The flotsam held in the currents all washes ashore on the Mustang Island Beach after the currents collide. The Loop Current pumps mega-tons of Sargasso seaweed into the Gulf in those years when hurricanes rip up the Sargasso Sea in the middle of the Atlantic.

Amos carefully differentiated between beach trash left by mankind and the flotsam deposited by the collision of currents – not a difficult task. Fluorescent light bulbs, for example, came from a ship or oilrig. Most domestic trash had "Made in China" on it. But occasionally something really dramatic happened, like the morning those rough-sawed planks of Honduras mahogany piled on the beach as far as he could see. Obviously, he concluded, a lumber barge sank somewhere in the Gulf.

Amos' theory said most things dropped into the Gulf of Mexico will end up on Mustang Island Beach. Two years of data began proving his thesis.

Next week was Fourth of July week and a very big deal on Mustang Island. The beach would be chockablock with beachers. This would skew his data, so he walked the extra mile to the Port Aransas city limits and took his beach trash data on a "normal" day as he went the extra mile. He continued about another quarter of a mile, since his wife, Dot, would come for him only when he called on his cell phone.

He spied something shiny near the top of a dune that didn't belong. He climbed the dune and recorded a silver-labeled plastic water bottle some barbarian had hurled into the dunes.

He saw a difference. The usual dune oats and sea daisies grew in profusion, but another strange plant waved an eight-frond greeting to him from over the dune. He took off his glasses and cleaned them with his water bottle. No question, it was cannabis, a sight he had not seen since his hippie days in Berkeley when they grew marijuana in flowerpots in the dorm.

At the top of the dune, he looked closer and stood transfixed. The field between the dunes and Highway 361 was awash with cannabis. Immediately on his left, a fountainhead of plants cascaded down on the field below, resembling the Amazon River with its tributaries rather than a sea of cannabis. A mainline trunk of cannabis plants fed irregularly through the field and at odd intervals other smaller lines of plants trailed off into the distance. Hundreds of pocket gopher holes dotted the shade of the plants where gophers lay about and scurried around playfully. Farther down the dunes, another fountainhead and tributary system of plants flourished. And past that, another, endlessly from where he stood.

He plucked a leaf and stuck his tongue to the brown sticky sap. ZAP! Yes sir, he thought, we've got the real thing here. How could such a huge crop of weed go unnoticed for so long? It must be almost six weeks old and beginning to flower.

***

Diggs lay beside his gopher hole situated to get the right angle of sunlight. Historically, the sight of people sent him panicked into a retreat down his hole. But he had breakfasted on Stuff, and the tall funny looking person standing on the crest of the dune wasn't particularly threatening. Diggs felt too fine. Besides, life was good these days.

Diggs' Stuff Mine and Emporium was doing well. Gophers could not get enough Stuff. There had been a couple of small setbacks. First, his inventory began depleting. Then another gopher, Dozer, struck another Stuff mine and opened his own business down the Great Sand Pile a ways. Business slacked off for a while due to competition before Diggs had his marketing idea. He simply ran around and dropped small packets of Stuff with his scent on it down the gopher holes, and his customers flocked back to the gopher that had discovered Stuff.

When Dozer became discouraged by lack of business, Diggs invited him over and offered him a partnership. Diggs suggested a change of name for the two locations to "D&D Emporium and Stuff Mine." Diggs would handle marketing and Dozer production. Diggs pointed out that discovering other stashes of Stuff farther down the Great Sand Pile might be possible. Dozer, it turned out, had a nose for Stuff like a coyote for gophers. They opened several new D&D Emporium and Stuff Mines while overlooking the down side of Stuff. Gophers disappeared at an alarming rate. The gophers spent a lot of time looking for missing friends and family. In the past this would have triggered great cause for alarm and mourning, but as a whole, the gophers stayed pretty apathetic about it. "They must be with the Great Gopher in the Sky," they would mourn.

Diggs would think, little do you know. Besides, the birth rate soared. Something about Stuff made a gopher feel so good he had to screw something – like another gopher. Diggs thought they might out-birth the rabbits if they were still around. He didn't complain about doing his part to help the baby boom.

The gophers wondered why the normally emaciated coyotes all looked fat enough to be pregnant.

***

Amos McAlister stood and pulled out his cell phone, squatted again, and took a close-up of the cannabis plant nearest him. Then he took a panoramic shot of the field of cannabis. He dialed Dot and told her he would be on the beach about a mile past Port A city limits

As a scientist, he now had a dilemma: turn home. Dot asked if he had a problem.

He answered, "I found something very disturbing on the beach."

Amos was never this reticent to discuss anything. So something so "disturbing" sent her imagination soaring. It must be either a beached whale or a landing party of Al Qaeda terrorists, she thought.

For some reason Amos hesitated about his usual trip to the Wisdom Table, so Dot made him a sandwich.

She spoke first. "So what exactly has you so upset?"

He looked up from his sandwich. "Do we have any cold beer?"

"Cold Beer – at noon? Why, you never drink at noon."

Amos got up, went to the fridge, and brought back a beer. "Sometimes a man needs a beer."

"This is one of those times I guess. There's obviously a reason."

Dot had returned to the table with a glass of ice tea and sandwich for herself. Amos looked up, and saw that she waited for an explanation. "Okay, I'll tell you what I saw today, but you can't tell anyone else about it until I decide how to handle the situation."

Amos's grandson, Jeff, was sitting at his laptop tweeting away with a college friend back in Dallas when he overheard his granddad through his closed bedroom door. He signed off and crept closer to the door, opening it a bit.

"You're aware," Amos began, "that I walked about a mile and a quarter past the city limits today, right? I climbed the dunes to log a piece of trash, and what I saw absolutely amazed me."

"What? What?"

"Wild growing cannabis, and I'm not talking a small patch. I'm talking acres and acres of cannabis."

"Cannabis?"

"You know the stuff we used to smoke at Berkley. Back then they grew it in flower pots in dorm rooms."

"You mean pot? Marijuana? . . . Growing wild on Mustang Island?"

"Acres of it. Here, see for yourself."

Jeff peeked around the door to see Amos pick up his cell phone from the table and call up the photos he had taken.

"My God, Amos, what should you do?" Dot rubbed her forehead with worry.

"I don't know how it got there or what I should do."

"You've got to call somebody, right?"

"Who? Chief Crump, the sheriff, DPS, EPA, DEA, FBI?" Amos' voice sounded puzzled.

"If word of this gets out, the Island could be overrun — with the wrong people. We really must handle this right."

Jeff had heard enough and casually walked from his bedroom to the refrigerator for a glass of milk. "How'd the trash survey go today, Gramps?"

"Nothing out of the ordinary, son. A great day, you should have gotten out of bed and gone with me."

"Maybe I will tomorrow." He sat down at the table, took off his bill cap, and laid it over the cell phone."

Amos and Dot looked at each other. "Jeff, honey, your grandpa and I are going outside."

Jeff nodded and watched them leave. He picked up the hat and phone and ran back into his bedroom and slammed the door shut. In a flash he plugged the cell phone into his computer and downloaded the photos. When he saw the panorama shot of the marijuana field he shouted, "Holy Shit!" With a few clicks of the keyboard he uploaded the photos onto his Facebook page under the headline: "Wild Growing Pot on Mustang Island, Texas."

Then he logged onto Twitter and sent the following tweet:

"Check my FBP dudes. Free wild growing pot. ROAD TRIP!" He returned the cell phone to the dining table, and when he saw his laptop, Twitter scrolled like the pinwheels on a slot machine. "Now that's what I call a viral message."

CHAPTER | 16

Harpoon stood on the dock and admired *Cordon Blues* as she rocked gently against her mooring lines and a sense of pride swelled within him. His and Krank's work put into cleaning, patching, and painting since her return to berth a week ago had paid off. They had even painted the mast and net booms, a rigorous job requiring lots of time in boson's chairs – not the comfy kind with padded seats and backs – only a board with a rope through each end. Re-rigging her took two days. They inspected and replaced each questionable cable, clamp, and clevis. Yesterday they had wound new cable onto the shiny new net wench and attached the net bag. The net was only a year old and still serviceable, but with barely enough money left from the felony funds they bought new teakwood net doors that hung like pieces of furniture from the end of each net boom. It's a shame they'll get torn up when we start shrimping again next week, he thought

He climbed aboard, entered the freshly painted cabin, put the key in the ignition, pressed the start button, and the new engine roared awake then settled into a smooth idle that approached purring. Harpoon smiled broadly and patted the cabin firewall like a kitten.

The sun had cleared the horizon and began to ascend into a cloudless sky. The hum of the bay fishing boats as they idled by after they launched at the end of the harbor filled the air with the excitement of expectation. A dead calm left the harbor and channel glassy enough to reflect the sun's rays over the tops of the harbor condos. The screech of gulls begging a morning handout for an easy breakfast punctuated the ambient noise. The moisture-rich air smelled of salt and primordial life: the remembered smell, imbedded since man crawled out on dry land: the smell that habitually pulled him back to his origin.

He turned and saw Krank leap aboard over the stern. "Have you ever heard such a beautiful sound?"

"Not since Coyote sang the Ridley Fight Song." Krank put his thumbs under the straps of his "Fear the Turtle" muscle shirt and flexed.

"Coyote's a Ridley Turtles Booster?"

"It might be that he loves the hot dog and hamburger pieces dropped under the grandstand during a game. I know he mentioned once he wished people would stick with catsup and mayo and cut the mustard."

"Since we're on our shakedown cruise, could you hold off on any tragic late breaking news Coyote shared this morning? I'd like a turd free day."

Krank shrugged and cast off the mooring lines.

It was the middle of the season and The Island Joynt hummed on Wednesday Breakfast Buffet All You Can Eat $4.99. The Reverend Hannibal Jones had led the charge on the buffet about 7:00 a.m. but still held forth at the Wisdom Table at 9:00 along with Chief Crump, Coach Bostich, Wiley Coots, who'd had a fishing charter cancellation, Mayor Riley Glenn, Justice of the Peace Quinton (Flip) Fonders, and the officers of the Rotary Club. Old Doc Elam sat at the head of the table enjoying his emeritus status.

The Rotary officers, all merchants, held a board meeting on

Wednesday prior to Thursday's actual Rotary Club meeting because of the buffet. They finally discussed the club's agenda, as they had only talked about the dismal tourist season in Port Aransas.

Reverend Jones looked up from his third plate and saw Amos McAlister approach with a plate that showed true appreciation for the buffet and smiled at a comrade in arms. "Amos, the world might spin out of control since you missed your beach trash inventory this morning. What brings us this honor?"

A murmur of surprised agreement arose from the others at Amos' unusual appearance for breakfast rather than lunch. Amos set his plate on the table and slumped into a chair. "I'm afraid there's a matter more pressing than island trash today." He definitely had their attention. "I made a discovery yesterday."

A second of silence followed as each thought back quickly and wondered at what Amos might have caught them. A general question then arose. "What did he discover?"

Finally, Wiley said, "Amos, it's hard imagining even a few things more important than beach trash."

Amos spoke above the laughter of the table, "I'm not sure we should even discuss it here in front of God and everybody."

"Brother Amos, there's nothing so deleterious we cannot share with God Almighty! And amen." The Reverend's pulpit basso rolled over the dining room, and every head turned toward the Wisdom Table.

Amos ducked at all the attention focused on the group. "That's what I mean. Until you know what I'm talkin' about, you must keep this thing among those of us here at the table."

The reverend's brow furrowed. "Is it a matter of moral turpitude?"

Chief Riley leaned forward. "Are we talkin' about some sort of crime here?"

"Is this something that might affect our business community?" Mayor Glenn asked.

"Yes." Amos' chest swelled with a sense of accomplishment as he leaned back.

Questioning faces frowned at each other trying to figure out his answer.

"Yes to all three questions." He finally put them out of their misery.

"Good God, man, tell us what you're talkin' about." Mayor Glenn's impatience showed through.

Amos leaned toward the center of the table and the others closed in with him. "Yesterday during my beach trash survey, about a quarter mile past the city limit, I found acres of cannabis growing wild between the dunes and the highway."

Their knowing expressions betrayed those whose past or present included marijuana, but the others held quizzical looks. Rev. Jones asked, "What's cannabis?"

"It's the plant that produces marijuana – pot – weed."

"The Devil's own issue? Growing right here on the Island?" Jones' voice reached pulpit level again, and with his head raised toward the heavens prayed, "Lord God of us all, deliver us from this evil lest we fall into the grip of the Devil's weed. And amen."

Chief Crump ran his hand through his hair in agitation. "How do you know it's growin' wild?"

Amos pulled out his cell phone and shared the panoramic view of the cannabis field. "It's too erratic to have been planted. The pot grows along certain features in the soil."

"My God, I'm lookin' at a lot of weed . . . but you say it's outside the city limits?" Chief Crump's face looked hopeful.

"Right."

"Thank goodness. It's out of my jurisdiction."

"Wait a minute, Chief," Mayor Glenn interrupted. "Don't think for a minute this isn't your problem. If the locals find out about free marijuana, there'll a smoky haze over our fair city rivaling Los Angeles. Half the town will be in the pokey."

Amos nodded agreement. "But that's the small part of it. If word of this gets off the Island, we'll be inundated with stoners from all over the country."

The eyes of the merchants brightened. One who owned

three T-shirt shops spoke up, "You really think this would bring people onto the Island?"

Amos nodded for emphasis, "Hoards."

Mayor Glen stood in a half crouch. "Now hold up here! We're a family tourist town. You think our kind of people will haul their kids here knowing the Island's been invaded by an army of pot heads?"

"Lookin' at my sales this summer, I haven't noticed them bringin' them here anyway," another merchant chimed in. All the merchants' heads bobbed in unison.

An ear-splitting trill rang out in the dining room. Coach Bostich had forgotten where he was, blew his whistle, and raised his hand as if he wanted quiet in the locker room. Heads swiveled and quiet reigned. Bostich shrunk a little in size. "Since I'm charged with the responsibility for some of our town's most rambunctious youth for a good part of their time, I don't see livin' in a pot garden as a plus for them personally or for their on-field performance. So let's cut the bullshit and figure out how we'll get rid of this stuff."

"Never fear, Brother Bostich. The mighty wrath of the Lord shall descend on this abomination." The Reverend's voice boomed. "My Christian solders will band together and march shoulder to shoulder through this field of iniquity. They will lay waste this scourge of the Devil. It will be as though fire and brimstone rained from heaven as on Sodom and Gomorra. Genocide Chapter 19, and amen. Righteousness shall prevail, sayeth the Lord."

Flip Fonders, Justice of the Peace, jumped in, his slightly built frame and Mister Peepers glasses belying the voice of authority. "Reverend, before you take the law into your own hands and trespass on someone else's land, we might want to know on whose property this cannabis is growing."

"God's Army recognizes no Metes and Bounds, Judge, save only those of the Pearly Gates themselves. And amen."

"Unfortunately, Reverend, the State of Texas does. As I

remember it, old Walt Greely's property ran from Beach Access Road 1 for about half a mile south. So if this the property in question, that's a real problem."

"Why so?" asked Amos.

"First, Old Walt had 'No Trespassing' signs all around the place. Second, he died about six years ago without a will. His six kids live all over the country. Since then there's a mountain of lawsuits, counter suits, quit claims, injunctions, and sale contracts among the siblings over who actually owns the property and whether to develop or sell it."

"But do you have 'just cause' for issuing a search warrant?" Mayor Glen asked.

"If the stuff is in plain sight, a warrant's not necessary," said Crump.

"True, but there's the matter of culpability. Since it's been determined the cannabis grows wild, you would be on shaky ground, entering the property without the owner's permission, unless he/she/they have been determined culpable in the growing. And like I say, nobody knows who the owner or owners are."

"Besides," said Chief Crump, "since it's outside the city limits, either the state or the feds would have to handle it."

"Now there's a great idea." Wiley Coots joined the conversation. "Let's notify the great Sate of Texas and the FBI and let them handle it."

"Don't get too hasty, here." The mayor squirmed in his seat. "If we call outsiders in on this, it will be on the local evening news, maybe even nationally. I mean, an outbreak of wild cannabis is news anywhere."

"Don't forget those Drug Enforcement Agency guys who race around havin' a grand old time rippin' and roarin' in that God-awful, noisy cigarette boat. I expect to see them water skiing behind it one day," complained one of the Rotary members who lived on the Corpus Christi Ship Channel.

"My God, I forgot the DEA. They'd love somethin' to do."

"Yeah, they'd jump on this with both feet."

Old Doc Elam spoke up. "The toxicology book lists cannabis sativa as poisonous."

"I like the way you're thinking, Doc." Flip stroked his little goatee while he thought. "An endemic outbreak of a poisonous herb can be grounds for condemning the property to protect the general health of the citizens and to prevent the herb's propagation. There can be no entrance or egress of condemned property by anyone, including law enforcement."

"You can do that?" asked the mayor.

"With no publicity?" asked Amos.

"Law enforcement agencies and the Greely kids might try removing the condemnation if they find out about it, but that's a long and difficult process."

The president of the Rotary Club gathered himself and spoke with authority. "Men, what we have here is a pretty good solution for a difficult problem. We're movin' into the dry season, and the stuff might wither and die on its own. Can we agree we will sit on this while Flip works his magic, and let Amos monitor the situation until we know how best to handle it?" The Rotarians nodded their heads enthusiastically in agreement.

***

Harpoon and Krank entered the dining room at the peak of the discussion, and when they saw the Reverend still in attendance, they made every effort to get through the buffet line and seated unnoticed. Harpoon glanced and nodded in the direction of the Wisdom Table. "If Rev. Jones finds out we have ol' Blues operational, he'll start up the business about a blockade of the channel at the jetties."

"Why blockade the channel?"

"He wants my help organizing a protest of the Coast Guard turning off the beacon at the Crystal Epistle."

"The beacon was good."

"For Rev. Jones it's 'God's Holy Light,' and he means to light up the sky again."

"With a blockade?"

"He means to take on the U.S. Coast Guard and possibly the U. S. Navy force them to reverse their ruling that the 'Beacon of God' is a menace to navigation."

"Brave man." Krank nodded in contemplation.

"Yeah, but he doesn't have a boat, so he wants all the shrimpers and off-shore boat captains to put their boats in the way of ocean-going tankers."

"Not many of those folks even go to church."

"Exactly! Includin' me. At least not up until we start playin' for the Epistle's Sunday service."

"It could be exciting."

"A little too exciting." Harpoon paused a moment for a bite of biscuit which he chewed with deliberation. "He's mentioned it several times, but I always tell him the Blues is out of commission."

"You can't say that anymore." Krank's face glowed with the pride of a perfect shakedown cruise. "She's good to go."

"Ship shape and never looked better."

Coach Bostich's whistle rent the dining room ambience. Everyone fell silent and gawked at the Wisdom Table. Bostich lowered his hand and head to conspiratorial height. He spoke passionately at a volume well below his normal, but still audible to nearby tables.

Krank watched Bostich for a minute. "Something's got Coach irritated."

"You have an amazing gift for understatement. The whole table seems in an uproar for some reason."

"They're never here this late."

"Something's sure got 'em stirred up."

A silence fell over their table as they slowed the pace of their forks and eyed the Wisdom Table. After a number of impassioned exchanges, the Rotary president half stood and spoke to the group, they all seemed to agree, and got up to leave. Harpoon knew he had made a tactical error when Rev. Jones saw them and waved. Once up and moving, he came immediately to their table and sat down without an invitation.

"It's good to see members of the Crystal Epistle Church of Everlasting Enlightenment brand new blues band out and about."

"Good to see you Reverend," Harpoon lied. Krank simply shook the Reverend's hand.

"The Wisdom Table seemed unusually excited this morning." Harpoon gestured toward the table.

"We're under attack, brothers. The Devil has sent a plague of his weed to infest our island. We needed the Lord's help to see the way, so I prayed, and He has shown us the light."

Krank frowned. "Devil weed?"

"Cannabis, Brother, marijuana . . . pot."

Now Harpoon frowned. "Growin' on the Island?"

"Growin' wild a little south of Beach Road 1—acres of it. Not to worry though, we have the problem under control." He rose and turned to leave, then turned back. "Be sure to tell me when your boat's back in service, Brother Harpoon."

Krank shook his head as he watched the reverend retreat. "Reckon we know where the marijuana's buried."

An hour later, Harpoon and Krank stood on the crest of the dunes lookin' down at the acres of cannabis "Maybe we should call it Happy Valley."

"Good for the peace pipe."

"After all the trouble and threats those assholes gave us the last six weeks, think we should tell Mako and the Goons where their weed went?"

"Fuck 'em!"

CHAPTER | 17

Jeff McAlister paced his bedroom and stopped periodically to send out a Tweet for a position report from his friend Ricky Stone in route from Dallas. His last report showed Ricky had cleared through Mathis, which meant he would be in Port A in about an hour, if his Volkswagen bus didn't break down. The bus, older than Ricky by several decades, was unaccustomed to road trips and often balked when it felt abused.

When Ricky got Jeff's Tweet yesterday about free weed on Mustang Island, he immediately set about gathering the necessary equipment for the road trip: a ragged old fly tent that attached to the back of the van, a couple of folding lounge chairs, a folding table, a somewhat moldy bed roll (even though the van had a mattress in the back), a grocery sack of T-shirts, shorts and underwear, an extra pair of flip flops, a beach towel, a Coleman gas lantern, a Coleman propane stove, a couple of pots and pans, his fishing gear, his conga drums and all his ganja paraphernalia, as he called it in the parlance of his SMU biology/premed major. An intimidating set of speakers and woofers installed so they opened to the world with the cargo doors constituted his only modern convenience. His 64-Gig iPod Touch plugged into this system could pound out sixteen thousand four hundred different musical renditions at a lethal sound level, and an app also connected him, through the mystery of digital microwaves, to most everybody and everything happening in the world.

He only knew pot through the consumer side, not production and sales. So he went on the net for a quick undergraduate study of all thing cannabis, especially on the quickest and best way to get cannabis into suitable form for the spiritual enrichment of man. Armed with his newfound knowledge, he collected kitchen utensils, a roll of aluminum foil, and his mom's fruit ripening bowl. Aluminum foil in the bottom of the fruit ripener and a good sunshiny day should get the cannabis going in less than an hour. He had an eye toward commercial enterprise, as the ability to get fresh cannabis buds quickly into usable form would be a marketable skill – something for which other stoners might pay a stipend that could support him for an extended period on the Port A Beach.

He texted his parents who were in Jamaica visiting family. Robert Stone, M.D., a Jamaican immigrant, had met his wife while he attended Baylor Medical School in Houston. They now both practiced in their own clinic in Dallas; he in proctology, she in urology and they laughingly called it "The Bottoms Up Clinic."

Ricky, their premed collegiate son, was the light of their lives. Handsome from birth and blessed with a joyous outlook on life, he was immensely popular in school, and was the size and muscular build that made coaches of every sport vie for his participation. His 4.0 grade average, his Reggae band, Stoned Cold Dreads, and the enjoyment of life seemed more important to him than busting his chops in athletic endeavors.

> Dear Mom and Dad,
> I couldn't get you on your cell. (He
> knew this lie would not hold up but
> felt it necessary). Jeff invited me
> down to Port Aransas for a couple of
> weeks. I've taken The Crate and a

> few things. We'll be spending some
> time on the beach. Text me on the
> Pod when you return. NO PARTIES
> WHILE YOU WERE GONE! YEAH!
> LUV
> Ricky.

Ricky had launched out at daybreak the next morning headed for the Promised Land. Bob Marley and the Wailers pulsed out Reggae on the Crate's sound system at a volume that menaced the old van's structural welds.

Jeff's grandparents, Amos and Dot, sat on the far end of the deck and talked in low tones since Amos's return from the Wisdom Table breakfast. Jeff assumed their secrecy directly connected to the dreaded marijuana patch he had advertised to most of the known world yesterday. But he needed his grandparents' Jeep immediately to go meet Ricky. He and Ricky had agreed to check out the ganja together and make their plans before all the other stoners clogged up Highway 361. In desperation, after he had waited an eternity for their conversation to end, Jeff approached them and asked about borrowing the Jeep.

"Where you headed, Jeff boy?" Amos asked.

"I met this cool tourist chick last night in the Flats, and told her I would give her a tour of the Island today and maybe grab a burger or something."

"A burger? This sounds serious. Maybe you should bring her by here so we can give our approval before things go too far." Amos chuckled at his infrequent attempt at wit.

"We should at least be at the fried shrimp stage, don't you think?"

"How can I stand in the way of young love? When will you be back?"

"Mid-afternoon I expect."

At noon, Jeff sat in the parking lot of the Circle K at the

corner of Beach Access Road 1 and Highway 361, the designated meeting place. He had hailed an older friend who bought a twelve-pack, and iced it down in a cheap styro cooler. His eyes moved back and forth between the cooler and the Official State of Texas Notice in the Circle K window that offered a fine and jail sentence for the consumption of alcoholic beverages on these premises. And that didn't include the additional problem of underage consumption. The thought of a tall cool one won out, and he popped the top of a Bud Light can as a constable's car pulled into the parking lot. Startled by impending doom, he poured half the can in his lap trying to conceal it. The constable went inside and returned walking toward his car with a package of cigarettes, pounding it against his fist before opening it. He waved at Jeff and walked toward the Jeep. Jeff scrambled and struggled while reaching for a beach towel in the back seat and felt the beer level in the Jeep seat creep up to his privates. He finally reached the towel and dropped it in his soggy lap and covered the beer can and his marinating crotch only seconds before the constable put his foot on the Jeep's running board.

"I didn't see Amos on the beach this morning. Is he okay?"

"Oh, yeah, he had some business in town." Jeff hoped the wind would blow the beer fumes away from the constable.

"Yeah, there's something goin' on in town. I got a call from Judge Fonders about coming to his office after lunch. Something about condemning a piece of property." He stood, stretched, and walked away, wheeled on his heel, pointed a pistol-like thumb and forefinger at Jeff, "Stay out of trouble now!"

Jeff almost wet himself. "Sure thing." His exhale sounded like a tire blowout. The constable walked away laughing at the teenager's startled reaction.

Still a little shaken, Jeff crawled out of the Jeep and soaked up the beer in the seat with the towel – the brew ran down his legs onto his flip flops. He had no quick fix for the shorts and skivvies – only a sticky drying process. He thought about a drive to the beach to rinse off in the surf, but he might miss Ricky.

He laid down spread-eagled in drying mode on the hood of the Jeep, and fell asleep, awakening not long after to pulsating music. Jeff raised his head and saw Ricky's ancient, psychedelic VW bus as it sputtered into the Circle K lot. The sixties paint job, since refreshed, showed the work of a talented artist propelled into soaring inspiration by industrial strength mind-altering substances. Ribbons of eye-popping colors streamed over the van's surface, swirling around every feature of the VW and occasionally pooling into spaces which held semi-representative depictions of sixties rock groups and hippie icons. Almost graffiti-like, Ricky had appliquéd a big current-day picture of Bob Marley over a rendering of the Grateful Dead, the edges of which leaked out around Marley's dreads. The Sixties banner above Marley's head still proclaimed "Give Love a Chance."

The van door opened and the woofer waves blew Jeff's hair back. He glanced at the Circle K and saw startled wide eyes peering out of the quaking plate glass windows. He gave Ricky a timeout signal and covered his ears.

Ricky nodded and killed the engine and sound system simultaneously. The air rushed back into the vacuum created by the sound waves. A handsome brown-skinned teenager clad in tight-fitting rainbow shorts and a Bob Marley tank top that covered only the upper half of his six-pack torso, jumped from the van. A red, green, and gold headband crowned a full set of dreadlocks and surrounded a smile bright as the sun.

"Greetin's ta me Bruddah, Jeff, dat greet pheelantropiss, who be sharein' his ganja stash wit all a mankind. Now ain't dat right, Mon."

"Holy shit! You've gone Rasta on me. Where in hell did you get those dreads?"

"Nowhere in Babylon be any dread shop equal ta da 'I and I´s House A Da Livin' Dread – Dreads While Ya Wait.' Real human hair – believe dat, Mon? Some poor Rasta down on his ganja done give up his dreads so da spirit of Jah be passed on tru da Tribe."

"I hope your dread operation is reversible."

"No problem, Bra. Possible some chick gone crazy in da trows of ecstasy be grabbin da dreads might snatch me bald. No doubt she be traumatized in da process. Caution be needed here."

Jeff held back from their traditional hug greeting. "I'd be afraid something'd crawl out of those things and bite off my ear."

"Not a problem, Bruddah, Da Livin' Dread be givin' a certificate dat nutin be livin' in da dreads. Most Important."

They hugged and Jeff paid close attention to the van for the first time. "The Crate made the trip. Amazing!"

"Da Crate's eternal, Mon. No doubt da Smithsonian be holdin a special exhibit for Da Crate one day."

Jeff stepped back and gave an overall look at his friend. "I'm not sure you're cut out for this Rasta thing. All the Rastafarians I've seen are black. You look like you've just been out in the sun too long."

"Not true, Bra. All a da chillin, Red an Yella, Brown an White alla precious in Jah's sight. Alla chillin in da worl."

"You learned that in Methodist Sunday School. And who the hell is 'Jah'?"

"Right, Mon. Jah, Ras Tafari Makonnen crowned His Imperial Majesty Emperor Haile Selassie I. King of Kings, Elect of God, and Conquering Lion of the Tribe of Judah, be God Incarnate."

"You be spendin' time on da Wiki, right, Mon. . . . Jesus, now you've got me doin' it."

"Education, Bra. Da Wiki be necessary for new Rasta bruddahs. But da Wiki don say nuttin bout da New Tower of Babel be right here on da Island, Mon. A Holy Place, Bra, dis Island. Ganja and da New Tower a Babel, most impressive.'"

"You're babbling. Ganja - holy? The Tower of Babel?"

"Da Holy Smoke, Mon, ascends Rastas straight to Jah. Important weed for sure."

"And the Tower of Babel?"

"Da Tribe of Judah built da Tower of Babel for ascendin'

to heaven. It be gone now, but da folks seein' it struck plum dumb and start thinkin an speakin different from each other ever since. No explanation, but praise to Jah, da New Tower a Babel back down da road a piece."

"It's the Crystal Epistle."

"No, no, no, Mon. Karma so strong Bra Marley drowned out by serious strong blues guitar wailing. I'm tellin' ya, Mon, Marly never ever drowned out in The Crate before. Da Tower's most powerful, indeed. Possible da Tower's Truth be revealed and folks be thinkin' and talkin all da same again. Jah, Mon, don't tink nutin bad about da New Tower a Babel."

"So I have to put up with this Rasta shit all summer?"

"Truly, Mon, when da tasty snowflakes start showin' up, day got no resistance for da Rasta. Serious abundance a snow-white booty. Besides, da Stoned Cold Dreads already be headed for da ganja patch."

"Your band's coming?" Jeff's smile reflected his appreciation.

"Ever las one. Got me congas in Da Crate."

"Dat be mos' righteous, Mon."

Jeff led the way in the Jeep as The Crate labored through the beach sand, grumbling all the way. At the point where he felt they were abreast of the cannabis, he stopped and motioned Ricky out of the VW. Together they climbed the dunes, and when they reached the top, they both shouted, "Holy Shit!"

"Praise be to Jah!" Ricky dropped on his knees and bowed to the ganja. "We be blessed beyond all possibility. Ganja into da next century,"

They had topped the dunes at Diggs' D&D Emporium and Stuff Mine #1 where the cannabis had almost matured. Ricky was eye-to-eye with the plants when he knelt, and he saw well-formed buds. He looked closely at the plants and buds and recalled an article he had read the night before about a new strain of cannabis developed in Mexico. Impervious to herbicides, it grew year round, matured in less than two months, this cannabis was essentially indestructible. Like the Low Ryder Strain, this new Mexican strain, called "Columbians," grew near the ground and produced as much marijuana on a football field as previously took over ten acres. As a budding biologist, he studied the plant and compared it to his recollection of the photos of Columbians. He leaped into the air shouting, "JACKPOT!"

Jeff had strolled down into the patch a ways and turned to see Ricky running toward him. "What's the problem?"

Ricky gestured all around. "I'm positive this ganja is a new strain grown in Mexico. The stuff 's indestructible, and produces tons of buds in less than eight weeks. Don't know how this stuff got here but this is a gold mine!"

"Where did the Rasta go?"

"Sorry, Mon, much excitement for sure. This patch be a ganja escalator straight to Jah for all Rastas. Most joyous indeed."

"When can we start harvesting?"

"How bout tomorrow?" Ricky ran full tilt through the cannabis leaping and shouting, gophers flying in every direction, until he stopped at a group of plants with well-developed buds. "We be startin' right here." He planned the harvest as he stood leafing through plants and buds.

***

Rudolfo Rattler had overindulged on stoned gophers and coiled up in the shade of a cannabis plant for his siesta. Well into his digestive period, someone rudely awakened him as he ran past his cannabis plant. His erotic dream left an itchy, amorous feeling that needed female scratching. Stoned on gophers as he was and with his poor eyesight, he couldn't figure out what stood in front of him, but he sensed warmth. Stealthily, he slithered beside it, raised himself above the cannabis, and rubbed this warm thing ever so gently as any lover would.

***

Ricky felt something more substantial rubbing his leg than cannabis leaves. It felt rough and a little scratchy. He glanced down the outside of his left leg and saw a rattlesnake smiling up at him with adoring eyes. "WHOOYEEE SHEEEHIT!" He cleared the cannabis by several feet and hurtled towards the dunes. He bounded like a gazelle and screamed, "VIPERS, MON! A PIT A HORNY VIPERS BE WANTIN TA FUCK YA SILLY! HOLY JAH, I DON SHIT MYSELF! MOST INCONVENIENT!"

CHAPTER | 18

Kicky's retreat over the dunes as he tripped, rolled, and tumbled down the face and across the beach stirred up enough sand for a desert storm. He screamed, "HEINOUS VIPERS!" as he ran until he waded waist deep in the surf where he quickly ripped off his shorts and skivvies and commenced cleaning himself. "Praise be to Jah for savin' da Rasta from horny viper fangs."

Jeff lacked Ricky's inspiration and fell behind, but eventually reached the surf, huffing and puffing. He waded in since he could use a little rinse off himself after his Constable encounter. "You get a bug up your ass, man?"

"No, Mon, a really big rattlesnake. The bastard rubbed up against my leg like I'm the hottest viper on the beach. Loosed my bowels and the poor snake still wonders what hit him, mon." Ricky shuddered visibly. "Snakes and da Rasta don't mix."

"I guess I forgot about the rattlesnakes in the dunes. They get pretty big 'cause they've got plenty to eat; gophers, mostly."

"Most disturbing these heinous vipers, mon. I swear this ugly bastard be horny for me."

"Well, you do have a certain charm about you."

As they completed their clean up and pulled on their shorts, an old rusty Honda Element moved slowly toward them on the beach. "Hook 'Em Horns" painted in orange adorned the sides and a set of Texas Longhorns crowned the windshield. Two surfboards strapped on the roof told something of the occupants, two teenage couples, who seemed hesitant about where to park the Element crammed with camping equipment. They paused at The Crate for a few moments and then moved on a few yards before backing up to The Crate again. The driver got out, waved, and trotted toward Jeff and Ricky. "Hey, dudes, that your hippie van?"

Ricky walked ashore. "Ya, Mon, da Crate be mine."

The driver relaxed and smiled at a kindred spirit. "You guys know anything about weed growing wild on the Island?"

"Most definitely."

"We thought there'd be a lot more stoners here, man, 'cause just about everybody in the world got a Tweet on it."

Jeff chimed in, "You're the vanguard, man."

"The beach be full soon, no doubt." Ricky made a sweeping gesture. "One grand party, mon."

"Where's the best spot for parking old 'Hook 'Em' over there?"

Ricky pointed about twenty yards past The Crate. "You'll have a front row seat if you set up camp over there next to the dunes. High tide covers about half the beach right now."

"But where's the ganja?"

"No worries, mon. Check The Crate tonight. All will be revealed."

"Thanks, hippie dudes." The three did high fives and knuckle bumps, and the driver jogged back toward the three expectant faces in the Honda. "Game on! PARTEEE!"

Ricky frowned at Jeff. "Why so far away, mon? There's two fine lookin' chicks in there."

"We're gonna need some city planning, or this thing will get out of hand."

"City planning?"

"If the Stoned Cold Dreads come, we need a place to set

them up and an open area for dancing, kegs, and to party, so we have to rope off a space." Jeff motioned an arc around the beach in front of The Crate.

"Yah, mon, great tinkin', but we best be hurryin' cause da stoners are on the move."

"You set up The Crate, and I'll go into town, get supplies, and borrow Granddad's generator for juice to run the band's amplifiers."

Constable Sherrill stared at the stack of flyers Judge Flip Fonders handed him:

Department of Safety & Permits

County of Nueces, Texas

Contact Numbers (361) 749-6405

Notice of Condemnation

NO: 369

DANGER: DO NOT ENTER THIS PROPERTY FOR ANY PURPOSE:

This property is condemned due to an infestation of poisonous herb. No one may enter this property at any time. Entry of and/ or removal of any vegetation from these premises is strictly forbidden and punishable by a fine and/or jail sentence.

Signed: Judge Quinton Fonders
Date: June 27, 2010
Time: 2:45

Do Not Alter, Deface, Or Remove This Notice Without Appropriate Authority

"Old Walt Greely's place condemned for an infestation of poisonous herb?" Constable Sherrill rubbed his forehead with the back of the hand holding his cowboy hat. What kind of herb could it be?

"Yeah, we need these notices up this afternoon." Judge Fonders handed the Constable a copy of the Greely property plat. "Use the staple gun and put one on every third fence post."

"How long do you think these will last outside?" He held up the paper flyers.

"I've ordered permanent ones, but they won't be ready until next week."

"One Hour Signs couldn't whip them out? Save putting 'em up twice."

"We live on Island Time, remember? 'One Hour Anything' takes a week."

***

Claude the Coyote's pups, now old enough to venture out of the den on their own, left him time alone with his mate. Up until recently she protected the pups and did not let him in the den. But when he laid gophers in front of the den, she got very sociable and came out to rub on him in the friendliest way. He couldn't wait for her to kick the pups out of the den for good. Maybe then she'd want good old-fashioned coyote coitus. With plenty of gophers for food, life was smooth as water on a calm day, but he still didn't understand completely why he felt so happy during this normally intolerable wait.

They had spent several nights together singing love songs, but nothing happened. Today was different. She had finished her gophers, herded the gangly pups out of the den, and immediately nuzzled Claude in all the right places. In the past he had to chase her down for sex. Not today. He let out a howl and set about delivering the goods in a way few coyotes could.

***

Constable Sherrill looked back at his handiwork and wilted a little when he saw he was only half finished stapling the notices along Highway 361. He had considered but rejected the South cross-fence running from the highway to the dunes. Ain't no way

136

I'm wading through all those rattlesnakes to staple up notices.

He wiped the sweat from his face and grumbled about spending so much time outside his air-conditioned patrol car. Besides, the recent rains left water standing in the bar ditches, and he got his boots wet and muddy. He imagined a rattlesnake behind every tuft of spartina and Johnson grass. He turned, leaned against a fence post, and lit a cigarette. His brow furrowed as he watched the traffic passing toward Port Aransas. This was not the usual late June, Wednesday afternoon traffic. First off, there were too many cars, and the number was increasing. Too few condo commandos' BMW, Lexus, and Caddies mixed in. The traffic had a very low percentage of fishermen's pickup trucks towing boats and too few Island Trash's rust buckets. Older model compacts, most with camping equipment strapped on the roof and occupied by teenagers and college kids took their place. Looks like Spring Break; almost like an invasion. At this rate the cops will be directing traffic.

He jumped the bar ditch and moved the patrol car up the road. He stapled flyers up Highway 361 to the Circle K corner, then turned up the Beach Access Road. When he reached the dunes he saw two coyotes balls-up in wild animal sex. They howled a duet in harmony he thought he recognized. He drew his pistol and took aim at the top coyote. "You fuckers ate my cat!" Then he thought better of it. Sure as hell some Greenie will see me and raise a shitload of stink about ruining the ecology. Besides, why interrupt anything having so much fun?

Jeff spent half an hour on his computer printing out signs and then spirited his granddad's Honda generator and gas can out of the garage along with a staple gun used in a recent condo reupholster project. He drove to a construction site of a friend with a home building business. When his friend saw Jeff, he crawled down from the roof. "What's up man?"

"Big party out on the beach a little past Beach Road 1, but we need a bandstand. Don't suppose you could borrow some lumber, come out after work, and throw something together. There's free beer and weed for you; oh, and lots of chicks."

"Wouldn't miss it, dude, but what's the occasion?"

"Wait 'til you see it!"

"Sounds kickin'. My *hombres* welcome?" He pointed at the other two carpenters on the roof.

"Absolutely." Jeff gestured toward the dumpster loaded with scrap lumber. "We'll use your scrap wood for a fire. I'll take some right now, if it's okay."

"We'll bring a load when we come. Saves paying for hauling the junk to the dump."

"Oh, since you're over twenty-one, maybe you could pick up a couple of kegs, and we'll pay you when you get there? Trust me. It'll be worth it. We'll set you up with free pot for life."

"That's all? You sure you can't think of anything else, *amigo?*"

"You're kidding, right?" Lottie's quizzical expression underlined her disbelief.

"It's what the Right Reverend said this morning. Seems the Wisdom Table spent most of the morning figuring out how the problem could be handled after Amos McAlister reported his findings." Harpoon and Krank had finished breakfast and gone back to *Cordon Blues* for a few repairs after the morning shakedown cruise; now they sat across from Lottie in the Joynt's bar and enjoyed a late beer lunch.

"So what are they planning?"

"They feel they can keep this a secret?" Krank almost smiled at the idea.

"Gossip's all this island produces. What are they thinking?" Lottie looked around the barroom and envisioned the tongues wagging once Islanders got even a hint. "How do you think this happened?"

"We're pretty sure the two Bozos buried the ganja in the dunes about six weeks ago, and the seeds must have germinated and started growing. How – I have no idea.”

Lottie shook her head, unable to comprehend the whole thing. “How will your buddy Mako react to free pot on the Island? It’ll hurt his business, for sure.”

“I don’t see how he can blame us for that. His idiots were the ones that buried it. Of course he might decide we stole it and planted it. Like maybe we’re going into competition with him.” Harpoon looked a Krank.

“That would be bad medicine for sure. The Powers are converging on the Island. Something big will happen.” Krank stared into the bar mirror and looked into tomorrow.

When Jeff reached The Crate, Ricky had positioned it so the doors faced the beach and the speakers quaked out Reggae music with the pull of a Pied Piper on the stoners. Twenty-five to thirty cars parked against the dunes on each side of The Crate as their occupants set up camp.

The Crates’ fly tent waffled in the breeze with the lounge chair set up under it. The table fronted the tent with the propane stove and cooking equipment set up for action, and lanterns hung from the tent poles. Ricky talked and gestured as he bent over a VW Beetle, probably giving instructions to the driver. The Beetle moved in the direction Ricky pointed. He stood and waved at Jeff.

“Hey, Mon, glad you’re back. It’s a full time job keeping folks from camping in front of The Crate. Most difficult indeed”

Ricky held up the signs he had printed:

WARNING!
DO NOT DRIVE HERE!
DANGEROUS LOOSE SAND

“We’ll staple these on sticks from the scrap lumber and stake out the area we need for the ‘Party Plaza.’ A friend’s bringing a couple of kegs, some wood for the bonfire, and lumber for a bandstand.”

"Most impressive, mon. Maybe you should run for governor."

"I plan to, but in the meantime let's get to work."

In addition to the bandstand erected in front of The Crate, the carpenters built a keg rack that was now the focal point for the campers. A sign announced, "Free Beer Tomorrow – Today Give It Up For The Kitty" hung from the handle of a cooking pot slowly filling with donated dollar bills.

The sun hung just above the dunes when Ricky ran up shouting, "They're here, mon!" They both ran toward a van with the garish words "Stoned Cold Dreads" scrawled on its sides, and a shout of appreciation arose from the crowd milling about the party plaza. Most of the stoners had partaken of their old stash and had mellowed out, but the topic of conversation always drifted back to "where's the wild ganja?"

The Crate pumped out the Reggae, and a few of the revelers danced around the bandstand while the Dreads set up for the evening. Ricky helped set up the band. He looked around and smiled broadly. The bonfire crackled as dusk settled over the beach. The cries of gulls winging their way back toward their nests punctuated a passive ambience. Smoke rose from grills in preparation for cooking evening meals. The aroma of grilled meat wafted in the breeze. A mellow scene, but one of expectation. Emboldened by a number of beers, Ricky took a microphone and shouted, "Fellow stoners, bring it on in here to da bandstand. Gather around. Da big question be, where's da ganja? Right, mon?"

The crowed responded, "Right!"

"Now all will be revealed. But ya got ta show respect for da ganja provided so freely by the great Jah. Care be most important also so we don't mess up the dunes, right. Each day volunteers be bringing in a harvest fresh to da Crate over there and processing it for your pleasure. It's yours for the taking, but make a contribution so things can keep going. Now follow me to the promised land."

He stepped from the bandstand and moved through the crowd toward the dunes. The crowd followed Ricky like he was Moses, mumbling questions as they all climbed over the crest. The sun touched the horizon, and the rays painted a calm bay with shades of yellow and orange ricocheting in a dazzling array of light and illuminated the marijuana field like a Chinese lantern.

The effect produced a sense of awe in the crowd of several hundred on top of the dunes. "Ooohs" and "Ahhhs" rained down on the ganja patch. Ricky looked at Jeff. "Only da great Jah could paint a picture of paradise like dis, mon."

A shout rang out, "PARTEEE!" The crowd turned on its heels and ran down the dunes whooping and laughing.

Two guys in one of the cars hung up in the traffic jam on Highway 361 looked at the hundreds of people on the dunes. One said, "We're definitely where it's happen'n, man.

CHAPTER | 19

"Who the hell's calling me at seven in the morning?" Harpoon's head struggled up from the pillow on the third telephone ring, and he stared at the clock. His head hit the pillow again recovering before reaching for the phone. He'd had way too much fun the night before. He and Krank celebrated a day early before going to sea for eight days the next morning. Actually, a night early to allow quality time with Lottie, the last night before shipping out. But more happened. The Joynt rocked with people he'd never seen before. "Parteee!" for sure, and all had a good time. He remembered endless talk about free ganja on the Island.

Then he heard what sounded like Lottie's voice from the phone still only half way to his ear.

"Come on Harpoon, you can do it. You can lift a phone. I've seen you." She sounded edgy, but her voice still lilted with a little residual good cheer.

The phone finally reached his ear. "Lottie, that you?"

"I knew my big strong man would come to the aid of a damsel in distress." She summoned up enough cheer for a tinkle of laughter.

"I didn't get much sleep last night, and you're losin' me.

What damsel?"

"Me, big boy. I'm in big trouble."

The thought of his own drug related problems flashed through his muddled consciousness, and he sat upright in bed. "What? What trouble are you in?"

"The Joynt's overrun with customers. Hungry mothers, all of them. They're eating me out of house and home."

"That's trouble?"

"Yeah, since we're running out of provisions. They called me in early this morning to help serve and cook, so I can't go shopping for more food. Sysco can't deliver until tomorrow, so would my big strong man go forage for food?"

After an extended pause, "Pilgrim, you there?" Lottie asked.

"Yeah, I'm getting myself together. Of course I'll help. You want me to shop the Family Center Super Market and get some groceries?"

"Hop out of bed, and hurry over to the Joynt. I have a shopping list. Move it, big boy." She hung up before he could respond.

Ten minutes later he walked through the bar door. Lottie rushed to him, and not even taking time for a hug, handed him the grocery list and some money.

She hugged him. "Thanks for the help. You're a life saver."

Harpoon looked at the list. "Eggs, bacon, bread, butter, ham, pancake mix, milk…"

"Oh, and I know we'll run out of shrimp and fish. Could you work a miracle with your shrimper buddies and come up with some for lunch and dinner? You'll be handsomely rewarded." She smiled wickedly.

"I can get this from the Family Center?"

"Not a chance. I called, and they're running out of everything themselves. I heard the ferry lineup goes all the way back to Aransas Pass. The Flour Bluff HEB might be your only hope. They may be far enough from this mob to still have food."

Harpoon enjoyed the beautiful, cloudless day as he drove down the Island past the Port A city limits. The heavy traffic headed toward Port A on a Thursday puzzled him. At the Circle K, he saw people lined up ten deep at the three Port-a-Potties. Behind Ol' Walt Greely's property, something peeking over the dunes looked like a telescoping mobile TV broadcast dish, and a man stood on the dune crest holding what looked like a shoulder-mounted TV camera. What the hell's going on? He rolled down his window for a better look and heard Reggae music from behind the dunes.

Farther down, he turned onto the sandy, potholed two-track and stopped at the head of Wilson's Cut and Krank's houseboat. When he walked up Kranks' gangplank, he could smell the sweet smoke of his peace pipe, so he knew Krank lay on his chaise lounge communing with nature and possibly with Coyote.

Harpoon walked around to the waterside of the deck, and before he could speak, Krank said without opening his eyes, "You're up early."

"I'm rescuing a damsel in distress."

"Lottie needs more food for the restaurant." Krank loosed a stream of smoke through the corner of his mouth.

"How did you know?"

"When the Powers converge, many people follow."

"That's for damn straight. The Island's crawling with them."

Krank opened his eyes and sat up. "Coyote's concerned about people invading his happy hunting grounds. Plenty of gophers, and when he eats them he feels right. Now people are everywhere, and he must be careful how he hunts. He's gone a day without a gopher and he's feelin' kinda low, especially since his mate won't put out without some gophers."

"If I don't get back to the Joynt pretty quick with these groceries, I might suffer the same fate."

"Then why you wastin' time here?"

"Why not ride into Flour Bluff with me and stock up provisions for *Cordon Blues* while I get Lottie's stuff? Maybe pick up anything you need for your houseboat, here." Harpoon gestured around the deck.

Krank sat up. "I need another propane bottle and a few things for Widow Jeffery while I'm at it."

Kranks's usual reticent conversation pervaded the cab of Harpoons pickup truck until Harpoon spoke up. "There's something bizarre happening back at ol' Walt Greely's place. The Circle K is swamped with people. there was a live TV broadcast going on, and the whole fence has condemnation posters on it."

"Coyote says lots of strange smelling plants are growing where gophers are easy to catch. No digging in gopher holes. They come out, sun themselves, and dance around. They're not even scared of coyotes or snakes."

"So we have happy gophers and happy coyotes after they eat the gophers. We have female coyotes who put out only after eating happy gophers, right?"

They rode in silence until Krank spoke, "Coyote's happy hunting ground must be where Gordo and Bozo buried the marijuana, and the gophers got into it."

"An article on the Internet talked about low growing, fast reproducing marijuana. Supposedly it can mature in six weeks." The two looked at each other knowing the time frame fit.

Lottie was right. A crowd mobbed the Flour Bluff HEB Store, but the shelves still held enough to make shopping look doable. They split up – Krank shopping for *Cordon Blues,* and Harpoon pushing two carts for Lottie. By the time Harpoon had loaded the staples in the carts, he had little room left for eggs – lots of eggs. Then he spied a mound of red fish imported from Mexico and local, individual size flounder and went for a third basket. He was pushing his train of carts to the checkout stand when Krank arrived equally loaded.

The checkout lady had a questioning expression. "You guys starting a restaurant?"

"Already have one, running low on food." Harpoon smiled.

"You must be from Port A. I hear it's getting crowded over there since the TV Broadcast about the wild growing marijuana."

"Wild growing marijuana?"

"Yeah, I saw the news on break. They showed acres of it."

Harpoon looked at Krank. "We've gotta get back to the Joynt quick."

"You finish checking out while I get my propane tank from the rack outside." Krank jumped over the adjacent counter and hurried out of the store.

They didn't talk on the return trip. Harpoon busied himself, dodging traffic while making time driving back to The Joynt. But as they approached the Crystal Epistle, Harpoon asked, "What time's the rehearsal Slidin´ Will told us about?"

"He said five o'clock, so we would have a couple of hours before the choir showed up."

"He said Sweet Bessie Thompson and her gospel singers will be there, right?"

Krank looked at the Crystal Epistle as they passed. "Backin' up Sweet Bessie will be a kick."

"I offered to give Fuck-'Em-All-Ted a ride, but Will said he would pick him up."

When they reached old Walt Greely's property, cars parked along both sides of the road caused the rubber-neckers to slow traffic to a crawl while they gawked at what was happening. Constable Sherrill had parked in the Circle K lot, and his deputies had positioned themselves along the fences, enforcing the property's condemnation signs.

With extravagant wheelwork, Harpoon squeezed through the clogged traffic and finally into The Joynt's parking lot. He said, "How about we unload here, and I'll clean these fish for Lottie while you head over and provision the Blues. Maybe you could check out some shrimpers to see if they have any frozen product left."

When Lottie saw the kitchen back door open, and Harpoon

and Krank lugging in the much-needed supplies, she let out a yelp of excitement and came rushing to help. In between trips, she hugged both their necks. "You guys are absolute heroes. I've never been caught off guard like this before. I don't know where all these people came from." Then she spied the fresh fish and shouted for joy. "Where did you get these?"

"They were stocking them when we got there, and I bought them all." Harpoon handed the receipts from HEB showing the red fish were imported from Mexico, as commercial fishing for red fish was illegal in Texas.

"You remember all the talk last night about free marijuana on the Island?" Harpoon ran his fingers through his hair.

"Yeah, but I didn't have time to think about it."

"A Live Eye TV broadcast this morning showed acres of wild growing marijuana down on 'ol Walt Greely's place. I don't know how people found out about it before, but somehow they did."

Lottie stood in thought for a moment. "That's where all these people are coming from?" She paused for a second. "This has something to do with the weed buried in the dunes, right?"

"I'm afraid you're right." Harpoon shrugged. "Apparently Coyote's been eating lots of crazy gophers lately that make him feel good."

Harpoon took out his wallet and handed Krank money, "Krank will provision the boat and look for shrimp."

Lottie hugged Krank again. " Krank, you're a sweetheart. I reckon I better bump up tomorrow's order from Sysco with all these folks coming into town. It's like the old days when we had really serious business."

Harpoon had scaled the flounder and had almost finished filleting the red fish when Lottie rushed into the kitchen carrying some papers. "You're a life saver for cleaning those fish. I've got to run to Rotary meeting. Why not come along? I'm not staying for the whole affair."

"Krank should be back when I finish up here, and we may have a couple of beers before I run him out to his house boat."

She kissed him and ran out the back door. "Beer's on me."

"You really think this wild growing marijuana will stir up Mako and the Goons?" Harpoon asked. He and Krank were on their second beer in the more-crowded-than-usual Joynt bar, particularly with shrimp season opening the next day.

"Maybe not."

"Why do you think that?"

"The goons visited the houseboat a few weeks back." Krank pulled a toke on his beer.

"My God, Krank, you never said anything. What did they want?"

"Payback for us kickin' their butt and to find out where their ganja is. But I counseled with them. They agreed they had no reason to bother us again. Convinced them we did not know where their marijuana was."

"How'd you do that?"

"An old Indian trick."

Harpoon's frown of concern still wrinkled his forehead as they headed for Krank's houseboat. The cloudless sky and slight landward breeze, ripe with the salty smell of eternity, should have calmed him, but the uneasiness of events swirling out of control had returned. He couldn't wait to get back out to sea and away from everything he'd initiated with his felony. They had dropped off the things Krank had bought for the widow Jeffrey and excused themselves from the slice of rhubarb pie she'd prepared from her garden and offered in gratitude. They bounced to a stop at the houseboat gangplank, and Krank jumped out and grabbed his propane tank.

Harpoon leaned over and asked out the passenger window, "You sure you don't want to get your stuff and come stay with me tonight? I still think those assholes will try for payback when they know they've lost their contraband for good."

Krank almost smiled. "You'll have plenty of company tonight. Tomorrow I'll go get iced up so you can have a little more quality time."

"You want me to pick you up for the rehearsal tonight?"

"Ugh." Krank nodded with a smile.

CHAPTER | 20

Chief Farley Crump arrived at police headquarters an hour late Thursday morning, mumbled something unintelligible at the desk sergeant, closed his office door behind him, and slumped into his chair. He pulled out the top right drawer, took a bottle of Excedrin, shook four into his hand, and gulped them with yesterday's coffee sludge. He had fought a good fight last night, but in the end, José Cuervo won, and now he suffered the defeat.

At retirement, overweight, and out-of-sorts with all mankind, he'd taken the Port Aransas job and hoped for a quiet, smooth existence, free of the foibles of his charges. Traffic tickets, tickets for glass containers on the beach, and No Beach Parking Permits were the order of the day except for occasionally arresting a drunk or an errant teenager.

But something in the air last night disturbed his peace. News of marijuana growing wild on the Island could not be good, and the level of activity and electric atmosphere as the town filled up with visitors set his teeth on edge. There would be trouble before all this passes, so he had consulted with José Cuervo in preparation.

He picked up the night shift Call Sheet, and trouble leaped out at him. Someone from Reverend Jones' Crystal

Epistle had called and reported the noise from the "Sodom and Gomorrah" on the beach was disturbing their Wednesday Night Prayer Service. Crump closed his eyes and groaned inwardly. "Good God, the pot field's a quarter-mile away from the Epistle." He rubbed his temples. "It's started. All these kids are headed for the beach and the pot field."

Chief Crump dialed the home phone of the officer who'd been dispatched to the call from the Crystal Epistle. A sleepy answer followed five phone rings, "Sorry to wake you, Fred, but I have to know what happened on the beach last night." Crump thought about another Excedrin to steel himself for the answer.

"Don't worry, Chief, I planned to come in early today and talk to you about it."

"What happened?"

"You won't believe it until you see it."

"Try me." Another wrinkle formed on the chief's forehead.

"It's past the city limits down in the No Beach Parking Permit Required area. There are at least a hundred cars, campers, and tents. It looks like an Afghan refugee camp."

"It's out of the city, right?" Chief Crump's furrowed brow relaxed a little.

"Yeah, but there's more. They had a reggae band with lethal amplifiers, kegs of beer, and they all looked stoned as the Rocky Mountains. Hundreds of stoners leaping up and down, singing, and shouting to reggae music. Man, I'm telling you it was one kickin' loud party."

"So what did you do?"

"I ask this Rasta lookin' fellow if they would hold it down."

"What did he say?"

"He offered me a joint."

"Constable Sherrill will have to deal with this problem, right?"

"Maybe with the help of the National Guard. You gotta see it for yourself. I'm just glad I didn't have to handle it."

Chief Crump leaned back in his chair and stared at the

ceiling in dismay and contemplated driving his cruiser down to the scene of the complaint.

The desk sergeant opened the door and stuck his head into the office. "I'm sorry about this, but J3's out here, and they want to see you."

The Chief thought about escaping through the back door, but said, "Christ in a handbag, what else can happen today?" His past meetings, both formal and informal, with the three DEA agents stationed on the Island had accomplished little. To him, Joe, John, and Jesús, dubbed "J3" by the Port Aransas Police, were fuck-offs who did little but hang out in bars and drink on Uncle Sam's tab. "Send the assholes in."

"Mornin' Chief," the three spoke almost in unison as they filed into the office.

Crump eyed them from under a frown as they made themselves comfortable. They wore their "deep cover" uniforms: long hair, beards, mirror sun glasses, faded jeans loose fitted to hide the gun strapped to their ankles, bill caps, and ratty T-shirts that announced "Go, You Ridleys," "Fear The Turtle," and "Legalize Pot."

"I didn't think you guys ever got out of bed before noon." Crump leaned back in his chair.

"We picked up a lot of chatter in the bars last night about someone growing pot on the Island. We wondered what you knew about it." Jesús spoke for the group.

"Don't know a thing about someone growing pot on the Island." Crump squirmed in his seat at his small omission about pot growing wild.

"Strange, man, 'cause there's gonna be a lot of bummed out stoners who've come here because of it."

Joe weighed in. "You don't know anything about pot growing on the Island? The stoners think it's free for the taking."

"I know there's no pot growing in the City of Port Aransas." Chief leaned back with a sense of pride.

"We didn't expect to find a vacant lot full of marijuana

plants." Jesús gestured toward the rest of the Island. "But surely you've heard something if these folks keep turning up from all over the state."

Crump stared at his hands for a couple of minutes. "I guess if the world already knows about it, it won't hurt to let you Bozos in on it. Amos McAlister found a giant field of marijuana growing wild out past the city limits. We're trying to keep it under wraps and prevent what's already happening from happening. I have no idea how all these people know about it."

"Where exactly is it?" J3 asked in unison.

"Drive down the beach. I reckon it's over the dunes from the tent city you'll find. Thank God, it's not in Port A. "Crump smiled for the first time that morning. "So it's not my problem."

"Doesn't sound like much of a problem. We'll find out if somebody's growing it. Whether or not, we'll spray it with herbicide, and the day is over, right, guys?" Jesús looked at the other J's who shrugged at the notion they might have to spray down a field of marijuana and rattlesnakes.

"It's a bit more complicated, boys."

J's two and three looked relieved, but Jesús said, "Why?"

"Judge Fonders condemned the property, and you can't enter the premises legally."

"Horse shit, man, we can go anywhere we want to. We're the DEA, man," J2 spoke up.

"Tell that to Judge Fonders when he issues a warrant for your arrest."

J3 looked at each other, their faces big question marks. Finally, Jesús said, "You think Crump's right?" They stood, shuffled their feet, and finally excused themselves. "We'll damn sure find out if this is right."

Chief Crump always drove Mayor Riley Glen for the Thursday Rotary Club meeting at Pelicans Landing Restaurant – a show of force of the executive branch of Port Aransas government. The cheerfulness of the early arriving Rotarians surprised him.

Smiles and goodwill abounded. They stood in circles, gestured, and slapped each other on the back. The gloomy expressions and conversations on the rotten business this season had vanished.

The group's attention turned to Crump and Glen, and one shouted, "Morning, Chief, Mayor, good to see you this bright and cheery day." The good spirits pervading the group puzzled the two officials. They paused for a moment. Finally, the mayor said, "You guys seem absolutely radiant today. What's up?"

The owner of the Circle K shouted, "Sales! That's what's up. We ordered special deliveries brought in to catch up on inventory. I could make a livin' off beer and toilet paper."

Lottie Langton rushed into the meeting room. "Sorry I'm late, guys, but they called me in to help with breakfast at the Joynt this morning. A hungry hoard descended on The Joynt and swamped us. I can't stay for the whole meeting because lunch will be slammed too."

Chief Crump looked around the room and spied Roly Odem, a smallish, owl-eyed man with wire-framed glasses. Roly knew the sad financial condition of about everyone in the room since he was both president of the Rotary Club and the only C.P.A. on the Island. Odem gaveled the podium. "Everyone please take a seat. We've got a lot to discuss, and I know you need to get back to work."

The roar of conversation hushed as the members moved toward their lunch tables. The level of conversation rose again once they were seated. Roly gaveled the podium again. "Remain seated as Reverend Jones leads us in the invocation."

The Right Reverend Hannibal Jones hefted himself from his chair, closed his eyes, and raised his arm until the ceiling fan brushed his fingernails, triggering a quick jerk back, after which he shook the offended hand, and exclaimed, "Christ!" But he quickly recovered and continued. ". . .Almighty God, Founder of the Universe, Healer of All Our Ills, and Forgiver of All Our Sins, we're thankful for all our blessings, but we come before you today with heavy hearts. We find ourselves under attack by Satan himself, Lord. He has spread his Devil's weed upon the sacred earth that sustains your loving flock. Infidels have erected Sodom and Gomorra right here on the Island. Carnal lust, sin, and degradation run rampant, and the problem grows, Sacred Father."

Crump looked around the room under his lowered eyebrows and could easily spy those members not privy to the marijuana event. Furtive glances traveled around the tables, and he saw one whisper question, "What's he talkin' about?"

Rev. Jones continued, "Give us strength, Father. Make us warriors for righteousness, so we can defeat this evil and drive it into the sea and cleanse our blessed island once more.

"God, protect us from the dunderheaded government bureaucrats that extinguished the Holy Lamp of God and give us the patience and determination to man the bulwarks of our channel blockade until God's Holy Light again brightens all our lives."

Wiley Coots turned to the charter captain next to him. "Good God. It's the blockade again."

Rev. Jones summed up. "Bless our food and keep us on the Righteous Road. Amen."

Roly echoed "Amen. All rise for the Pledge of Allegiance."

After the din of chairs scooting around ceased and the members sat down, Roly announced, "We have a guest speaker today, Jasper Oats with the Environmental Protection Agency, who will to speak to us on preservation of our Island wetlands." A perceptible groan rose from the land developers. Another quick gavel. "Lottie will now read the minutes of the last meeting."

Lottie stood and passed out sheets of paper. "Here's a copy of the minutes which you can read at your leisure, but they mostly contain our bitching about how bad business is. The only important thing is the motion to form a committee to work with the Chamber of Commerce to come up with ideas on how we can get more people to come to the Island."

One of the members shouted, "Well, by God, that worked."

The room rocked with laughter and applause. Chief Crump squirmed in his seat at the mention of the surge of Island visitors.

Roly gaveled silence and introduced Jasper Oats, a tall thin man whose facial expression gave the impression that something smelled bad. He had dressed down to Island style with a "Save the Whales" T-shirt, which, along with his unkempt blond goatee, were the only remnants of his Hippie days at Berkley.

Crump rubbed his forehead in a futile attempt to relieve his headache before Oats' rhetoric intensified it. He only hoped the speaker would keep it short. Blessedly, Oats seemed to understand that his subject would not hold the group's attention for long, so he quickly reviewed the importance of maintaining the fragile ecosystem on the Island and then outlined the importance of the wetlands. He summed it up with. "Gentlemen, it's of the utmost importance for us to refrain from the use of pesticides and herbicides that could damage the wetlands flora and insect population. We all know what a nuisance mosquitoes can be, but they're an important part of the food chain in the ecosystem."

He sat down to a polite rustle of applause. Wiley Coots said to his table, "The only good mosquito's a dead mosquito."

When Roly called for new business, hands shot up all over the room. The first speaker stood. "I think the thing about new business is that we finally have some." The room again erupted with laughter and applause.

Another member stood and asked, "What the hell is all this Satan and devil talk Rev. Jones spouted off about?" A chorus of shouts agreed with the question, while Chief Crump flinched.

The group went quiet and waiting for an answer. Roly hesitated to call on Rev. Jones to explain himself, but Mayor Glen stood. "Roly, let me speak to this issue." He paused for a moment until he had their attention. "On Tuesday, while on his Beach Trash Survey, Amos McAllister found a giant field of cannabis growing wild on 'ol Walt Greely's property south of town."

Somebody spoke up, "What's cannabis?" A rustle of laughter circled the room from those more familiar with the ways of the world.

The mayor explained, "Cannabis is marijuana, pot, weed, ganja or whatever you want to call it."

Some of the members gasped.

Mindful of the ceiling fan, Rev. Jones hoisted himself again, raised his hand tentatively, and shouted, "It's Satan's own seed. Devil Weed!"

Someone asked, "What are we gonna to do about it?"

"I think we need to eradicate it as quickly as possible, but in the meantime we tried to keep it quiet long enough for Judge Fonders to condemn the property because of a poisonous weed infestation. We didn't want the Island overrun by the wrong kind of people."

Someone in the back shouted, "You mean the kind of people spending a ton of money here right now?" Heads bobbed everywhere.

Chief Crump shifted uneasily in his seat. He sensed things going the wrong direction. Mayor Glen soldiered on. "Now wait a minute people, let's not forget that our tourist trade is family-oriented, and if we get a bad reputation the tourists won't come."

Someone in the back spoke up. "You're talking about all those tourists that haven't been here the last few years?" Laughter echoed from the rafters.

Several asked, "So you say all these people that showed up yesterday and today knew about the marijuana? How did they know?"

Crump, unable to stand it any longer, leaped up. "We have no idea how they found out about it, but it would not surprise me to see television cameras. Then we're really in a pickle."

"What kind of pickle?"

"The Island will be overrun with people." The Chief paused and in a brief reflection knew he had said the wrong thing. The room erupted into yammering.

Lottie headed for the door. "I'm surprised you haven't heard. Channel 3 broadcast live from out there this morning."

The Circle K man turned to the man next to him. "I've got to get out of here and order more inventory."

Rev. Jones stood again. "We want to know what you're doing about this problem, Chief Crump."

"Well, Reverend, the whole thing's out of Port Aransas's jurisdiction. So there's not too much I can do. However, J3, I mean the DEA boys, came to my office this morning all excited about it and threatened to spray the whole area with herbicide."

"Herbicide!" Jasper Oats leaped from his chair. "Are these people crazy! Ruin the whole ecology over a little harmless cannabis?" He looked like he'd like to take the word "harmless" back, but rose instead to leave.

Roly gaveled out of habit. "Where're you going Jasper? The meeting's not over."

"I'm headed for the courthouse in Corpus Christi to get an injunction filed against the DEA." He stormed out of the meeting room.

The owner of three T-shirt shops on the Island stood. "Listen, people, we need to cool down here. Let's not get in too big a hurry. We need to let things unfold and take care of the problems as they come."

Rev. Jones tried to leap up with no success and hoisted himself up one more time. "Sir, are you saying we do nothing? That we allow the Devil's own seed and Sodom and Gomorrah to flourish here on our island while we 'let things unfold'? Beware, brother, 'Procrastination is a waste of time', sayeth the Lord. First Theseochronicus 13:15."

An audible "Huh?" could be heard over chairs sliding back. Members rose and formed groups of discussion for the like-minded. Roly gaveled a few times, and finally announced, "Meeting adjourned."

Crump turned to Mayor Glen, "Well, I think we know how the business community feels about our marijuana problem."

CHAPTER | 21

"Mako, I'm tellin' you, man, they showed acres of marijuana growin' on Mustang Island." Goon Two still favored his gimped knee where Krank had kicked him, so he sat down on the torn vinyl Naugahide of an ancient sofa. Mako sat behind a ratty desk and leaned back in a wooden office chair that creaked from age. They hung out in the backroom of an abandoned auto repair garage on Highway 44 past the Corpus Christi Airport. The room festered with the detritus of human low life. A single lamp, its crooked shade torn in three places, gave only a glow. The daylight that filtered through a bed sheet nailed over a small, barred window added little additional light. The stale smell of old ganja smoke hung heavy in the air. A window air conditioner mounted through the concrete block wall behind Mako's desk rumbled into action, but halted almost immediately with a hiss.

The chair groaned as Mako leaned forward and menaced Goon Two. "You're telling me there was a TV broadcast about a field of marijuana growing on the Island? Our marijuana's growing on the Island! The ganja you idiots couldn't find?"

Goon One spoke up, "Think about it, man, the shrimper and his Indian hid the stuff and then planted it. They planned to go into business for themselves and got caught. We owe the Indian bastard some serious pain."

Mako wasn't sure. He had always stayed small, stuck to marijuana, kept mobile, kept a low profile, and made the right payoffs to survive. He was most proud of the purchase of an old Salvation Army collection truck he had converted into his processing room. He bought the ganja in rough nugs because they were cheaper but still needed cleaning, seeding, and packaging. Slender fingers with long nails did the job best. Illegal alien women were less likely to talk to authorities, and they cost less. He hired them to process the marijuana blooms. They worked inside the Salvation Army truck chugging around Corpus Christi. They wore only their undergarments while they worked on the ganja to discourage them from hiding marijuana in their clothes. At about two hour intervals the truck pulled into the old garage to allow the women to use the restroom and to warm up or cool off, depending upon the season.

Mako's market area extended north to Port O'Conner, west to Victoria, and south to Kingsville. His dealers worked every university, college, and community college campus in the area, and along the tourist coast towns. He wanted to expand his operation to include the border towns and maybe even part of Houston but feared that any intrusion into the big boys' areas could be life-threatening. Port Aransas represented a thriving market with the locals as well as tourists. He also had a wholesale connection arranged with the major dealer in San Antonio who now hounded him daily for product Mako could not deliver.

He had checked the storeroom behind the fake wall in the garage and found the cupboard bare after six weeks without new product. After he paid for product he never received, a cash crunch limited his ability to reorder, and now he heard that ganja – his ganja – grew wild on the Island. Something had to be done to restore order to his world.

He flicked open his cell and dialed his Port Aransas dealer. "So what's happenin', man?"

The voice on the other end of the conversation said, "Mako, the Island's crawlin' with stoners, but nobody's buying anything. They say they can get stoned for free."

"There's no such thing as free product, man. What you talkin' 'bout?"

"It's growing right here on the Island, man. I've been out there and the shit's blooming everywhere. Come on out and see for yourself. I'll meet you at the Circle K."

Mako flipped the cell phone shut. "Load up, we're goin' hunting."

After the drive to the Island, Goon One pulled the black GMC Yukon XL into the Circle K parking lot and took on an additional passenger who gave directions. "Take the beach road and turn south. It's crazy man. You ain't gonna believe it."

An occasional fair weather cumulus floated by in a brilliant clear sky. The surf rolled up on a beach free of breaking waves that children and adults shared with a few fishermen. Mako viewed this perfect beach day and shook his head. "Why do these idiots come down here and get sand in their crotch, saltwater in their eyes, and sunburn when they got air conditioning back home?" Within a few hundred yards they passed vans, tents, RV's, and even makeshift structures made of sticks and old cardboard boxes – all populated with severely laid-back occupants. Mako turned to his Port A man. "You tellin' me you can't sell shit to this bunch of stoners?"

"No, man, they say they can get pot free. Besides, I don't really have much left to sell anyway."

Ricky Stone smiled out at the half-dozen expectant faces in front of the Crate's tent and processing table. "Ya, Mon, demand done outstripped supply. Most necessary to rely on your own stash 'til tomorrow."

The group looked disappointed and milled around aimlessly. "We heard there's plenty for the taking." The tallest of the group voiced their displeasure.

"Me buddy be hurtlin' toward us as we speak with new equipment for processin' nugs faster. Come around tonight an dig some Reggae from da The Stone Cold Dreads, soak up some brew, and PARTEE!! Ya, Mon, an tomorrow tings be much brighter, ya."

Ricky looked north and hoped to see Jeff's Jeep returning with the two hairdryers and the plastic tub from which they planned to make a high volume ganja dryer, but instead an ominous black SUV plowed through the makeshift village toward him. A tingle of dread trickled down his spine in anticipation of the DEA returning. He considered ambling down to the water for a swim as an evasive action, but he waited too long and the SUV stopped a few yards from the Crate. A short, sleek black-haired guy stepped down onto the sand. The yellow trousers blue sports coat, and cream-colored silk shirt with an unbuttoned collar took Ricky by surprise. Gold chains flashed around his neck, and all of his eight fingers glistened with gold rings and colored stones.

The guy walked toward him. "You in charge here?" The SUV and the golden guy drew a crowd of the curious. When Ricky didn't answer immediately, the guy asked again gruffly, "You with the pigtails, you head man here?"

"No, mon, only the Great Jah be the Head Man."

Mako could hardly hear over the Crate belting out Bob Marley's "Red Red Wine." "Who the fuck's Jah, and where is he?" Mako hollered and gestured at the gathering crowd. Goons One and Two now stood behind Mako and looked nervously around at the crowd surrounding them.

"Great Jah be everywhere, mon."

"Look, asshole, turn the fuckin' music down, it's giving me a headache. I want to know who's stealin' my ganja, or we're gonna start shootin' people." Mako pulled back the coat to reveal the Glock automatic on his belt. A hush fell over the crowd close enough to hear Mako.

"Whoa, mon, shootin' be really bad karma. Nobody stealin' nothin', mon. Great Jah sent the Holy Smoke for all

mankind to enjoy. Besides you best be gettin' in line for de ganja as the lawman and the DEA already beat ya here dis mornin'. Ya runnin' late for sure."

"The law's been here?"

"No doubt about it."

Goon Two stepped forward. "You guys workin' for the shrimper and the Indian?" Mako elbowed the goon in the stomach for his intrusion and doubled him over.

Mako looked around at the gathered crowd, and thought for a moment. "Okay, here's how it's going down, Pigtails: we'll be coming around at twelve noon everyday to pick up two-thousand dollars or the equivalent in ganja nugs. Got it!"

"Should we invite the law to join in on the fun?" Ricky was so pissed off he forgot the accent.

"Why you little shit." Mako whipped out his Glock and raised it to club Ricky, but the closest bystander grabbed Mako's arm and twisted it so the elbow rested on his shoulder. He jerked the arm down. An audible snap drowned out the music for an instant. Mako screamed and fell to his knees.

Goon Two reached for his gun and felt a foot slam into his compromised knee. "God, no! Not again." He roared and collapsed in a heap. Goon One jerked his arms over his head in surrender. The Kung Fu guys collected the guns, removed the magazines and disassembled them. One walked to the surf and sailed the parts out into the saltwater.

Goon Two groaned on the ground. "Jesus, I'm goin' broke buyin' guns."

Ricky looked at the two Kung Fu guys in amazement. "Hey, dudes, I haven't seen anything like that since 'Kung Fu Panda'. Much appreciation. Where'd you learn that?"

"No problem, man, we're Navy Seals home on leave," the one said as he dragged Goon Two back to the SUV. He stopped, looked back at Goon One, and said, "Grab golden boy there and bring him along."

Jeff swung the jeep onto the beach and saw the grille of a black SUV right in his face. He jerked his steering wheel to the right and avoided a head-on collision by inches as the Jeep careened into the dunes and stalled. Jeff stood in the front seat and waved both middle fingers. "Screw you! You miserable assholes." He had stuck the jeep and got out to see how badly. Sand covered the front bumper and buried the back axle. "Damn!" He walked around the Jeep once more. "I might as well try it." He climbed back into the Jeep, started the engine, and shifted into four-wheel drive. The tires slipped slightly before gravity took over and helped push the jeep down the dune and onto the beach. He patted the dash of the Jeep. "No wonder we won WWII."

"Ya, mon, ya missed the excitement for sure." Ricky ran up to the Jeep before Jeff could get out.

"Excitement?"

"Goldfingers himself showed up saying da ganja be his an we gotta to pay him thousands of dollars for it. He had two Bozos with him an plenty of guns, mon. Big trouble until two Kung Fu dudes kicked the shit outa 'em and threw the guns in the ocean and the crooks back into their vehicle. Be truly amazing man, ya shudda seen it."

"Were they in a big black SUV?"

"Truly, mon."

"The assholes almost killed me when I turned onto the beach. I ended up in the dunes to save myself."

"Bad fellows for sure. Maybe 007 be comin' to save us from Goldfingers."

"Sounds like the Kung Fu dudes did a pretty good job. Unless you think the bad guys will be back."

Ricky shook his head. "I don't know, mon. Maybe after they get outta the hospital." Ricky looked in the back of the Jeep and saw the five-gallon plastic tub and two boxes with pictures of hair dryers on them. You got the stuff, mon. Best news today."

Jeff pointed to the large holes drilled in the bottom and top. "I went by to get my carpenter buddy to build a frame and drill some holes in the ganja dryer from hell, so I'm a little late"

"Ya, mon, but what be all those little holes in the sides?"

"Major engineering, mon." Jeff smiled. "They let the dryer air out so all the pot gets dry at the same time."

"Quite amazin', mon. Be totally necessary you run for President and fix all dat's wrong, for sure."

Goon Two stretched out on the back seat and held his knee. "I'm telling you, Mako, the shrimper and the Indian have put together a hellava crew. They got the law guarding the field plus those two enforcers. Who knows? Pigtails might be in the Jamaican Mafia. Those evil bastards kill people before breakfast. It's big time, man. We got to do something about the Indian fucker and quick."

Mako started to turn in his front seat and gesture with the damaged arm but instead let out a scream. When he recovered, he shouted, "Will you shut up?" He looked at Goon One and said, "Can you go any faster? I need to get to a hospital before my arm falls off."

He lapsed into silence and thought about a call from his source several days before. They had offered him stronger stuff. He had left the door open, but said he needed to think about it. Occasionally a guy could catch a break for dealing ganja, but cocaine was something entirely different. His mantra, "stay small, and fly low," really didn't leave much room for "snow" much less black tar heroin. Besides, to buy in he'd have to use his getaway cash he kept in a safety deposit box, and he swore he'd never do that. He had no pot, the marijuana market sucked, and he was low on money. He had to make a move. The pain ricocheted around in his head like a motorcycle wall-rider and stoked the fires of resentment and defensiveness. People used to show him respect for the kind of guy he was. They moved out of his path and didn't want any part of him. They scored their pot and scurried away like a bunch of rats. Now he and his crew had no hardware, and the pain of a broken elbow given to him by a couple of hippie stoners made him sick with rage. Things had gone in a bad direction ever since he did business with the shrimper and his Indian. Maybe those two assholes had caused all his troubles.

***

Diggs, the pocket gopher, was in a funk. He saw the whole complex in a shambles as he traveled the tunnels and shafts between Stuff mines. Gopher crap that nobody ever cleaned anymore lay around everywhere and really stunk up the place. The gophers' joie de vivre was fun and all, but things had changed while the Emporium and Stuff Mines did a lively business.

For one thing, the roots the other gophers traded for Stuff tasted a lot like Stuff. He actually preferred the tender roots of the plants from around the people boxes lined up in rows. But the gophers got lazy and harvested only the closest roots. Stuff really didn't taste good until after the first bite or two then nobody really cared. But the taste pervaded the new roots no matter how much he ate. He stayed hungry all the time, and he had to admit he had gained a little weight eating all the roots the other gophers brought to the Emporium and Stuff Mine. He could still get a little loving, but it was more difficult.

The new plants had grown up and now shaded the whole world. Soaking up some rays took some looking for an unshaded spot. Many gophers had returned to their old habit of digging tunnels and shafts at night. Snakes and coyotes seemed hungrier than normal, and they could hide in the new plants very easily. Gophers seemed to evaporate these days.

Something on the other side of the big sand pile shook Digg's world and caused tunnels to collapse. The "Boom! Boom! Boom!" went on almost day and night. At first the beat made him dance after eating Stuff. Now the noise annoyed him, Stuff or no.

Lots of people crawled around in the new plants at night and looked for something. They stayed very quiet, but occasionally he'd hear frantic shouts of "SNAKE!" or "HEINOUS VIPER!" followed by pounding feet, receding over the big sand pile. His world had gotten really crowded what with coyotes,

snakes, people and these damn bad tasting plants blocking his sunshine. Not so much after he ate Stuff, but sometimes, he wished he could have his old life back.

CHAPTER | 22

Slidin' Will Pickens picked up a case of Dry Creek Vineyards Old Vines Dry Creek Valley Zinfandel 2007 in the storeroom of Good Pickens Bait Shop, Wine Bar and Blues Emporium – Affordable Boat Rentals and set it on the bar. The usual smell of last night's cigarette smoke, acrid wine, and the redolent reminder of bait tanks pervaded the emporium. The wooden overhead fan blades thunked away but couldn't homogenize the air into something more satisfying for the olfactory senses. He heard the front door open and the bell ring. Only the beer signs on the walls lighted the Blues Emporium's bar room, but in the half-light he saw Dick Walzem, minister of music at the Crystal Epistle Church of Everlasting Enlightenment as he stood just inside the door holding a sheaf of papers. The boats were rented, the bait seined and sold, and the fishermen had already purchased all those tackle items necessary to catch the big one, leaving the two men alone.

"Morning, Preacher, what brings you out so early?" Slidin' Will headed toward the bar with the box of wine.

" 'Preacher' might be a little strong, but I thought we might visit a few minutes about the rehearsal tonight. I mean, if you have the time." Although dressed confidently in a light blue, button-down collar, oxford cloth, long-sleeved shirt with a striped club tie, starched Docker Khakis, and Rockport boat shoes, Walzem still seemed as hesitant and unsure of himself as if he were walking on ice.

Slidin' Will set the case of wine down on the bar and walked around behind. He slid back the ice box top. "How about a cool one to start the day?"

"A Coke maybe?"

In deference to his guest, he pulled two Cokes from the ice chest so cold the humidity condensed into droplets that soaked into the napkin in which he carefully rolled each bottle. The whoosh as the bottle lids snapped open sent a tiny plume of mist swirling above each.

Slidin' Will set one smoking bottle in front of Walzem. "Glad you came by, Reverend. I've been doin' a lot a thinkin' about this whole Epistle blues band deal."

Halfway through a big pull on the frosty coke bottle, Walzem choked and coke bubbles spewed out of his nose while he coughed.

"You okay, Reverend?"

After he recovered, Walzem gasped, "You're still doing the gig, right?"

"Oh, yeah, but I had some questions how the thing's goin' down." Slidin' Will looked at the panic in Walzem's face and chuckled. "Don't get all choked up, Reverend."

"Oh thank you, Jesus! Reverend Jones is dead set on starting our new music program this Sunday." Walzem's eyes begged for agreement.

"Now that's a problem. Shrimp season opens tomorrow and Harpoon and Krank go out for ten days."

"Christ Almighty! . . . Sorry. There's gotta be a way around this."

"Maybe you could make holdin' off 'til Sunday afternoon worthwhile."

Walzem thought for a moment. "They're getting paid anyway. Maybe we could sweeten the pot."

Slidin' Will looked at the little insecure man in front of him reeking of aftershave in his Christian-friendly clothes and coiffured hair. He wondered how Walzem had ended up in a bar on Mustang Island at the whim of Reverend Hannibal Jones. He almost felt sorry for him. "You might be on the right track there."

Walzem nodded his head in reflection.

"So what's up, Reverend?" Slidin' Will arched his bushy eyebrows.

"First of all, is everyone coming for rehearsal tonight?" Again, the anxious look.

"It wasn't easy, but they've all committed. We got guitar, sax, harmonica, tom-toms, and Fuck-'Em- All-Ted on the organ. He's unpredictable. I'll pick him up myself so he doesn't go sideways. What about Sweet Bessie and her crew?"

"She'll be there with three backup singers. Ahhh . . . you think we could call him 'Ted'?"

Everyone had used the name "Fuck-'Em-All-Ted" so long it now held no more particular meaning than just "Ted." "I reckon 'Ted' would be more fittin' in the Epistle environment."

"Have you thought much about the music?" Walzem held out the sheets of paper.

"You read my mind." Will looked at the papers, each with the lyrics of religious songs. "There's a lot of repetition in these lyrics."

"These are praise lyrics, and you're right they have a lot of repetition. But don't you use repetition in blues lyrics also?"

Slidin' Will unlocked a cabinet behind the bar and took out a guitar case. He always smiled when he saw the glistening steel body of the 1927 National Steel Guitar – a thing of beauty with its chrome plating and brass fittings. The beer signs reflected from the shiny surface like a kaleidoscope as he tenderly removed it from the case.

Walzem's eyes widened as the National appeared from the case. "I've never seen this kind of guitar."

"They're rare. Most folks think of a steel guitar as a

horizontal contraption used in Country &Western music with electric resonance fretted with a steel bar. But these modern gadgets got their name because they made the same sound as this original National Steel Guitar." Slidin' Will tuned the guitar as he spoke. He stuck the wine- bottleneck glass slide on the little finger of his left hand and strummed a chord while he slid it up and down the strings and produced a glissando effect, radiating out into the bar room as only a steel guitar can.

"My goodness, you can almost talk with this thing."

Slidin' Will hit another chord and moved the slide up and down and out came a very audible, "Oh, yeah." He picked up a sheet of lyrics entitled "Why Do We Live Without Jesus" by Steve Green and studied the lyric while he tapped out the rhythm with his foot:

Every heart is filled with longing

To be free from all life's pain

Every heart is filled with longing

To be free from all life's pain

But all the earthly pleasures

Are going to always end the same

Slidin' Will adjusted the guitar's position. "Let me see somethin' here" and he ripped into:

You ain't nothing but a hound dog

Been snoopin' round my door

You ain't nothing but a hound dog

Been snoopin' round my door

You can wag your tail

But I ain't gonna feed you no more.

Walzem waved his arms. "Will, Will, don't you think that's a little too aggressive."

"No question about it, but now listen." He clamped a capo on E minor and tapped a slower tempo but strummed the same melody. He played through once using his bottleneck slide while he accented all the pain in the song. Then he sang:

All of our heart's a longin'

To be free from all life's pain

I said, our heart is longin'

Gotta be free from Satan's pain

But ol' Satan's pleasures

Are gonna burn ya jus' the same.

"Sweet , Jesus, your singin' the blues. How did you do that?" Walzem stood on tiptoes like a cheerleader. "Can you convert all the verses and other songs?"

"Hard to say without seeing 'em, but I'll look at them today." Will placed the National back in its case. He looked at the grinning music minister who vibrated with enthusiasm and wondered if this was one of the few times a Walzem idea might work and actually make a difference. He thought the song leader might break out into a Jesus cheer.

They shook hands with Walzem's heart felt "thank you, thank you, thank you" poured over his shoulder as he danced out the door. The door reopened and The Crystal Epistle music minister shouted, "See you tonight."

As Walzem drove away from Slidin' Will's place, he remembered his close call with Rev. Hannibal Jones. He'd felt certain the meeting where Jones gave him the change music ultimatum, meant the jig was up once again. His last three gigs had ended similarly: a summons from the preacher, a confrontation, and unemployment. He knew in his heart he was a good, even Godly man. He loved Jesus, but he seemed to love sopranos more. Altos, not so much. Just sopranos.

At his last church, he'd broken his own ironclad rule – never dally with an unmarried soprano. Married sopranos were discreet and had both their family and their reputation to lose. One single, beautiful soprano bedded him before he knew what hit him. He later learned during choir practice she had indiscreetly suggested she had a thing going with old Dick to another soprano.

Dick had noticed restlessness in the soprano row. Frowns and unpleasant facial contortions rained down on him like a chromatic scale. After choir practice they exchanged or offered none of the usual pleasantries. No invitations for a cup of hot chocolate, no furtive glances and smiles – only bitterness. He had no idea of the extent of the problem, until the preacher summoned him two days later and confronted him with a majority of the unsmiling soprano section.

It seems these treble clef singers had, in closed session, determined he was pounding pretty nearly all the under-thirty sopranos like a pile driver, with no one the wiser. The preacher offered Dick a six-hour head start before he loosed the, until then, unsuspecting husbands on him.

When he answered the ad for the Crystal Epistle Church of Everlasting Enlightenment, Dick knew he was near the end of the road. He must change his ways, and for the first time, he wanted to change his ways. "Lord, if you'll give me one more chance, I'll be a new man. I'll dedicate my life to the glory of God in song."

He'd omitted this last employment debacle from his résumé as he knew the church where he'd served previously had an entirely new staff. He hoped he could finesse at least an employment confirmation from the new group. No one could have been more surprised than Dick, when Reverend Jones hired him on the spot at their first interview.

As luck would have it, the Crystal Epistle Church of Everlasting Enlightenment's church secretary, a truly cute and perky brunette named Jane, also sang in the choir – a soprano. As staff members, they found themselves thrown together daily as they executed their duties over the past year. Dick Walzem had felt his resolve fade and trouble loom on the horizon – trouble her oilrig roughneck husband might compound.

Harpoon did not often visit the Crystal Epistle, but on those rare occasions when he approached by car, usually to talk with Krank while he did his yard work, he was impressed by the soaring aluminum and glass spire topped by the moribund beacon light. The spire sparkled in noonday sun like a giant crystal. But at five-o'clock, as Harpoon approached, the sun softened in the west and reflected off a high, thin cirrus cloud layer, the spire took on a tinge, which later darkened and radiated an orange glow like burning mesquite coals.

Krank had gotten the Crystal Epistle yard in shape for the rehearsal. The smell of fresh cut grass filled the air, and the flowerbeds were weeded and edged. Harpoon smiled as he looked around the Epistle's yard where Krank's efforts produced hundreds of hibiscus blooms and an azalea hedge, a blazing mound of dark pink blossoms. Krank, you're amazing, with all the things you do for other folks at your own expense, he thought.

Harpoon couldn't remember ever entering the sanctuary before, and he looked around, surprised. The size seemed excessive for a town population of less than two thousand inhabitants. The ceiling stood high enough to accommodate a balcony. Harpoon thought, Ol' Rev. Jones can seat the whole Island at one time. Lots of folks must drive from other towns for the services, since most islanders like me never darken the door.

The octagonal shape continued up into the roof and finally formed the base on which the crystal spire rested. The eight-sided configuration allowed a great view of the podium from every seat in the auditorium, including the balcony that wrapped around five of the sides. The room was not lavishly appointed, but had tasteful accents of dark wood and maroon velvet pew cushions and dark wood trim on the podium and choir loft. The potential for hurricanes probably had eliminated the windows. The crystal spire gave the only natural light that radiated into the auditorium. With no other lights turned on, the brilliant lights over the podium and choir loft made them glisten like a jewels in the semidarkness of the room.

The podium and choir loft occupied one whole wall of the octagon and two white, smooth plastered walls flanked them. Above the choir loft, a small set of slide-back curtains looked as if they might occasionally have a Punch and Jesus Puppet Show. Harpoon laughed when he saw an actual Hammond electric organ built into the end of the podium. It's not a pipe organ sort of place. They've probably amped-up killer speakers to fill this auditorium. Fuck-'Em-All-Ted will be giggling when he finds he can rock this room.

The air conditioning system had filtered out the natural smell and sound of the Island: salt air, sea life, gulls, the surf, and people who played on the beach. The sanctuary captured the essence of eternity, making Harpoon uneasy, though the feeling was not totally unpleasant.

Halfway to the podium, voices of others who entered the foyer echoed behind him. The rattle of Krank's tom-toms was unmistakable. A door opened on the left side of the choir loft and Dick Walzem stepped through, followed by a very pretty brunette. Dick started visibly when he saw Harpoon, but recovered and spoke too loudly, "Harpoon, welcome to the Crystal Epistle. Have a seat in the front row. We need a short business meeting before we rehearse."

They both reached the front row at about the same time and shook hands. Dick pointed at the brunette. "Oh, this is Jane. She's the church secretary and also sings soprano in the choir. We're running off copies of the music we're going to adapt for performance."

Harpoon looked at the perky, smiling young woman who held out her hand and wondered where the copies were. He'd never seen her on the Island. She was someone he wouldn't forget. "A pleasure ma'am."

"Oh, I think the pleasure will be all ours, Mr. Harpoon."

By now, the rest of the group arrived at the front and introductions went all around, except for Ted who spied the Hammond Organ and had already slid his faded jeans across the seat. Harpoon thought Slidin' Will had probably forced Ted into a clean white T-shirt instead of the threadbare "T" he normally wore. Some joker had given Ted the shirt imprinted across the chest with "Fuck 'em all!" with "Ted" added below right as if the inscription came from the "Great Book of Ted." Harpoon noticed Ted's beard, normally an unkept mass hanging below his waist like a clump of Spanish moss, was shorter and neatly trimmed and combed. Maybe there's hope for Ted yet, Harpoon thought

Ted limbered his fingers and mumbled under his breath, "Hammond. Heh, heh. Hammond. Fuck 'em all. Heh, heh." He flipped the switch, pulled some stops, and noodled a little shuffle rhythm on the base pedals.

Dick turned toward the organ. "Brother Ted, could you join us here for a short business meeting before we play?"

Ted reluctantly inched his way off the bench and moved toward the group. "Brother Ted? Heh, heh. Brother! Fuck em all. Heh, heh."

Sweet Bessie and her three backups occupied the middle four seats of the front row. Bessie wore a turban made from blazing colors of intertwined silk scarves while the singers all wore the big hats with floral decorations they normally wore on Sunday, as if they all believed women's hair should be covered in church.

Slidin' Will, Harpoon, Krank, and the sax man sat on their left, but Ted sat on the other side and couldn't take his eyes off the organ. Jane, whose hair seemed a little tousled, sat in the row behind.

Dick Walzem radiated good cheer and fronted the group. "I am really excited about our new musical program, and it's great you came tonight. I thank you." He raised his arms. "Praise the Lord!"

Sweet Bessie and her backups sang in harmony, "Aaaa ah men!"

"Thank you, Sweet Bessie. Now let's keep this business meeting short because we only have tonight and Saturday's rehearsal before we go on national television on Sunday."

Harpoon and Krank looked at each other with knotted brows. Harpoon said, "Dick, I think we have a problem here. Krank and I leave tomorrow morning for the first day of shrimp season, and we'll be gone for ten days."

Walzem's benign expression signaled he was not caught off guard. "Slidin' Will told me as much, and I have prayed and possibly have a solution." He pointed up and down the row of performers. "We will pay you each fifty dollars for tonight, one-hundred dollars for Saturday's rehearsal, and one-hundred-fifty dollars for the Sunday morning service. A total of three hundred dollars each per weekend."

Sweet Bessie and the girls held up their arms and sang, "Praaaaise da Lord."

Dick said to Harpoon and Krank, "You think you could hold off shipping out until Sunday afternoon?"

Harpoon and Krank looked at each other and calculated how many shrimp they must catch to clear three hundred bucks each in two days. Krank spoke first, "The shrimp will grow bigger by Sunday."

Harpoon nodded agreement. "My feelings exactly. We could shrimp from Sunday afternoon until Thursday noon and be back in time for rehearsal."

"Plenty of time for the widows' yard work too."

Harpoon looked at Walzem. "Count us in."

Ted covered his mouth and mumbled, "Heh,heh. Three hundred bucks. Heh., heh. Fuck 'em all. Heh, heh." The backup singer beside Ted turned arched eyebrows toward him.

Walzem could barely contain his excitement. He pointed toward the sheets of paper Slidin' Will held. "I think Slidin' Will has material for us to look at and practice, but let's talk about problems. First, the congregation has sung most of the music except for a choir number and usually a solo by a choir member or myself."

Sweet Bessie spoke up, "We always sing with the choir and the congregation jus' joins in."

"True, but our congregation doesn't know much gospel music."

Jane spoke up, "Why can't we have the AV people show the lyrics on the screens like we do now? They'll catch on."

Harpoon pointed at the two blank walls. "You project stuff on those two walls?"

Jane nodded her agreement. "The AV department projects graphics, song lyrics, Bible verses, and announcements."

One of the backup singers spoke, "Bessie and us can sit in the choir tonight and work wit'em on the music and the moves."

Walzem looked puzzled. "The moves?"

Sweet Bessie frowned. "Wha'? White folks got no moves?"

"Heh, heh. Can't jump either, heh, heh. Fuck 'em all." The lady beside Ted raised her purse like she planned to take his head off.

Walzem said, "Now, Ted, We can't say those words in here. It's offensive for the ladies and disrespectful to the Lord."

Ted lowered his head, covered his mouth, and mumbled.

"Slidin' Will, I know you blues men are performers and both sing and play instrumental solos. Church music is more about the lyrics than the music itself. You have any ideas about the instrumental solos?"

Slidin' Will thought for a moment. "I know we'll have no trouble backin' up Sweet Bessie, the choir, and the congregation. Maybe we could replace the choir number and the soloists with a couple of our numbers with some of these lyrics here?"

Harpoon added, "What if Sweet Bessie and her singers, and maybe even the choir riffed out behind our instrumental solos. There will always be lyrics for the congregation to hear. They might even join in."

Walzem's eyes lit up. "I think this will work."

"Got no problems, Reverend. We do it all a time with our church band." Bessie and her friends nodded like chickens in a granary.

Walzem turned and pointed out the microphone stands. "Why don't we take our positions and get in some practice before the choir comes in at seven-o'clock. Slidin' Will, you guys take the mikes beside the organ and Besse and the singers stand in the center of the podium."

Bessie and the ladies went up the steps first. "What we gonna sing, brother Walzem?"

"Pick three of your favorite gospel hymns, and we will start with them so the band can get up to speed on backing you up."

The four ladies circled up and discussed song options. In less than a minute Sweet Bessie said, "Maybe we start out wit a 'ol spiritual like 'Swing Low Sweet Chariot' everybody knows. Maybe start slow an' then jump it up a little."

One of the other singers said, "Then we do 'I Never Heard a Man Speak Like This Man' kinda mild and mellow. Then a little up-tempo with B. B. King's 'He Brought Me Water'."

There always came a time when Dick Walzem questioned his judgment. He wondered if he'd made a mistake. Was there any hope of this working? Had he done something wrong? Had his carnal sins come back to haunt him? Should he pray for forgiveness or for survival? Now his pinball life made him wish he had taken up selling bibles. He closed his eyes and said a silent prayer. "I'll leave it up to you ladies. Let's try it." He looked at Jane. "Write down the words as we go. Oh, and be sure the AV folks come up with some good graphics as backgrounds for all the lyrics."

Sweet Bessie counted off, and a slow perfect harmony floated out into the sanctuary:

Swing low sweet chariot

Comin' for to carry me home…

Krank set up a "call and answer" rhythm on the tom-toms and Slidin' Will and Ted picked up the musical key and started a riff behind the singers. Harpoon and the Sax joined in with an embellishment on the basic theme. Sweet Bessie finger snapped a two-four double time rhythm. Krank jumped it up, and she swung into the first verse

If you get there before I do…

The singers and the band answered:

Comin' for to carry me home…

Walzem raised both arms and danced in a circle. "Praise Jesus! I'm coming home."

The rehearsal progressed more slowly when they worked on "I Never Heard a Man Speak Like this Man" and "He Brought Me Water" because the music was less familiar for the band.

Walzem wanted to see how the blues praise music sounded. "Okay, Slidin' Will, let's hear what you've put together for the band."

"We'll do a quick run through on the song we discussed this mornin' and then we'll try something I worked on today." Slidin' Will showed the lyrics to Harpoon. "This is a slow version of "Hound Dog" in E minor." He ran through the melody one time on the steel guitar, then nodded, and one by one they fell in behind him. On the second verse they all joined in with Slidin' Will as he sang the verses and Harpoon sang the refrain.

Walzem felt superfluous and sat down in the front row and listened while these professionals worked. *They must read each other's minds.* When Will took the first instrumental solo. Bessie and the singers swung into to a vamp behind him:

Our heart's a longin'
Free from all life's pain.

He sighed with satisfaction after each solo. These people have taken a song about a woman kicking a worthless lover out of her house into a passionate plea for a closer relationship with Jesus. His eyes glistened with emotion as he stood and cheered after the song.

Harpoon leaned toward Slidin' Will. "When'd you start playin' an acoustic and a electric guitar all at once?"

"Man, I'm only playin' one, but I'm sure enough hearin' two. Sounds a lot like Stevie Ray Vaughan, right?" Slidin' Will looked at Ted. "Ted you got a guitar stop pulled on that Hammond?"

"Heh, heh. Guitar Stop. Heh, heh Nope! Fuck 'em all, heh, heh."

Harpoon spoke first, "What are we gonna do if this guitar man wails on out on his own?"

Slidin' Will could see the concern in Harpoon's eyes. The whole thing could take on the look of lip-sink-orama. "I think we gotta back him up."

"What's next?" Walzem asked.

"Well Preacher, I kinda like "Because of Your Love." We can do it in a Willie Brown/Muddy Waters format."

"What's that?"

"Show him guys." Slidin' Will sang:

Woke up this mornin'

The band answered with the same tune and rhythm

Looked all 'round the room

The band answered with the tune and rhythm.

"'Because of Your Love' fits the rhythm pattern exactly. What do you think?" Slidin' Will was not sure how Walzem would go for such a basic blues idiom. "Maybe it's a little low down for church folk."

Walzem stood and paced for a minute and wondered how far he could go with the blues format. Maybe we should stick with gospel. Finally he looked up at the band and said, "Let's try it."

Slidin' Will said to Ted, "We're in a key of C, so give me a wailin' high C note and work on down to middle C and then play under the lyrics, and the rest of you answer, okay?" He pointed, and Ted struck a soulful high C and Slidin' Will sang a glissando supported by a single string slide down to middle C as he sang :

Jeeeahhhzzus

You endured my pain...

The band and singers answered

Because of Your love

You bore all my shame

Because of Your love

I said You felt all my pain

Because of Your Love

And You bore all a my shame

Because of Your Love

Sweet maker of the universe

Because of Your Love

Broken for the sins a the earth.

Walzem stood in rapture as Will, the band, and the singers worked their way through two more verses. Rev. Jones was right. How could anyone not understand the sacrifice Jesus made for our sins from this?

The choir members had drifted in and taken their seats in the choir loft, and joined with Dick Walzem's enthusiastic applause at the conclusion of the song. An elderly lady with a tape measure around her neck and a clipboard in her free hand showed visible pain as she pulled herself up the handrail and podium stairs one at a time. She approached Slidin' Will when Walzem spoke up, "This is Mazie Hartung, our choirmaster who will measure you for choir robes."

Ted looked at the tape measure like it was a snake. "Heh, heh. Choir robes? Heh. heh, fuck 'em all. Heh, heh.

As the choir loft filled, Walzem could see their unrest. He climbed onto the podium and addressed the choir, "You probably wonder why there's no music issued for tonight's rehearsal." The choir mumbled and nodded their heads. Dick looked around the choir and saw the predominately over-forties welcomed the change. The sprinkling of younger singers might not appreciate the older music, and of course a handful of "Good Christian" racists would resent the black singers and their music.

"Rev. Jones is changing the focus of our musical outreach. So we've brought in Sweet Bessie Thompson and her gospel singers and we've formed a blues band headed by a man most of you know, Slidin' Will Pickens, the former recording star and current bait shop owner. We've had a run-through on this Sunday's music with the singers and the band, and now let's work on combining the choir into the music. I really think you'll enjoy this."

Harpoon carried a tom-tom as he and Slidin' Will walked down the Epistle steps on each side of Krank while Ted followed behind, mumbling to himself. "Dick Walzem seemed pleased with the rehearsal." Harpoon looked around the group for agreement.

Krank gave one of his rare smiles. "Choir needs more work on its 'moves'."

Slidin' Will shook his head, trying to understand what this invisible presence could be. "To tell you the truth, I was concerned about the whole thing, but everything's all right. I wonder if the electric guitar will show up all a time. I'm tellin' you the cat's got some licks." "The spirit will remain with us until the end." Krank made one of his pronouncements and Harpoon's stomach turned a little queasy.

Harpoon had told Slidin' Will about Krank's psychic pronouncements, but this was the first one Will had heard first hand." You talkin'bout the Stevie Ray Vaughan spirit you guys been seein'?"

"Krank, man, you're always sayin' stuff like 'the end' like it's really 'The End'."

Krank put one of the tom-toms in the back of his truck

and took his other one from Harpoon. "Everything must end."

Slidin' Will looked back and forth between Krank and Harpoon, motioned to Ted, and said, "See you over at the Emporium. I think we need to blow some things outa our heads."

CHAPTER | 23

The Joynt bar had standing room only for most of the night, but with a different crowd. Lottie noticed the young stoners from the days before, who'd inquired about the free pot, were gone and replaced by voyeurs come for a look at the event broadcast on TV stations statewide. The cannabis patch and stoner beach colony had become a tourist attraction like the Haight Ashbury district of San Francisco back in the sixties. This definitely was a better crowd for the Joynt.

The stoners only drank beer, seldom ate in the restaurant, and walked the check whenever they could, while this crowd migrated from the restaurant into the bar for mixed drinks and conversation about the ganja gig. Both the men and the women wore T-shirts void of clever sayings or commercial logos – only little alligators or country club logos monogrammed over the pockets. These were neatly tucked into Bermuda shorts accompanied by either tennis shoes or loafers, and a bill cap monogrammed with a country club logo. Several wore socks with their sandals.

Lottie thought, new blood in the tourist scene could be a really good thing for the Island's economy. Real estate values might even improve if they invest and hang around.

The noise level between the music and laughter prevented

any sort of normal conversation. A pall of smoke hanging in the air above the crowd made the perennial Christmas tree lights look like maritime navigation lights in fog. She saw Harpoon through the dim light and haze as he squeezed past the crowd toward the bar. He'd called earlier and said he and Krank weren't going shrimping until Sunday afternoon; he knew she'd be busy, and he'd explain later after jammin' at Slidin' Will's Wine Bar and Blues Emporium for a couple of hours.

A couple stood as Harpoon reached the bar, and he took one of the seats. Lottie greeted him with a napkin clad Shiner Bock. "It must have taken a deep religious experience to keep you and Krank in port tomorrow."

"Three-hundred dollars."

"Three hundred dollars can give a couple of guys a religious experience?"

"Each!"

"Six-hundred dollars can produce an even more moving experience."

"We're playing for this Sunday's service. It's televised nationally."

"I wonder how many listen?"

"I don't know, but I'll bet Rev. Jones has the week's Nielsen TV ratings right under his Bible."

"I reckon quite a few listen and contribute if the Epistle can pay you guys that kind if money."

"Dick Walzem said the good reverend feels the new music will bring back the viewers lost over the last year when they started singing "praise music."

Harpoon surprised Lottie by staying pretty much in control even after two hours at Slidin' Will's where the musicians drink free. Obviously music trumped beer tonight. Harpoon was so depressed since he confessed his involvement in drug trafficking, he spent a lot of time drinking. Her concern was how to help him. But tonight he seemed completely upbeat and happier than she'd seen him in weeks.

Harpoon was a good man. Even so, she could not picture him playing in church. Folks could depend on him, and up until his illegal activity, he always stayed part of the solution rather than part of the problem, but a churchgoer – no. Yet, here he stood in front of her, joyous, as if his venture into religion had made a difference.

"I don't know how long the church gig will last but I'll enjoy it as long as they want me." He gave her a meaningful smile. "You and I blocked out some quality time for tonight since Krank and I planned to ship out tomorrow, but a little thing like staying in port shouldn't stand in our way, right?"

She untied her apron and headed around the end of the bar. "I'll tell the manager I'm leaving. Why don't you meet me at my house?"

Harpoon raised his eyebrows and made a fake lunge toward the door. "Last one there sleeps on the bottom."

Krank had gone home from Slidin' Will's, intent on going to bed, but the sound of the stoners' reggae party raging on the beach across the Island lured him onto his deck chaise with his peace pipe. Before he dozed off, he heard rustling in the spartina grass across the Cut. In the almost-full moonlight he made out the shape of Coyote. The wind calmed, and the beach party sounds faded gently away. He communed with Coyote. *It's pretty late.*

Coyote looked at him. *"It is late. The time is at hand."*
"I know."
"Are you ready?"
"There are things I will miss – friends, mostly."
"Maybe you will see them again."
"That would be good."

Krank awoke as a brilliant sunrise peaked over the dunes. A light breeze blew landward and wrinkled the surface of Wilson's Cut. He looked around and saw he had spent the night on the chaise lounge. "Thank goodness a breeze came up and kept the mosquitoes away." He picked up the peace pipe resting on his chest and sat up, stretched the muscles cramped by the cool night air, and thought, "I've got to get going if I'm gonna get all my Island widows' yard work done by Saturday afternoon rehearsal."

The first of the fishermen rumbled down the two-track road pulling a small aluminum boat toward the launch afforded by the Cut's natural slope into the water. He knew Coyote would not show up this morning with fishermen already arriving. Krank wished he had because he wanted to discuss what must have been a dream. He got up, moved inside, washed his face and hands, made a ham and cheese sandwich for lunch, and loaded his yard work equipment.

Before lifting his head from the pillow on Lottie's bed, Harpoon reached behind and felt her side empty. He sat up. "Lottie, you still here?" Silence. He swung his legs over the side of the bed and went into the kitchen where coffee waited, and a note invited him for breakfast. He looked at his watch and wondered if the invitation would hold for lunch. He pulled on his clothes, drove home, showered, dressed in work clothes, and drove back to the Joynt – more to see Lottie than to eat.

His mind wandered as he drove through the town now bustling with tourists, but Lottie drifted back into his consciousness. Lottie, what am I going to do with you? You're truly habit forming. I wonder if we have any hope of a permanent arrangement? Lots of problems, though. He knew his business always teetered on disaster. God forbid he get convicted as a dope dealer. She would probably gladly support him financially, but the thought didn't thrill him. Many shrimpers escaped south to countries requiring no turtle excluder devices, and diesel fuel sold at a fraction of the cost in Port Aransas, where shrimpers could still make a living.

He snapped out of his reverie when he pulled into the Joynt's parking lot, and saw several of the Wisdom Table's regulars as they made their way through the parked cars toward their mid-day rendezvous. He waved at Wiley Coots and Coach Bull Bostich, probably involved in an animated conversation about the upcoming football season. A gust of wind off the harbor brought all the nautical smells and sent the quiver of anticipation though his soul that always heralded shrimping. Sunday seemed a long time off.

Inside the Joynt, he immediately saw trouble looming. A large group of tourists had commandeered the Wisdom Table, unaware of their social blunder. Chef Crump, Wiley Coots, Bull Bostich, and a couple of others of the Wisdom Table hierarchy milled about like the sheep in the "Dog in the Manger" story.

Lottie spied the problem from the kitchen and rushed out to Harpoon. "Would you help pull tables together in the bar and make a substitute perch for the city's finest?"

She rounded up the lost souls and herded them into the bar. "No problem men, we've made a special table for you in the bar where you can talk without interruption. After all, we would not want the city to halt for lack of a Wisdom Table, would we?"

She noticed grumbles and looks of dissatisfaction, but they dutifully followed her into the bar. "Here you go, gentlemen." She pulled back a chair for Wiley Coots, and the others followed suit. "All the comforts of home, right? And a beer on me if you want. I'll get Cindy in here right away for your orders."

She didn't know Rev. Hannibal Jones had arrived and stood behind her. She stepped backwards, bumped into the rotund reverend, caromed off, and apologized. His good-humored voice boomed into the room. "The pleasure's all mine Sister Lottie; however, dragging a man of God into a din of iniquity might tarnish his reputation. But faced with the problems besetting our island, we must take extreme and expeditious measures, and amen!"

When she saw Rev. Jones in his invocation pose, Lottie backed out of the bar into the restaurant where she slammed into Harpoon. "I feel like I'm in a pinball machine today," she said as she waved Cindy toward the bar.

Harpoon loosed his grip on Lottie. "I'm getting out of your way. I've got a few things to do on 'Ol Blues. Then I have to cut my grass since it'll be a couple of weeks before I get the chance again. I might even cut yours."

"Last night that good? Let me think. There may be a few more chores on my honey-do list." She knew she had made progress if lover boy was offering yard work.

"Like the Good Book says, 'Tit for tat."

"I'm not sure that came out of the Good Book, unless it's in one of Rev. Hannibal's mystery Bible books." Lottie kissed him on the cheek and rushed back into the kitchen.

Chief Crump watched the makeshift Wisdom Table fill quickly. Wiley Coots, Coach Bull Bostich, two T-shirt shop owners, a restaurant owner, a motel manager, a bank president, Amos McAllister, Judge Flip Fonders, J.P., Constable Sherrill, Roly Odem CPA, and another table was added for Mayor Riley Glenn so they all could be seated. Crump looked around the table at the uneasiness of the group hiding behind the façade of good humor. This might be the first time Wisdom Table attendance pushed one hundred percent. The group dressed casually in blue jeans and khaki pants with T-shirts or open collared sports shirts. This must be Casual Friday since the banker's not wearing a necktie. I bet there weren't two dozen neckties on the whole Island, and they only got worn two at a time by the two bank presidents. 'Casual Friday' on the Island. He chuckled to himself. What could possibly be done to make Friday more casual than the rest of the week? He caught sight of Rev. Jones. Well, maybe a few preachers wear ties on Sunday.

He knew the restlessness of the group came from the paradox of their economic condition. "You're all making a shitload of money off the cannabis patch," he thought, but you're too hypocritical to campaign overtly in favor of breaking the law. You know the law will ultimately crap in your nest, but you'd like it later rather than sooner. This will be a truly interesting discussion."

Rev. Hannibal Jones stood, held his arm in the air, and delivered an invocation, "Lord God, Creator of Us All, Healer of Our Ills, Forgiver of Our Sins, and our Bulwark Against Evil, we come today with heavy hearts. We are beset with the devil weed, Satan's own seed. We ask forgiveness for our sins and for your divine guidance as we rid ourselves of those infidels who now infest our Island. Bless the food and strengthen the Army of God for carrying out your Holy Purpose . . . oh, and smile down on Coach Bostich and the Fighting Port A Ridley Turtles this coming football season, and amen!" The whole table chanted in unison "Go, You Ridleys!"

Football practice started in a couple of weeks, and Coach Bostich knew the Wisdom Table was getting antsy about what they should expect on the gridiron this season. All of the Port A lifers remembered the old glory days when Krank lit up the scoreboard like a slot machine, and dreamed of their return. Coach had trod a razorblade between building enthusiasm for ticket sales and maintaining expectations within achievable limits. The humdrum football seasons had dragged on year after year with the occasional hope of a district title, always trampled like a bug in a parking lot by the Beeville Jones High School Trojans. Occasionally a winning season lifted Ridley spirits, but then the doldrum 5 - 5 and 4 - 6 seasons always set in until some of the opponents stunk up the football fields even worse, and the Ridleys would squeak out a 7 & 3 with a shot at a title. With little good news, Coach Bostich rose and made his report. "Thank you Rev. Jones, I appreciate your invoking the higher powers on behalf of the Fighting Port Aransas Ridley Turtles."

"Go, You Ridleys!"

"Actually, we may need divine intervention this season. As you know, the Ruger family moved away this summer and took our quarterback with them. If a bunch of hard-working inspired boys who will give their all can win us some games, then we're okay, 'cause we have plenty of those kids. What we lack is talent, particularly at quarterback. Our best hope is for a family to move onto the Island with a really gifted youngster. Still, good honest effort on the gridiron, a will to win, and a little luck can often overcome more talented teams. So I think we can at least provide our fans with real excitement this season."

Wiley Coots shouted, "Fear the Turtle!"

The table erupted into another, "Go, You Ridleys!"

Chief Crump knew, in a normal season, the remainder of lunch would be devoted to telling old football stories, prognosticating on the coming season, and general hype about how this could be "our year." But the more pressing issue hanging over the group like big city smog quashed the chatter into an uncomfortable silence. They looked around at each other and each wondered who would broach the subject of how they might keep the Island humming and the money pouring in as long as possible. Crump took the leap before Rev. Jones pontificated on moral issues. "It's been a while since we've all come together. I expect you want to discuss how we can continue the prosperity the Island's currently enjoying." His cohorts looked like a collection of bobble-heads. "Constable Sherrill, you're the only law enforcement present in whose jurisdiction the pot field abides. How about telling us what's happening on the side of the law."

"I reckon there's three or four-hundred stoners camped down on the beach, and they operate like an anarchy. There's this Rasta lookin' fellow at the center of activities, but they've set up an underground self-serve distribution center where anyone can pick up a little weed for free. The closest thing to paying's a donation bucket for the toilets, fuel for the generators, and something for the band. Texas has not decriminalized small amounts of pot like some other states, so all of them are subject to arrest on possession charges."

One wide-eyed T-shirt shop owner spoke up, "You mean you'll arrest them?"

"The sheriff sent a deputy over from Corpus Christi, and a Texas Ranger's on his way down from Austin. But I've told them unless they bring the National or State Guard, don't bother. We could end up with something worse than the Waco disaster if things get out of hand. Besides there's not enough jails in Nueces county for them."

Judge Flip Fonders joined the conversation. "Since they took up residence in accordance with the law on the 'No Permit Required' beach, Constable, you could argue the finer points of the law requiring a search warrant for each tent or camper. My office would take weeks creating a hundred-fifty or so warrants, particularly if 'just cause' must be proven."

A collective sigh of relief issued from the business community at the idea their bonanza would continue for several weeks.

Amos McAllister jumped into the conversation. "We're moving into the dry season, the plants will dry up, and there's a finite amount of cannabis buds. Between plants dying and the demand for cannabis created by the horde of stoners on the beach, the problem might solve itself."

A literalist asked, "You're saying once they harvest all of the buds and the plants die; the stoners will leave and the tourists with them?"

"Very possibly."

The group emitted an audible groan.

Chief Crump offered, "You mentioned Waco. The good news is the DEA boys have held the FBI at bay by insisting it's a matter for their agency, and the drug bust, their very first, would fall in their column, and not the FBI's."

Mayor Glen wondered how politically expedient admitting a mistake in judgment might be. Finally, he found the politically correct phrasing. "At first this whole episode appeared to tarnish our reputation as a family tourist destination. Now just the opposite. Teenagers all over the state beg their parents for a vacation here in Port A. Amazingly, the parents happily oblige. The town's booming with shiny new faces all apparently enthralled with the joys of Port A."

The motel manager who had recently transferred into Port A from California said, "It's a shame Texas hasn't passed medical marijuana legislation like some other states. We could keep this boom going for years. Maybe we can think up another way."

The silence of the ages fell over the table. The newcomer looked around and knew had he farted like an elephant trumpeting in The Cave of Winds; he could not have committed a more egregious social blunder. All eyes turned toward the Right Reverend Hannibal Jones as he hoisted his girth from his chair.

Rev. Jones stood for an interminable minute with chin on chest as if praying. He raised his head heavenward and bellowed, "I feel like a stranger lost in a foreign land, surrounded by Philistines. Who are you people? Are you not the good God-fearing Island folk I've loved over the years? The people with high moral values who stood for right and against all evil?"

Wiley Coots looked around the table and wondered if this included him.

The Reverend looked deep into the eyes of each person at the Wisdom Table "We have in our midst the very essence of evil. Had Satan himself risen from the bowels of the earth and blossomed here on the Island we could not be more in peril. The devil weed has already corrupted our very moral fabric and left us scheming ways to prosper like the greedy moneychangers Christ Himself scourged from the Temple of Jerusalem. A modern Sodom and Gomorrah wallowing in wanton pleasure, intent on drunkenness, debauchery, and fornication, as in the Genocide Chapters 18 and 19 biblical accounts, has sprung up, and we turn our backs. Woe unto us if Jehovah God rains down fire and brimstone once again to cleanse our souls. Yea verily, I say unto you, think not on how to perpetuate the cancer that is eating the heart and soul of our island but make haste and rid us of our potential destruction, and amen. ”

Rev. Jones lowered himself into his chair with some effort. Wiley Coots turned to a T-shirt seller beside him and whispered, “How do you follow an act like that?”

Harpoon had stopped by Bilmore & Sons for a case of engine oil for the Blues and the Family Grocery Center for four more cases of Shiner Bock, a different form of lubrication. He decided that buying the produce for the galley on Saturday might insure its freshness. He mostly wanted to check the refrigeration unit on the Blues and make sure the perishable food Krank had stored the day before was still okay. He heard footsteps on the deck while down in the engine room and galley stowing the oil and beer. He climbed the ladder and saw Mako with Goons One and Two leaning against the sorting table.

He hesitated for a second imagining what these assholes wanted. Surely they had figured out where their pot was by now. A sling on Mako’s right arm supported a cast and hid all the gold hanging around his neck. His blue sports coat held his other arm. The goons wore their usual double-knit gangster finery including fedoras. Harpoon climbed out on the deck, grabbed the ice shovel, and strode toward the drug dealers. “I don’t remember giving you permission to come aboard. Get off my boat!”

Goon One moved into protective mode in front of Mako while Goon Two with his damaged knee looked menacing; his hand behind his back gripped the Glock in his belt. Mako shoved them aside and took a defiant stance. “Drop the shovel, cowboy. We got business to discuss.”

“I’ve got nothing to discuss with you idiots.” Harpoon’s head swiveled around as he wondered how many branches of law enforcement saw Mako on the deck of his shrimp boat in broad daylight wearing yellow pants and a blue sports coat. The whole island’s in turmoil over drugs, and I’ve got the local drug lord standing on the deck of my shrimp boat. This is just wonderful. “Like I said, get off my damn boat – NOW!”

Mako walked past him. "Shut up and get into your wheelhouse. NOW!"

Harpoon cocked his right arm to lay a haymaker on Mako's jaw when he felt the cold steel of a pistol on his temple.

Goon Two hobbled into sight. "Where's your Indian friend, tough guy?"

"Maybe he's down in the hold gettin' the AK-47."

"Maybe he's not, since we watched your boat before you got here."

Mako turned as he reached the wheelhouse door. "Forget the Indian. We'll deal with him later. Get the cowboy in here. We need to talk." Mako opened the door, moved inside first, and sat in the pilot's seat with great difficulty. No help came from the arm in the cast, and the chair stood higher than his butt. After three tries he finally landed one cheek of his ass on the edge of the seat and leveraged himself into the prominent position, while the Goons herded Harpoon into the cabin behind him. "Let's make this short. You're making another pick up for us on Tuesday night."

Harpoon stared at Mako in disbelief. "You're out of your mind. I'm not doing anything for you guys. In fact I seriously wish I'd never heard of you, and I don't plan to see you ever again. Now get off my boat and don't come back."

Mako leaned back in the pilot's chair with the casual air of a gambler with good cards. "I don't see you have a choice. I'm not asking. I'm telling you, and I'm offering the same pay."

"Well, I'm telling you to go straight to hell!" Harpoon turned to leave, but Goon One blocked the wheelhouse door.

Mako ignored Harpoon's comment. "We're not pickin' up ganja this time. You've completely screwed up the marijuana market."

"I haven't screwed up anything. I made a mistake and hauled some bales of pot your two bozos carried away in their pickup. That's the last I saw of it."

Goon Two spoke up, "We've figured out you and the Indian

dug up the pot and planted acres of it."

Harpoon laughed out loud. "I'd expect this level of intelligence from an idiot who wears a size five hat."

The cast on Mako's arm dampened the menacing gesture. "You two shut up. I'm movin' up to bigger things, and the package we pick up will be much smaller this time."

"What part of 'I'm not picking up anything for you assholes do you not understand?"

" I don't see you goin' to the law with this, since you got a lot to lose there." Mako slid from the chair and stood nose-to-nose with Harpoon. Actually, more like nose to chest. "I'll call you Monday and work out details." He turned and walked out of the cabin followed by the goons.

"Yeah, and maybe I'll bake some cookies for the trip, assholes!"

Ricky Stone and Jeff McAlister sat inside the Crate and watched the ingenious ganja dryer tumble the night's harvest. A wooden frame held two hair dryers inserted through holes the size of their barrels in the ends of the plastic drum and circulated hot air into the revolving drum. A bungee cord belt around the drum and a record turntable kept the drum spinning like a giant record.

The marijuana THC escaping with the dryer's hot air had relaxed Ricky to the point of almost dozing. His fake dreads looked a little tired, and the air in the Crate became stifling when the dryer ran, plus they both could use a good bath. "Completely ingenious, Mon. We be crankin' out da ganja before da stoners wake up. We dry the nugs, and the stoners do da cleaning and seeding. Very efficient, for sure. High volume even."

"We're at risk though."

"What da risk, Mon?"

"While we're drying the pot before the stoners get it, we're holdin' a felony amount of marijuana. Not good when the law shows up."

"But we're not sellin' it, Mon."

"Doesn't matter. We can't possess, transport, use, sell, or probably know anybody who does. Small amounts sometimes get probation, but ten pounds of pot, man, can alter our lifestyle for a decade."

"Very short sighted of da law. A mon should be able to enjoy the Holy Smoke undisturbed, right? It's religious freedom, Mon. Anyway da last few days be worth it. Never has there been such a party. Chicks by the dozens, the Stoned Cold Dreads pumpin' out reggae, plenty a beer, and Jah's Holy Smoke. Very spiritual, Mon."

"NOW LADIES AND GENTLEMEN I MUST WARN YOU. YOU MAY SEE DISTURBING CONDUCT ON THE BEACH TODAY. NUDITY, CARNAL LUST, OR EVEN GANJA CRAZED STONERS. SO BE READY TO SHADE YOUR EYES TO ANYTHING YOU FIND OFFENSIVE."

Ricky and Jeff sat up, wide eyed.

"What be this talkin' I hear? Most disturbin'."

Jeff slid The Crate door open. "Good God, it's a sightseeing tour." He leaped out and ran in front of a battery-powered dune buggy, belonging to a fleet of electric dune buggies for tourists in Port A. They normally resembled brightly painted lady bugs, but this family version fitted with three seats held five people plus, in this case, the owner of the rental operation who sat behind the wheel with a microphone in his hand.

"SEE, THERE'S A GANJA CRAZED STONER NOW."

Jeff put his hand on the fender and grabbed the microphone from the driver's hand. "Dick, what the hell are you doing?"

"I'm selling sightseeing tours, man." He pointed to the five anxious faces behind him, all with perfect teeth, wearing T-shirts with little alligators monogrammed above the pockets stuffed into Bermuda shorts, and sandals with socks.

"Are you out of your mind? Sightseeing tours? Get out a here!" Behind Jeff several of the stoners, rudely awakened by the sightseeing announcements and apparently offended by their content, had gathered. Suddenly, a beach-sand "mud ball" exploded on the canvas roof of the tourist wagon and showered sand down on all sides. One splattered on the windshield, exploding like a hand grenade, and the next one hit upside Dick, the driver's, head.

Jeff held the microphone to his mouth, "LADIES AND GENTLEMEN YOUR TOUR HAS BEEN CANCELLED. PLEASE GET YOUR REFUND BACK IN PORT A."

Dick became the busiest man on the Island as he tried to back up and get the cumbersome vehicle turned around. One of the alligator shirts leaned out of the wagon and shouted, "Hey, man, where can I score some pot?" Another fusillade of sand-balls cut his query short. Finally, with three tries, Dick retreated down the beach as the wide-eyed tourists looked over their shoulder wondering if the stoners were chasing them.

Ricky watched with Jeff as the defeated sightseeing buggy faded away. "I think it most intelligent stowing the ganja at the distribution point, so I carry out dis mission."

"Good thinking." Jeff looked around the beach encampment. "It looks like a big night tonight again. Let's go into town, so I can report to my grandparents, who probably wonder where I am, since my cell phone battery ran out yesterday. We need some gasoline and kegs of beer. There's probably enough money in the bucket for the expenses plus a couple of juicy burgers."

"You tink maybe this Rasta might score a bath at your grandparents? Some chicks be thinkin' I'm a little ripe, if ya know what I mean."

"You'll have to lose the Rasta dreads and accent before we get to their beach house."

"No problem. They're itching like crazy."

Jeff looked out on the beach village scene from the hammock hung under the fly-tent attached to the Crate. A calm, serene scene with little activity except for those frolicking in the surf. The beer kegs had been iced, and the generator fueled up with a backup gas can on standby. The nighttime revelry, followed by the after-midnight ganja harvest and drying left little time for sleep. Many of the stoners needed an afternoon siesta, including him and Ricky, who already snored inside. The Crate's sound system was blissfully silent for the first time.

Since the grandparents were not home, he had had no embarrassing questions. The note he left them said he was staying with Ricky on the beach and everything was fine. He started to mention the Jeep, but thought better and opted against problematic issues. His last thought before he drifted off in the hammock was: how cool is this?

A sense of movement and the smell of meat smoke brought Jeff back into the realm of the living. The sun still shone forth on the beach scene, but settled near the crest of the dunes. The ganja city was awake and on the move. A hundred or so charcoal grills sent burnt offerings of everything from steak to wieners into the heavens. The smell reminded Jeff his noontime burger had worn thin.

A stoner approached from his camper a few hundred feet down the beach. "Hey, man, we've cooked up a lot of roasted corn, sausage, and stuff. Why don't you and the Rasta come on over and help us eat it up?"

"Best idea today! Be over as quick as I can get the Rasta up and moving. We'll bring along some beer." Jeff shook the stoners hand. "Thanks, man."

When Ricky and Jeff arrived back at the Crate, they saw a cache of driftwood piled in the center of the plaza by some enterprising stoners. The sun slid behind the dunes, and the reflection on the scattered clouds gave the impression of luminescent cotton balls. A cool breeze blew off the water and washed surf up on the beach with susurrant sighs. The air, now cleansed of sacrificial smoke, took on the pungent hint of cannabis. The Stoned Cold Dreads did their mike checks that punctuated the growing dusk. Someone doused the driftwood with charcoal lighter, touched a match, and the party was on.

Ricky looked over the assembling crowd. "This be the way Great Jah means life to be. Most appreciated, for sure."

The Stoned Cold Dreads cranked up the lighthearted Bob Marley tune, "Don't Worry, Be Happy," and the crowd bobbed around the bonfire in reggae rhythm. We better enjoy it while we can, thought Jeff. "They're playing our theme song."

The fire now glowed as coals while the Dreads loaded up their equipment. The crowd still milled around the plaza, but many drifted toward the beach and enjoyed the psychedelic dance of the full moonlight among the waves. The moon had crossed the "yardarm" of the dunes when the harvesters moved out into the Ganja patch. They crawled on hands and knees and clipped off the nugs as they found them. They now could distinguish between the ominous rattle of the unstoned and the Cha Cha Cha beat of the friendly gopher-stoned snakes.

Their harvest complete, they assembled at the Crate and consolidated their illicit produce. Much of the camp slept, but a few of the seriously stoned still sat transfixed on the beach. Harmonious howls of coyotes in the dunes broke the silence. Jeff moved for a better view. "They sound an awful lot like the Backstreet Boys."

The group of harvesters stood by Jeff and observed the songsters. Four coyotes grouped together serenaded the moon, silhouetting them perfectly atop the dunes.

One of the harvesters said, "Man, that's some creepy coyote shit."

"Nah, mon, da coyotes be nothin'. What's creeping me out is the dude in a flat brimmed hat, standing beside 'em playin' the guitar."

CHAPTER | 24

Dick Walzem had addressed the Mazie Hartung problem shortly after his arrival at the Crystal Epistle Church of Everlasting Enlightenment a year ago. Reverend Hannibal Jones had told him neither he nor the previous minister of music had a solution, as Mr. Hartung's insurance policies left her quite well off, and Mazie contributed generously to the church.

Reverend Jones had explained, "Mazie lives to sing in the choir. Her friends are all choir members, and her life revolves around the choir."

It took only one choir rehearsal and one Sunday service for Walzem to understand the problem. Time had not been kind to Mazie. At age seventy her eyeglasses still resembled paperweights even though the optometrist had sold her the new thin-style polycarbonate lenses. The eyeglasses had achieved some improvement in vision, but on sheet music apparently a "quarter rest" still resembled a "quarter note." To Dick's dismay, this often left Mazie's crackling voice singing when the choir was not.

The decibel level of her speech must have increased as her hearing faded. At Walzem's first service, Mazie "whispered" to a fellow choir member during Rev. Jones' sermon, when the

Reverend paused for effect. Mazie's voice echoed throughout the sanctuary with, "I fry mine in butter."

Dick hated that her diminished hearing had also affected her pitch and singing and made her discordant clunkers the butt of many congregation jokes. Walzem had moved quickly and had asked Mazie to visit with him in his office. He invited her to sit on the couch and sat next to her.

"Mazie, you're loved and respected by all here at the Crystal Epistle, and in these few short days I've grown to share in these sentiments." Dick reached for her hand and patted it.

"Why, thank you, Brother Walzem. I'm flattered." She smiled and nodded appreciation.

"Mazie, yesterday right here in this office I prayed on my knees and thanked the Lord for all the choir members and most especially for Mazie Hartung, and the Lord spoke to me as clearly as I speak to you right now."

"How blessed you must have felt, Brother Walzem." Mazie's eyes lit up in amazement.

"I was filled with the Holy Spirit, and I asked, 'Lord what would you have me do?'"

Mazie's eyes looked as big as quarters. "And what did the Lord say?"

"The Lord said, 'I have a special plan for Mazie Hartung to reward her for her complete dedication and devotion to the choir." Dick patted her hand again.

"A special plan?"

"That's right Mazie. The Lord said, 'From this day forth, Mazie will not sing in the choir, but instead is elevated to the position of choirmaster.'" Walzem broke out into a broad grin. "It's just wonderful, Mazie."

"Not sing in the choir?" Mazie's lips quivered slightly.

"Mazie, the Lord thinks you're much too valuable for singing in the choir."

"But what does the choirmaster do?"

"Mazie, we'll give you the little office under the choir loft

stairs. You will have full responsibility for the choir robes; you will be the music librarian, and you will act as choir secretary. It's a very important job, Mazie, or I'm sure the Lord would not have promoted you to it."

"But can't I sing in the choir also?"

"No time for that, Mazie. You'll be much too busy as choirmaster." Brother Walzem slid off the couch and knelt facing Mazie. "Pray with me, Mazie, that the Lord's will be done."

Walzem's quick dispatch of the Mazie problem had made Reverend Jones ecstatic. Dick, himself, felt gratified over the last year at the diligence and conscientiousness Choirmaster Hartung exhibited, even though she often admitted to friends she missed singing in the choir. In fact, she missed being in the church at all. They had wired a cable TV into the choir dressing room so she could watch the services.

Mazie had Saturday off since the choir normally had no function. But the new gospel singers and the band members all needed choir robes. When she'd come on Friday to select the robes, some were soiled. She took them to One Hour Martenizing for a quick dry cleaning, to be picked up Saturday morning, so they would be ready for a fitting at the special Saturday rehearsal.

She was surprised when she saw Dick Walzem's and Jane's cars parked in front of the church when she arrived. She drove around to the back where the door led directly into the choir room. She unlocked the door, and then returned to the car to get the robes.

Dick Walzem felt absurdly giddy with anticipation as he and Jane entered the choir room from the sanctuary. They climbed the stairs leading to the baptistery above the sanctuary choir loft. Jane, a modest person, suggested they use separate dressing rooms to disrobe and don baptismal gowns resembling white nightgowns with little bowstring ties at the neck. Dick and Jane were descending into the baptistery when Mazie entered the choir room with the cleaned robes.

Mazie sensed motion at the top of the baptistery stairs and looked closer. She thought she saw Brother Walzem and Jane in baptismal robes as they entered the baptistery. She was completely confused. Her eyes played tricks on her these days, and she often thought she saw things that were not there. Could this be one of those times? She knew the baptistery had no water in it, and the curtains were drawn covering the opening into the sanctuary. Why did they need baptistery robes? Why would Brother Walzem and Jane get into the baptistery in the first place? After all, they both had been baptized already. She thought she should climb the stairs to check more closely, but this was a bad arthritis day. I just don't know what to do.

Mazie hung the choir robes quickly, fled to her car, and almost drove away when she swerved back and parked at the sanctuary entrance. She got out and walked up the steps. Halfway down the aisle she took a seat, clasped her hands, and bowed in prayer. "Lord, I'm old, and I don't often understand everything I see and hear. I try not to interfere when I'm not sure what's happening. I'm very confused right now, Lord, and I hope you can help me understand what I should do."

A two part heavenly chord (A-augmented 11th) filled the sanctuary from behind the baptistery curtain – **"UUUUUUHHHHHHH!"**

Mazie jumped at the sound. She opened her eyes and raised her head and looked around the sanctuary for the source. "Lord, I've never felt you so close before. It's like you're speaking to me directly. Could this be true?"

Another ethereal chord (B plus 11th) a whole tone higher and increasing in volume **"AAAAAHHHH!"**

Mazie lowered her head again and clinched her eyes, "Lord, I've never felt so blessed. That you would speak directly to me – with all my senses – person to person. I can't thank you enough, but Lord, I need your guidance. I think I saw something that isn't right. I mean why would Brother Walzem and Jane climb into the baptistery wearing only robes? I mean, there isn't even any water in it. Lord, I need to know if I should tell Reverend Jones about this. I don't want to cause a problem, but should I tell people what I saw?"

Another angelic chord (Inverted A augmented 11th) a full tone higher and at full volume **"YAAEESSS!"**

Jesús of the J3 DEA talked on his cell phone with the Coastal Bend Crop Dusters whom he had contracted to spray the cannabis patch on Mustang Island. John and Joe had come back inside after a smoke break and sat across the desk from Jesús, their supervisor, in the little room allocated to the Port Aransas' "3J's" in the Corpus Christi DEA Office. The gray ambience of the government office, accentuated by a flickering florescent light, did little to lift any occupant's spirits. The agents wore DEA T-shirts with their badges visible and their side arms in plain view. Their chagrin at the delay required to requisition and get a fifty-gallon drum of herbicide spray delivered to the crop duster intensified their current attack mode. "Goddamn bureaucratic bullshit," Jesús had called it. He clicked his phone closed. "He says the wind's okay for spraying. So let's mount up."

John gathered up the documents and the plat map of Mustang Island to show Coastal Bend Crop Dusters where to spray. "You know Saturday's a busy day on the Island, and now with the stoner colony we might be sprayin' a lotta folks."

"We've got to get this done before somebody messes up our first big drug operation." Jesús disappeared out the door. He knew the drive to the crop duster would take about thirty minutes. The duster operated from a small airfield on Farm to Market Road 1604 a little north of Corpus Christi Municipal Airport, whose director of aviation wanted no part of the dangerous chemicals handled by the dusting operation.

Jasper Oats of the Environmental Protection Agency had a pipeline from the DEA into the EPA, since his girl friend worked for the Drug Enforcement Agency. He had expected it, but still felt scandalized to learn from his mole that Jesús was only waiting for delivery of herbicide and windless conditions to carry out their plan to spray the cannabis. Jasper sought out a fellow member of the Sierra Club, District Judge Carol Sanchez, to get an injunction specifically forbidding the DEA or their assigns from any form of herbicide spraying on the Island. Jasper knew who would do the spraying, the crop duster's location, and that the DEA hoped to carry out their operation on Saturday. Jasper went to the Nueces County Courthouse early Saturday morning and convinced the Nueces County Sheriff to accompany him to present the judge's injunction. Their siren screamed and lights flashed as the two hurtled toward Coastal Bend Crop Dusters.

The three agents arrived first and went in the office with the plat map, and showed the pilot Old Walt Greely's property where the offending cannabis grew.

The pilot studied the map for a moment. "A pretty small patch of ground you're talking about. What's on the corner there?"

They answered in unison, "A Circle K."

The pilot looked up. "A Circle K? You're kidding! There's no way I can spray there with the fixed wing duster. I'll spray half the Island with that rig. Circle K will sue me before I can get back here and land."

Jesús ground his teeth before he spoke, "You telling me you can't do this job?"

"Yeah, I can do it, but I'll have to use the helicopter. The down draft from the blades will force the spray onto the cannabis and not leave the stuff floatin' around in the air for everyone to breathe."

They all looked a little non-plused while they remembered the Viet Nam aftermath of the Agent Orange spraying reported widely in the news. Jesús looked a little unsure. "You think it'll be alright to use the helicopter?"

"If I'm very careful and hover low to the ground." The pilot paused. "You know, you guys could spray those few acres by hand. The helicopter will cost you twice as much as the Piper Cub."

"The Justice of the Peace on the Island condemned the property because of poisonous vegetation, and the constable's deputies patrol constantly keeping anyone out," Jesús explained. "Besides, we're not too excited about wading through rattlesnakes to spray it ourselves."

John spoke up, "Twice the price? Do we have enough in our budget?"

Jesús' brow furrowed and his teeth clinched. "We'll get this job done today if it kills us."

One of the others added, "Yeah, and everyone else too."

As they walked out into the hanger to pump the herbicide into the helicopter spray tanks, the Sheriff's cruiser blasted onto the tarmac and headed straight for the hanger. The pilot and the drug agents stood riveted in place as the sheriff executed a broad slide with his cruiser; smoke poured from under the screaming tires, and came to a rocking halt directly in front of the helicopter. The cruiser lights transformed the hanger into a rave hall, with the siren echoing like techno-music.

Joe said, "Boy, all we need are some babes and something to drink besides herbicide."

The sheriff opened the cruiser door after extinguishing the siren and lights. He unfolded his great frame from the vehicle, and stood for a minute and surveyed his surroundings. He concentrated on the Piper Cub and helicopter rigged for crop spraying. The distance to the four who stood by the helicopter took so few strides that Jasper Oats trotted to keep up.

Jesús saw Jasper and the envelope in his hand. "What the hell's going on?"

" I reckon you're the DEA, judging by your T-shirts, so you must be with Coastal Bend Crop Dusting." The sheriff stood a few feet before the three and pointed toward the pilot.

The pilot shuffled his feet for poise. "Right, sheriff. How can I help you?"

The sheriff took the envelope from Jasper, opened it, and removed two legal documents. "I'm serving you and the DEA with an injunction signed by District Court Judge Carol Sanchez forbidding the DEA or any of its assigns from spraying herbicide of any kind on Mustang Island." He handed a document to Jesús and the pilot.

Jesús, Joe, and John gathered around the document and studied its contents. Jesús spoke up. "Hey, wait a minute. This is a state district court injunction. We're enforcing federal law here. This judge has no authority to do this."

A smile flickered across the sheriff's face. "Son, you're in Texas. My advice: Don't mess with Texas!" He turned on his cowboy boot heel and in a few strides stood beside his cruiser. "You comin,' Oates?"

Oates made the peace sign to the DEA boys who stood, looking like they had feathers in their teeth. "Sorry, guys, looks like Mustang Island is saved for another day."

The remaining four watched the sheriff's cruiser blast out of the hanger with lights blazing and siren howling. Jesús looked at the pilot. "This guy's full of shit. They have no authority in this case. So we goin' sprayin' or not?"

The pilot laughed. "Only if you're flyin' the helicopter."

***

Diggs, the pocket gopher, and his partner, Dozer, had spent the day traveling between each of the Stuff Mine & Emporiums checking inventories of Stuff and the general condition of the facilities. The gophers lined up, trading their roots for Stuff at each of the Stuff mines. They all looked faded and in need of a boost.

In the tunnel between Nunber 4 Stuff Mine & Emporium and Number 5 Stuff Mine, they ran head first into a visiting rattlesnake. "Holy shit!" Diggs jumped back so violently he flattened Dozer. Neither had eaten any Stuff since the night before, and in their heightened awareness, a snake was a snake – Cha Cha Cha or no Cha Cha Cha. It lay there and smiled with its eyes closed.

Diggs approached the snake with great caution and found it comatose. "It must have crawled down the surface-shaft beside Stuff Mine Number 5 and gotten stuck because of a big bulge in his middle. It's totally zoned out for some reason."

The fright on Dozer's face relaxed a little. "This is too good to be true. We might rid ourselves of one gopher-eating devil snake."

"I like the way you think." Diggs dug a tunnel around the snake while Dozer packed the sand and sealed off the old tunnel right up to the snake's head. When they reached the Number 5 Stuff Mine and Emporium, Diggs dug a new vertical surface shaft while Dozer packed the sand and sealed the old tunnel right up to the snake's rattle.

"There! One buried devil snake." Dozer's voice squeaked with excitement.

Even with all the euphoria Stuff created and with all the exciting time above ground, Diggs had never forgotten about tunneling into "The Great Burrow in the Sky" and the coyote there. Gophers often talked about the "The Great Gopher in the Sky" living in the Great Burrow. Some seemed adamant they knew everything about the Great Gopher – who he was; what he was; where he was; and what to expect when they reached him. Diggs wondered if he had really dug into The Great Burrow, after all. What if the "Great Gopher" wasn't a coyote as he thought? It didn't make sense for the Great Gopher to be a coyote, waiting there to pounce on unsuspecting gophers coming His way. The Stuff mines seemed to be in good order, but he felt there must be more to life than munching out on Stuff, feelin' right and dancin' around. What if I could finally find out the truth about the Great Gopher in the Sky and tell it to the other gophers? That's it! I'll dig in search of The Great Gopher.

***

Early in the morning Coyote already sat in the spartina grass across Wilson's Cut when Krank stepped out on the deck with his peace pipe. *"You're early today."*

"There is conflict."

"Conflict?"

"Balance requires sacrifice."

"It's true, I guess, but who must sacrifice?"

"All will be revealed."

Krank had wanted to discuss his dream, but Coyote turned and trotted away as a fisherman towed his boat into the two-track leading into the Cut.

Krank still thought about his coyote conversation Saturday afternoon as he pulled up to his houseboat after completing the yard work for the Island widows. His cell phone rang as he unloaded his lawn mower. Harpoon's voice asked, "Hey, good buddy, can I pick you up for the rehearsal on my way out?"

From his voice, Krank knew Harpoon needed a visit. "I've got to clean up, but why not stop by?"

Krank took his bar of soap and dove into Wilson's cut. He treaded water while he washed himself and left a halo of soap bubbles, expanding on the water in concentric rings. The water refreshed him after a day-and-a-half of yard work in the July sun. He dove underwater and rinsed the soap from his long hair, swam back to the houseboat deck, and pulled himself up. He wrapped a towel around his mid section. Behind a screen, he removed the towel, drew a dipper of rainwater he'd collected in a cistern, and rinsed off the salt water. Towel wrapped, he went inside and dressed.

Krank heard a truck, grabbed his tom-toms, and went out to meet Harpoon. He threw the drums in the back and crawled into Harpoon's cab. Silence hung in the pickup until they reached the highway.

As Harpoon turned onto the highway, Krank broke the silence. "Coyote says there's conflict on the Island."

"Boy, he's got that right." Harpoon continued looking straight ahead. "I had visitors on the Blues."

"Our friends, the dope dealers?"

"How did you know?"

"It seemed about time."

"While I stowed oil and beer below, Mako and the Goons came aboard."

"They want another pickup?"

Harpoon turned toward Krank. "Maybe you should tell me what happened."

"Did they threaten you?"

"One drew a pistol when I was about to cold-cock Mako. He wants us to pick up a small package Tuesday night at the same location. Apparently it's important enough he's making the trip himself."

"You didn't agree?"

"I told him to go screw himself. He left saying he'd call Monday to work out arrangements. I didn't tell him we'd be gone tomorrow afternoon. " Harpoon smiled at Krank, pleased with his oneupmanship.

"Coyote says 'All will be revealed'."

"Ah, come on, man. Your Coyote cramps my ass sometimes."

Harpoon and Krank stayed deep in thought for the remainder of the trip out to the Crystal Epistle. As they pulled into the parking lot, Harpoon said, "Looks like the choir members have all showed up, judging by the cars."

"We've aroused interest."

"So it seems. A bunch of strangers invading their music probably doesn't sit well with everybody, though."

"We're about to find out."

Mazie Hartung greeted Harpoon and Krank in front of the podium and escorted the singers and musicians down into the choir room for their robes. Ted initially showed resistance to the idea of the choir robe and mumbled something under his breath best not heard by Mazie. Slidin' Will helped Ted dress while he assured him the robe would not smother him. Mazie felt good that Sweet Bessie and the girls wore choir robes like they grew up in them. Not so with the musicians. They had misgivings about playing their instruments, tripping over them, and of course how silly they looked.

The five of them stood in a circle and eyed each other. Slidin' Will started to say something but burst out laughing instead. The others followed suit until their laughing could be heard up in the choir loft. Will recovered first. "God, if we're not a ridiculous looking bunch of blues musicians."

Ted looked around and found no one in hearing range. He lifted his robe knee high and let it drop and again drag on the floor "Hey, Hey. Choir robes. Hey, hey, Fuck 'em all. Hey, hey."

Harpoon said, "Ted, I think you could take two steps before your robe moves."

"There's no way to keep this a secret since we'll be on national television." Slidin' Will held his robe out in front. "But none of our friends'll watch a church program, anyway."

The sax man's robe sleeves got in the way while he fingered his instrument. "Man, playin' in this thing I'll sound like a junior high kid practicin'."

Dick Walzem stuck his head down into the choir room from the stairs. "How about everybody coming on up so we can get our meeting started."

The choir sat in the loft, and the singers and musicians in the first row of the auditorium. Jane passed out the programs for tomorrow's service. Walzem said, "We need to go over the Order of Service so our new associates know how things happen. We begin the service with the Doxology. I'll lead the choir and congregation singing a cappella."

Ted looked at Slidin' Will. "Hey, hey, a cappella? Hey, hey."

Will looked down his nose at Ted. "That means without us."

Walzem said, "Since you'll be at the organ, Ted, it'll be best to sing without instruments since you don't know the music. The congregation will feel more included also. Rev Jones will give an invocation and welcome the congregation and our new singer and musicians. Why don't you come on up and take your places so we can rehearse the rest of the service?"

Once Sweet Bessie, the singers, Will, and the musicians were in place, Walzem continued. "We'll then open with 'Swing Low Sweet Chariot' with the choir and congregation. So let's do a run through." Walzem nodded with pleasure at how well the choir, singers and musicians moved into a groove on the spiritual.

"If you look at the program, you'll see Rev. Jones will give a scripture reading and another prayer, followed by the offering – which means we need an offertory." He turned to Sweet Bessie. "Bessie, do you and the ladies know 'Cast Your Bread Upon the Water'?"

"Brother Walzem, you ain't never sung in no gospel choir less you know 'Cast Your Bread Upon the Water.'" The ladies all nodded agreement. "You gotta get the folks of a right mind when the plate's bein' passed."

A light came on in Walzem's eyes. "Would you ladies give us a couple of verses?"

Sweet Bessie gave a down beat, and the four singers moved into the introduction and first verse:

There are people who think they're not receiving

Anything from God at all.

Oh, they are shaken from their believing

When they don't see results quickly fall.

But don't you waver, just keep on living

In the way God wants you to.

Don't get discouraged, just keep on giving

And soon it will come back to you.

Keep on casting

Your bread upon the water.

Keep on casting

Your bread upon the water.

Soon it's gonna come back home in everyway.

Slidin' Will and the band fell in behind the singers and answered each phrase, and Walzem cued the choir who joined them, as they practiced their moves.

By the time the singers finished two more verses the band and choir were rocking and the sanctuary pulsed with the energy needed to pry open pocketbooks.

Walzem beamed. "I'm amazed at how great you guys all sound. We've got a good thing going here."

The singers nodded agreement. "Amen, Brother Walzem. Right on!"

Ted covered his mouth and mumbled, "Hey, hey. Amen. Hey, hey. Fuck 'em all."

"We're using Slidin' Will's version of "Because of Your Love" as the special music, so let's run through that." Walzem was truly gratified at the progress the choir had made with their moves while backing up the singers and musicians.

At the completion of the rehearsal, Walzem held up his hand. "Let's bow our heads and give thanks for what we've accomplished here today."

The prayer caught Slidin' Will, Harpoon, and the other musicians in mid-stride half way down the steps to the sanctuary floor. They looked around at the choir and each other and tried to recover a little poise as Walzem prayed. "Lord we want to thank you for bringing these wonderful singers and musicians into our lives. With your help tomorrow we will 'make a joyous noise unto the Lord' and exalt the glory of God. We thank you for all your blessings, and we pray in Your wonderful name."

Slidin' Will looked at Harpoon and Krank. "It seems kinda strange leavin' here and headin' over to the Blues Emporium, but it's Saturday night and you guys would all be really welcome."

Before anyone could answer, Ted, who accidently stood on the bottom of his choir robe, took a step, and did a pratfall down two steps onto the sanctuary floor where he rolled back up and stood a bit disoriented. "Hey, hey. Busted my butt. Hey, hey. Fu . . . er . . . Bless 'em all."

Harpoon dropped Krank off to pick up his truck, and the two went to *Cordon Blues* for a last onceover before they headed out tomorrow. Satisfied, after about an hour of fine-tuning, Harpoon said, "We deserve a few brewskis for all we've done today."

"It's time." Krank jumped over the stern gunnel and headed for his truck.

When Harpoon and Krank approached the Island Joynt bar, Lottie greeted them with, "You two look a little more righteous, but are you actually 'going down to sea in ships' tomorrow?"

"First, our church work, then we're out of here like a herd of Ridley turtles." Harpoon eyed Krank. "Right, Krank?"

"Go, you church goin' Ridleys!" Lottie chortled.

"Plans change." Krank stared into the back bar mirror with a stoic expression.

"Uh oh." Lottie looked at Harpoon. "Sounds like our soothsayer's antenna's up."

"We got no choice, Krank. We're outta here soon as we get finished with our church gig."

Lottie arched her eyebrows. "What does that mean? 'We got no choice.'"

Harpoon stuttered when he tried not to tell Lottie about the Mako encounter. "I mean we really need to go shrimping sometime before the season ends." Krank's face betrayed nothing.

Lottie smiled but didn't buy it. She grabbed a towel and wiped the bar rather than pursuing the issue. "So we have one more depraved farewell night?"

Harpoon grinned. "I think I have one more left in me."

Jeff McAlister watched the sun slide behind the dunes, leaving purple shadows creeping over the beach. The stoners gathered around the bonfire. The conflagration sent sparks skyward like luminous insects. The sweet smell of ganja drifted on a landward breeze that tickled the Gulf water into slight, rollicking undulations. The Stone Cold Dreads had completed their mike checks and were about to launch into their first reggae tune, when Jeff jumped up on the bandstand. "Hey, guys, I need to make an announcement if I can borrow your mike." The Dreads mumbled in agreement. Jeff took the microphone and announced, "Greetings, Stoners. Glad you're up for another big night of fun with the Stone Cold Dreads. Don't forget the donation jug for the beer and the band." He saw Joe and John from the DEA in their undercover garb in the audience. He pointed to each and continued, "Joe, John, glad to have The DEA represented here tonight. Any other lawmen here? Please hold up your hands." A rustle of laughter arose from the crowd. "Hey! About 10:30 tomorrow morning a bunch of us will walk up the beach and catch the jumbotron at the Crystal Epistle. Bring a towel, and you can lie out and hear the local blues band play at the service. If you get right, I can tell you watching the jumbotron's a trip, so check it out tomorrow."

Wisps of Jeff's announcement carried on the breeze to Krank across the Island. He stood on the deck of his houseboat, and smiled when he heard about the 'local blues band' will play at the Epistle tomorrow. "Maybe we will do some good tomorrow," he said aloud. He looked at his chaise lounge and shook his head. Early to bed so I can get up and take the Blues over to Aransas Pass and get iced down before church.

Harpoon and Lottie met at her house about eleven-thirty. She brought a container of soup from the Joynt that they shared before they retired to the connubial couch. Lottie may have felt their lovemaking had lacked urgency following Harpoon's return from a couple of weeks of shrimping but not this time. Really nice, took time to do it right. Yeah, Really nice. Harpoon's tender caresses had made her eyes misty, and she pulled him closer in her embrace.

While she drifted gently asleep, she thought about the hole left in her heart each time Harpoon went down to sea in ships.

Harpoon awoke about two o'clock and wondered why. Already awake, he went to the bathroom and then ran a glass of water at the kitchen sink. As he lifted his glass, the full moon outside the kitchen window high lit a black SUV stopped in the street with its lights off. He could make out two people in the front seat, but when he turned on the sink light, the vehicle moved slowly away without lights.

Krank awoke with a start and heard a car coming down the two-track toward the Cut. He rolled out of bed and crouched as he made his way to the deck door. Almost prone, he crawled out onto the deck and listened. The car stopped outside his line of sight, but the engine still idled. He heard no door sounds. The sound of crunching oysters shells inched closer. A full moon cast a phospherant glow that illuminated the whole area, and he moved forward and strained to get sight of the car. His first glimpse showed the car move slowly toward the far side of the Cut, and when in full view, he saw a convertible with two people in the front seat. The car climbed the tallest spoil bank and the convertible top whined open and let the moonlight flood onto its occupants. The boy and girl obviously intended a little moonlight madness as they crawled into the back seat. Krank chuckled, and went back to bed.

CHAPTER | 25

It surprised Harpoon when he could not find a parking place in the Crystal Epistle Church of Everlasting Enlightenment lot at the prescribed ten o'clock arrival time. As he looked for a space, he also watched for Krank's pickup truck and hoped icing down the Blues had not taken him more time than expected. The crowded parking lot indicated most of the Crystal Epistle members got their money's worth by attending Sunday school before the eleven o'clock service. He saw someone pull out of a parking place on the dune side of the lot and with dexterous wheelwork he grabbed the space.

Ten 'clock was too early for Harpoon, so he leaned on the front fender of his truck and admired the beachfront scene. Clear sky, light breeze, clean beaches, blue water, and sand dunes stretching into next week. A few beachers already occupied spaces in front of the jumbotron where they could multitask and soak up both rays and religion. A couple of fishermen's surf rods stood at attention as their lines sagged out into the water, while three sport fishing boats waffled in the surf, positioned for a good view of the jumbotron. I reckon Jesus' disciples were fisherman also, he thought as he filled his lungs with fresh salt air.

His reverie was interrupted by, "Shame we can't have church out here." Krank's pickup idled behind Harpoon. "The

Blues wasn't the only one needing ice."

Harpoon smiled as he approached Krank. "I figured you'd gotten jammed up. It'd be a shame if you missed our debut."

"What's a blues band without tom-toms?" Krank motioned toward his pickup bed. "I came straight from the boat, so I'll need to get my duffel bag on the way back to the Blues."

"Getting a parking place will take you longer than that."

Jeff McAlister looked back at the group trudging up the beach toward the Crystal Epistle. The crowd had grown to about a hundred, and all wore bathing suits of every type, including bikinis, and carried beach paraphernalia: mats, towels, chairs, and umbrellas. "Stoners on their way to church in swimsuits." Jeff laughed. "What's this world coming to?"

"Ya, mon. Most interestin'. Wonderin' why I'm here myself," Ricky chucked Jeff playfully in the ribs. "But a Rasta can find Jah anywhere, right, mon?"

"Just needs a little weed." Jeff cupped his hands over his mouth and shouted at the crowd following. "Better pick up the pace. Don't be late for church."

The musicians had set up their instruments on the sanctuary dais and descended into the choir room. The choir members busily donned their robes, and the arrival of the band attracted everyone's attention, even Sweet Bessie and the singers, already dressed in their robes for the service. Slidin' Will and the musicians saw the division between those for and against the new music as the parting of the Red Sea. Those excited about the change were friendly, gracious, and some even seemed in awe of Sweet Bessie, the singers, Will, and the musicians. Those who still felt blues to be the Devil's own music, stood back as if the band members smelled of burning sulfur.

The apprehensive tension between the unharmonious chorale members dissolved when Dick Walzem bounded halfway down the stairs from the sanctuary and unleashed a hearty,

"Praise the Lord! Standing room only, and the service doesn't start for twenty minutes, and the beach is overflowing with Jumbotron worshipers. What a glorious day for us to 'Make a joyful noise!'"

"Amen!" The gospel/blues side of the choir room cheered.

"Don't be nervous, 'cause God's on our side, and we've rehearsed our program thoroughly."

The stairs groaned as the Right Reverend Hannibal Jones moved down behind Walzem and pinned him against the handrail, rendering him a little breathless. Rev. Jones held his hand high, and the choir fell silent. "Lord Jesus Christ almighty God, we thank you for these wonderful people dedicated to spreading the Word through music and song. Lord, we hope and pray for great things today, and we ask you to put your loving hand on the hearts of all those within the sound of our voices today and bring them a blessing of pure joy. We are empowered by your strength and mercy, for which we give thanks. And amen!"

"Go, You Ridleys!" Ted shouted before he realized his shout was out of place.

The praise music side of the choir recoiled in righteous indignation while the gospel/blues group let out a whoop of laughter.

Rev. Jones laughed and shouted, "Fear the Turtle!" and with difficulty turned on the stairs and climbed back toward the sanctuary.

The a cappella doxology went better than Dick Walzem had hoped as the congregation joined in a zesty rendition. "Swing Low Sweet Chariot" was an obvious hit and a few of the parishioners swayed with the music. Walzem noticed Rev. Jones had a hard time sitting still and patted his foot and swayed to the beat. Sweet Bessie and the singers along with the band and choir now rocked out on "Cast Your Bread Upon the Water" as the offering plates passed through the sanctuary. A technical problem developed when the plates overflowed before they reached even half the faithful. The deacons passing the plates looked confused until a lady produced a garbage bag from her purse. They hurriedly emptied the plates into it, and then moved on to the rest of the congregation. Rev. Jones was in absolute rapture as the chairman of the deacons carried the black sack of booty from the sanctuary.

The stoners down on the beach settled in and became enthralled with the Jumbotron's blinking lights and the rock concert sound system, pumping out the gospel and blues music. Jeff McAlister looked over the crowd and felt a sense of satisfaction that the Crystal Epistle show did not disappoint. One stoner said, "Jeff, hey, man, this church thing's super cool – I mean frigid. Like, how'd you know about this, man?"

With the offertory complete, Rev. Jones stood and approached the podium then looked back at the singers and musicians. "Praise God and halleluiah!" His basso boomed out over the congregation. "What a magnificent outpouring of God's message in music and song. Can I have an amen?"

The congregation burst forth. "Amen!"

"I know some among us have reservations about our new music program Brother Walzem assembled for our worship services. But I say to those who feel blues music has no place in church: be of good cheer, for the Lord is with us and has shown us the valuable lessons to be learned from the blues.

"You see, there's a pervasive persona in blues music, and this persona's not godly. This person's more like Satan himself. And who is this evil one? This wickedness is called 'Mah Baby'!" Now let me tell you, people, Mah Baby's not someone you want to know. Why? Because blues is filled with Mah Baby's wickedness. Just like The Good Book is filled with Satan's wickedness.

"Consider this, folks. 'Mah Baby done done me wrong.' Like Satan always does us wrong, Mah Baby's always out to get us." The reverend's thump on the podium reverberated out over the faithful, up the Crystal Epistle Tower of Power and out into TV land. "Now hear this people: Jesus don't do us wrong. Jesus is always on our side. Jesus is our friend. Jesus looks after us and guides us to our Heavenly Father, and amen!"

"Amen!" Rattled the walls.

"Oh, yes, and 'Mah Baby' done left me.' That's right, folks, Satan will leave you to suffer eternal damnation in the Lake of Fire — but not Jesus. No sir! Jesus will never leave us. Jesus loves us and wants us to love him. Jesus will stand by our side through trouble and temptation. Through good times and bad, Jesus is the one we can count on to lead us home.

"Oh, people, my heart breaks when I hear "Mah Baby don't love me no more." Mah Baby, the great prevaricator. Satan the great deceiver! The Evil One who pretends to love us while putting temptations in our path. Temptations to lead us astray – down the path toward sin and degradation. I ask you, 'Is that love?'"

"No!"

"Does anyone here believe Satan ever loved us?"

"NO!"

"And amen!"

"Amen!" The place rocked.

"But thank God for his Son, Jesus Christ, who loved us before, loves us now, and will love us throughout eternity. Who loved us enough to die on the cross to save us from our sins, and give us eternal life in Glory. And there will never be a time when Jesus don't love us no more. Can I have an amen?"

Several jumped from their seats shouting, "Praise God and amen!"

Reverend Jones turned to Slidin' Will Pickens and Sweet Bessie. "Now Sweet Bessie and Brother Pickens, I know you can work with me on this."

Questioning glances darted between Sweet Bessie and the singers and among the musicians who instinctively grabbed up their instruments. Ted, either in a trance or close telepathic communication with the reverend, struck a grace note to a high

C which he held for several seconds and then began a chromatic glissando and slowly worked his way down to low C as Rev. Jones belted out in his basso profundo:
Woke up this morning with a Bible by my bed

The band answered him musically:
I said I woke up this morning with a Bible I never read

Sweet Bessie and the singers answered:
A Good Book he never read

I said, Great God in Heaven, How'm I ever gonna know what Jesus said.
Know what Jesus said.

The reverend turned to the singers, "Take it, Sweet Bessie."
Bessie stepped forward:
Woke up this morning with Jesus on my mind
Jesus on my mind

Woke up this morning with Lord Jesus on my mind
Jesus on my mind

I knew Sweet Jesus is the only peace I'll ever fiind.
Sweet peace of mind

Reverend Jones stood at the mike:
Woke up this morning Mah Baby's nowhere to be found

The congregation jumped its feet clapping and swaying:
No where to be found

That's right folks work with me on it:
I woke up this morning and Ol' Satan's nowhere to be found
Satan's no where to be found

Cause I'm livin' in Jesus on his hallowed ground.

Harpoon glanced at the reverend as he enjoyed himself with complete abandon. Jones danced back to the mike:
Satan spread his devil weed upon our land
Upon our land

I said, 'Ol Devil spread his scourge upon our land
Scourge upon our land

But he'll be defeated if in Jesus Christ we stand.
In Jesus Christ we stand

The reverend kicked up the volume and modulated a key. Ted and the musicians slid in behind him:
The Devil's weed makes us all a fool
Makes us all a fool

Smoke the weed and be the Devil's tool
The Devil's tool

Join the fight 'gainst 'Ol Satan, so Christ can rule.
So Christ can rule.

"Take one, Will." Will hesitated but moved to his mike and instead of words, loosed a guitar solo of such profound emotion many of the congregation rushed to the front, waved their arms, and danced – completely oblivious to anything but their current state of mind.
Reverend Jones grabbed the mike:
We all know Jesus' teaching, now it's up to us to be saved.
We've got to be saved

You know we're headed for God's glory

Headed for God's glory

When we trust in Jesus and believe in his story.
Believe his story.

The band took solos and rocked out while the congregation clapped, danced, and shouted.

Slidin' Will and Harpoon exchanged amazed glances when a second guitar joined in and launched into a solo of such intensity that the audience became frenetic in their ecstasy. Both Will and Harpoon shrugged and backed up the mystery musician.

When the excitement died down, Reverend Jones added, "Now I know there are those among us here, out there on the beach, and out there in TV Land with heavy hearts who want to lay their burden down. I say lay all your cares at Jesus' feet, and be blessed. So come on down to the front and kneel with me, and let's get our hearts right with God." He beckoned to the congregation and many left their seats and moved, mesmerized and joyful, to the front of the sanctuary.

Down on the beach, the guy next to Jeff stood as best he could in his diminished condition, and staggered toward the dunes.

"Where you goin' man?" Jeff looked up at the slender figure.

"I'm goin' down to the front, man. I want some of this Jesus thing."

As they hung their robes in the choir room, Harpoon noticed a larger crowd than before around Sweet Bessie, the singers, and musicians. Apparently a few of the praise music contingent had converted to the blues.

Harpoon took a couple of Krank's tom-toms, and they headed for their trucks. He felt excitement bubble up inside, whether from the prospect of shrimping or from the church service, he didn't know.

"I thought Stevie Ray's guitar solo added something." Harpoon glanced sideways and checked Krank's reaction.

"He has a plan."

"Actually I don't think I've ever played for a better audience. I mean, these folks really get into it."

"They feel the Powers."

"The Powers?"

"Powers have been collecting on the Island for many days." Krank waved his arm in an all-encompassing gesture.

"Krank, sometimes you give me a headache." Harpoon shook his head almost in disgust.

"Coyote says, 'All will be known soon.'"

"I hope he doesn't lay another chunk on the doorstep of my life."

Harpoon followed Krank out of the church driveway and north on Highway 361 toward Port Aransas. He waved out the window when Krank turned left opposite the Sandpiper Condo onto the road leading to his houseboat.

Over two-dozen boat trailers parked along the road in and around the launch area awaited the return of their boats. Krank wove his way through all the vehicles and pulled in at the end of his gangplank. He gathered his tom-toms, walked up the plank, and opened the door.

The extra propane bottle sat in the middle of the room with what looked like bars of Playdough and a cell phone duct-taped to it. He dove for it and struggled to his knees holding the gas bottle. The cell phone rang . . . and the world disintegrated.

CHAPTER | 26

Harpoon's truck swerved when the blast's concussion hit. He righted the truck and saw the column of smoke, rising from Wilson's Cut in his rearview mirror.

"Holy shit, what's happened?"

Smoke billowed from his tires as he stood on the brake pedal, sliding to a stop. The truck almost rolled when he turned around. As he accelerated back toward Krank's, Harpoon puzzled at the cloud rising from the Cut. The wind was dead calm, but still he knew the smoke was way too perfect. It resembled a huge black cylinder swirling from the ground. He turned off the road at the Cut as the cylinder left earth and ascended rapidly toward heaven. Oyster shell gravel sprayed in all directions when he stopped. He gazed in wonder as the cloud rose out of sight.

His tires spun out, and his truck ricocheted between uprooted boat trailers as he made his way toward Krank's houseboat. Gone. One oil drum floated stoically among the tips of a few deck timbers. Nothing! The houseboat had vanished. He saw Krank's truck upside down against a spoil bank about twenty-five yards down the Cut. Harpoon leaped from the car and ran stumbling over spartina grass until he dropped to his knees and looked inside the cab. Empty. "Where the hell's Krank?" He jumped up and ran like a deranged person back toward the head of the Cut. Someone had called 911 and sirens and flashing lights hurtled toward him from both directions. The shoulder of highway 361 filled up with cars whose occupants ran toward Harpoon. Crystal Epistle members, townspeople, and tourists all came running. Figures rose on the dune crest and disappeared. The stoners arrived soon after.

Constable Bubba Sherrill arrived, followed closely by Chief Crump and the Port Aransas Volunteer Fire Department. The large crowd burbled about what happened. Several constables and policemen set up a perimeter for crowd control.

The Nueces County Sheriff's siren howled as his cruiser made its way to the front of the crowd. The sheriff unfolded from the vehicle and strode toward the collection of officialdom. "What's happened?"

Constable Sherrill looked around the group and spied Harpoon. "What's happened here, Harpoon? Krank's houseboat exploded, right? You know if he was home?"

"We'd come from playing the service at the Crystal Epistle. Krank stopped here for his duffel bag before we went shrimping. A gigantic explosion blew up Krank's houseboat, and I can't find him!" Harpoon pointed at the upside down truck. "He's not in his truck, so he must have been in the houseboat. God, what a horror." Harpoon ran both hands through his hair and messaged his skull as he tried to force some understanding inside it.

Chief Crump jumped in. "Krank used propane on the houseboat?"

"Yes. He bought a new propane bottle last week." Harpoon felt dizzy and squatted to regain his composure. Nausea overcame him, and he leaned forward on both hands and barfed.

The explosion had blown out any fire that might have started, but the grass smoldered and tried to light again. The firemen pulled their hoses and sprayed it. Harpoon watched acrid smoke and ashes rise, and the calm air filled with the smell of what had been, but would never be again.

The sheriff surveyed the scene: overturned trucks with boat trailers twisted behind them, Krank's pickup must have rolled until it hit the spoil bank, the distance from the detritus of the blast and the location of the vanished houseboat. "This seems like a bigger explosion than a propane bottle." He looked at Harpoon, still squatted on the ground. "Any possiblity he wasn't in the houseboat?"

"I don't see how. Everything happened so fast." Harpoon felt another wave of nausea and leaned forward dry heaving.

"Ok, we've got to find the occupant; what's his name?"

Chief Crump said, "Krank."

"Krank who?"

The group of locals exchanged glances and all shrugged. Crump said, "Just Krank."

A few strides put the sheriff back at his car, and he pulled a microphone through the open window. The speaker boomed. "Listen up people." The crowd quieted. "A houseboat exploded with an occupant inside. We have to see if we can find the occupant or any remains. We need volunteers. If you want to help, form two lines, shoulder-to-shoulder from here to the highway."

The crowd milled around for a few minutes but finally fell into two lines as instructed. "Ok, walk slowly arm-in-arm in both directions and keep searching the ground for anything that might be human remains. Be diligent and report even the smallest item you find. Search out to about a hundred yards."

He reached inside the car and flipped a switch. "Unit one to base, come in."

The short wave sputtered and a voice answered, "Come in sheriff."

"There's been an explosion on a boat at Wilson's Cut about nine miles south of Port Aransas. Get the zodiac and a couple of divers over here pronto!"

"It'll take some time, but we're all over it."

"Hurry! Unit one out."

The two lines of volunteers began their march across the fields separating Wilson's Cut from Highway 361. They parted as a car swerved off the highway and bounced over the two-track potholes and ruts at an exaggerated speed and halted at the police-tape barrier. Lottie leaped from the car and ran toward Harpoon.

"A restaurant customer told me something happened to Krank. Is he alright?" She squatted beside Harpoon and put her arm around him.

Harpoon could not answer for a few seconds. "His houseboat blew up and we can't find him."

"I've found something!" The yell came from a guy in the middle of the line moving south. The volunteers broke ranks and bunched up for a look.

Harpoon stood to move toward the excitement. Constable Sherrill put his arm on Harpoon's shoulder. "You should stay here until we know what it is."

The sheriff pushed his way through the crowd until he stood beside a small mound of possible animal tissue. Squatting, he took a stick and carefully lifted an edge and saw fur. After he studied it further, he stood. "Ok, let's keep up our search. It's the remains of a cat, probably eaten by a coyote. Be thorough, and report anything you see like this man did." He patted the man on the shoulder.

Harpoon slumped at the news. "It's crazy. The explosion happened within minutes after Krank turned off the highway. A couple of minutes and the best friend any man ever had disappears."

Words of encouragement failed Lottie, so she pulled her man closer and held him. She looked at the volunteers and thought this amalgam of mankind, all of whom tried vainly to help, was so different from the splintered groups of the past weeks: Reverend Jones arm-in-arm with stoners and members of his own flock, stoners beside law enforcement officials, townspeople next to tourists. Amazing.

The two lines of searchers had traveled about a hundred yards in both directions. A barbed wire fence hampered the group that searched to the south, but they renewed the effort on the far side. Neither group reported any new findings. About half trudged back toward their cars while the remainder continued poking around under the brush and weeds and hoped to find anything that might confirm what had happened to Krank.

The arrival of the county's zodiac and divers provided a diversion for Harpoon, who still hoped for a miracle. He watched as the boat and divers began at the head of the Cut and worked their way out and scoured the spoil banks and bottom for any confirmation of Krank's outcome.

As the afternoon wore on, Harpoon and Lottie sat on the tailgate of his truck and awaited any news from the search. The television news had come and gone after they interviewed the sheriff and Harpoon. The crowd had dispersed except for a handful of parishners and Reverend Jones, who now approached the two.

"We have to get back to the Epistle for the evening service, but would you join us in a prayer before we go?" Reverend Jones put a hand on Harpoon's shoulder and raised the other in supplication. "Lord God Almighty, we've suffered a tragedy here today; an inexplicable disaster that leaves us distraught and full of doubt. Our friend Krank has disappeared, and we know not what has become of him. If in your infinite wisdom you have chosen to pluck him from among us, please give us the grace and wisdom to accept your divine plan. And we pray, Lord, that you especially comfort his special friends Harpoon and Lottie, for theirs is the greater loss. We pray in your name. Amen." He put his arm around Harpoon for a moment, and then left without another word.

The sun approached the horizon, and a slight landward breeze kicked up and sent a chill through Harpoon and left him shivering. Lottie moved closer and wrapped her arms around him as tears streamed down his face.

The divers had beached the zodiac after a fruitless

search. The circle of law enforcement officials stood at a distance and mumbled among themselves. Finally, Constable Sherrill approached the two and doffed his cowboy hat. "Harpoon, Lottie, I'm not sure what to say. We've found nothing to confirm Krank's alive or was killed in the blast. We've never seen anything quite like this. It's as if he vanished into the air. Is there any chance Krank left with someone else before the blast?"

"I wish that could be true . . . but . . ." Harpoon's voice trailed off to silence.

"It'll be dark soon, so we're calling off the search for tonight, but we'll be back tomorrow with search and rescue dogs. Meantime, why not go home and get some rest?"

Lottie slid off the tailgate and stood by Harpoon. "I'll take him home soon, Bubba. Thanks for all the help today. We'll keep hoping for a miracle."

Harpoon sat trancelike on the tailgate and stared down the Cut. He had sent Lottie home at dark. "I need to be by myself for awhile." She had acquiesced reluctantly. As he stood by his truck and watched her taillights recede into the darkness, a sense of deep, abiding loneliness flooded over him. "Krank, where have you gone?"

The full moon rose and cast a glow over the landscape, as the breeze rustled the grass, and the smell of eternity invaded the salt-marsh aroma. The Cut's surface shimmered in the moonlight as if subdued by the day's events. Possibly he had dosed, but he came to at the sound of something crawling through the Spartina. The sense of optimism that pervades all the bereaved, hoping for a better outcome, brought him to full alert. "Krank! That you?"

On the far side of the water Coyote materialized as he moved toward the tallest spoil bank. Silhouetted by the full moon, he raised his head, and loosed a guttural howl of sadness and misery so profound Harpoon sagged in grief.

Krank was gone.

CHAPTER | 27

Harpoon awoke with Stevie Ray Vaughan wailing out on " She's My Pride and Joy." He fought through the confusion of a deep sleep induced by weariness, depression, and a sleeping pill administered by Lottie when he'd arrived at her home the previous evening. He finally focused enough and realized the sound came from his cell phone in the pants pocket of the clothes he still wore from the day before. He dug the phone from his jeans with difficulty, he saw the time was ten o'clock, and the caller ID showed only "Wireless caller." "Hello?"

"I'm sorry about your Indian friend's accident." An unmistakable voice.

"How did you get this number?"

"I usually get what I want. Which reminds me, don't forget our little trip tomorrow. We leave about three o'clock for a rendezvous at dark, right?"

"You're out of your mind! We're not going anywhere tomorrow . . . How did you know about Krank?"

"I watch the news."

"Ok, here's a news flash for you. I'm more likely to sprout wings and fly than take you out on a drug run." Harpoon stood beside the bed and screamed into his cell phone.

"I can understand you're upset, what with your Indian friend's accident and all, but you must understand these kind of accidents can happen to anybody."

Harpoon stood in silence and crushed the phone into his ear. "That sounds like a threat. You telling me you killed Krank?"

"From what I understand his propane bottle blew up."

A longer silence. "Yeah, it blew up . . . when he entered his houseboat."

"It's a terrible thing, an accident. Let's hope no accidents happen to any of your other friends."

"You miserable cocksucker. If you had anything to do with Krank's death . . ." Harpoon's knees felt weak, and he sat on the edge of the bed. "I'll . . ."

"Let's say it's very much in your interest for your boat to be ready at three o'clock tomorrow." The phone clicked off.

Harpoon sat for a few minutes, his mind whirred at the thought of Krank possibly murdered and the veiled threat toward his other friends. "LOTTIE!" He jumped from the bed and ran into her kitchen. A note beside the coffee pot read "Short a cook and I've gone in to help with breakfast. Be back about ten-thirty. I love you." He looked at his watch – ten-thirty and no Lottie. He punched the speed dial on his cell.

"Island Joynt, how can I help you." Cindy's voice rumbled into his phone.

"Cindy, Harpoon. Is Lottie there?" He tried to steady the tension in his voice.

"Harpoon, listen man, the Krank thing really breaks me up. I'm so sorry."

"Thanks for you concern, but I really need Lottie." He couldn't keep fear from creeping up his throat.

"You sound bad, man, I'm really sorry . . ."

" Cindy! Can I just talk to Lottie? It's really important."

"That's the thing. She said she'd help with breakfast, but she never showed. It's not like her." Cindy registered concern. "Is there a problem?"

"She never showed?" Harpoon shouted.

"Harpoon, are you okay?"

"No!" He clicked off and punched Lottie's number.

"Hi! I'm out of pocket so leave your message. Or . . ." The cell went dead.

His hand visibly shook as he stared at the phone. "SHIT!" He crammed on his Nike's and ran to his truck. It didn't start on the first try. "SHIT!" The engine coughed into life on the second try, and he blasted out of the driveway and sped toward the Joynt. The truck slid to a stop at the front door. Inside, he looked in every direction.

Cindy came toward him, arms full of breakfast orders. "What's wrong, Harpoon?"

"Did Lottie ever show up?"

"Not yet." She stood still and shook her head as Harpoon ran out of the restaurant.

An SUV almost broadsided his truck as he ran the red light at Cotter Street but managed to avoid a collision by running up into a real estate office parking lot. At the Family Center, he leaped out almost before his truck stopped. Inside, he ran up and down the aisles looking to see if Lottie had stopped for short items at the restaurant. He bumped into the manager and knocked him back into a sun tan lotion display. Brightly colored tubes and bottles splayed in every direction. "Have you seen Lottie this morning?"

The manager's arms and legs flailed without gaining traction. A tube of sun screen on which he landed blew off its top and sent a stream of SPF 40, splattering onto an over-weight customer's butt. The lady let out a whoop that turned heads all over the store.

"Jesus, Harpoon, what the hell's going on?"

"Lottie, have you seen her this morning?"

"No! Not today, okay?" Before he could say anything further about the display scattered around him or the anointed butt, Harpoon was already halfway to the door.

He leaped into his pickup and roared out of the parking lot before he realized he had no idea where Lottie might be. Maybe she'd gone to the supermarket in Flour Bluff or Aransas Pass, but which one, and why hadn't she told the restaurant where she planned to go? She wouldn't be at a friend's if she had promised to help with breakfast. He swung right onto Cutoff Road and headed toward the ferry when he took his foot off the gas pedal and let the truck coast to a stop. Ahead he saw the Port Aransas Municipal building with the police department. The truck inched ahead when he downshifted and eased out the clutch. His mind churned over what he should do, but finally he accelerated and turned into the municipal building parking lot.

"Is Chief Crump in?" he asked the receptionist.

The woman's face filled with compassion. "I'm so sorry about Krank. I know he was like your brother. Let me see if the Chief can see you."

Chief Crump followed the receptionist out to get Harpoon. "Harpoon, I thought you'd be out at the cut."

"I wanted to, but I have a problem you can help me with." Harpoon shook the chief's hand. "What did they find?"

"They've searched for three hours with dogs and haven't found one trace of Krank. It's the damndist thing I've ever heard of." Crump shook his head in disbelief. "Krank's completely vanished."

"I'm afraid he's gone for good." Harpoon's eyes glistened at the thought. "But I wonder if you would help me with another problem?"

"Absolutely. What's up?"

"A creep's been bothering Lottie the past few days, and this morning I can't find her. It's probably nothing, but what with Krank and all, I'm very concerned. Would you help me with the phone company and get a location check on her cell phone? I'd feel a lot better knowing where she is."

"You're making a really unusual request."

"I know. Losing Krank's probably made me over protective,

I guess. But it'd feel a lot better."

After a long silence Crump asked, "Harpoon, is there something you want to tell me about?"

"I guess I've not totally returned to reality. Anyway, It'd really be a huge favor if you could help me."

Crump didn't answer, but picked up the phone and dialed the phone company. He frowned as he jammed his stubby finger into the dial pad after every telephone prompt. Finally he got a human voice on the other end. "Chief Crump of the Port Aransas Police Department, and we have a missing person. I'd like a position report on the cell phone for Lottie Langton." He looked up at Harpoon. "What's her number?"

"361-322-3365." Harpoon had to steady his voice.

The chief repeated the number and waited for a response. After several minutes he said, "Ok, thanks." He looked up at Harpoon. "They say her phone must be turned off, so they can't get a fix. Does she often turn her phone off?"

"No, never."

"You sure you don't want to tell me something?" Crump's face showed lines of concern.

Harpoon smiled as best he could with his guts churning. "No. I know she's as broken up about Krank as I am. Maybe she wanted to be alone without being disturbed by the phone." He slowly backed out of the Chief's office as he spoke. He waved as he disappeared out the door. "Thanks for your help."

Back in his truck, he pounded his fists on the steering wheel as he considered his options. The truck finally snorted into life, and he drove slowly to Roberts Point Park and parked out of hearing distance from the other park visitors. He did not recognize the number of the last call received on his cell phone. Mako answered on the third ring. "I thought I might hear from you."

"Where's Lottie, you miserable shit?"

"She's safe. Comfortable even. But I'm afraid you won't see her until we return tomorrow night. She'll be waiting for you in her house when you get back with a bunch of money in your pocket. Now with your past drug trafficking and all, don't even think about the cops, man. Know what I mean? But if we don't return tomorrow night with the goods in hand, I'm afraid another accident might happen – to her, that is."

CHAPTER | 28

His truck engine idled as Harpoon sat and stared out at the Corpus Christi ship channel and the jetties beyond. The nonday sun projected splotches of dark shadow from marshmallow cumulus scudding overhead. A spanking breeze kicked up whitecaps in the channel as oil well tenders and gleaming sport fishing boats coursed their way in and out between the jetties. He rubbed his temples with his thumbs and tried to erase the pained indecision. What to do? He mulled the idea of confessing his drug run to Chief Crump in the hope of enlisting police help in finding and rescuing Lottie. But they know less than I do about Lottie's whereabouts, and Mako might carry out his threat to kill her.

"God, what can I do?"

Time passed rapidly as he sat frozen in place. Shadows grew longer when he felt the warm blanket of resolve envelope him. I caused the problem. I have to fix the problem. He turned the key in the ignition, and the screaming grind of a starter motor thrust into an idling engine brought him to full attention. The truck moved slowly toward uncertainty.

He must not raise suspicion about Lottie. Avoiding restaurant employees, friends, and, most of all, Chief Crump was the best way. Rumor and news traveled fast on this small island. He drove below the speed limit and followed back streets to his house. Quickly inside, he knelt next to his bed. He fished the nickel-plated Colt revolver his father had given him and the box of cartridges from under the bed. He had taken the gun, normally hidden on *Cordon Blues* in case of an emergency, home when his boat went in for repairs. It was wrapped in oiled paper to protect against salt-air corrosion.

His duffel bag was already in the back of his truck, and he slipped from the house and into the truck for the trip back to the Blues. He parked well away from the boat and carried the duffel with the revolver to the dock. Harpoon tried not to attract attention as he heaved the bag over the stern and scrambled aboard. Then he crawled over the deck and down into the sleeping quarters.

The hatch was opened a crack for fresh air, and he cranked up the air-conditioning unit to cool the cabin. On the edge of his bunk, he removed the revolver from the duffle and unfolded the oiled paper. The nickel gleamed in the bare-bulb light and cast reflections around the room as he slid six rounds into the revolver. He sneaked up into the wheelhouse and hid the unwrapped gun under the firewall deck next to the wheel.

Back in the sleeping quarters with time on his hands, he felt hungry. He hadn't eaten in over twenty-four hours. A rummage through the galley cabinets produced two Payday candy bars and a package of Tom's Peanut Butter Crackers. The refrigerator held the fresh meats, produce, and fruit Krank had stocked on Saturday. Harpoon reached into the ice chest next to the stove and grabbed a Shiner Bock. "Livin' large on peanut butter crackers and beer."

***

Diggs, the pocket gopher, dug furiously. He had tunneled through a lot of ground in search of the Great Gopher and His Great Burrow in the Sky. In fact, the comfort of the D&D Mines was a distant memory. He was near exhaustion and craved a little Stuff to lift his spirits, but he kept on digging a circuitous route so as not to miss the Great Burrow. A terrifying event brought him to his senses when he was about to lose faith there actually was a Great Gopher and a Great Burrow. The ground shook with such force it bounced him around and collapsed his tunnel. It left him buried alive. What could possibly have caused this? He thought, as he lay in the suffocating darkness barely able to move. Could it be the Great Gopher? Maybe I'm getting too close to the Great Burrow, and He sent me a warning. A warning to come no closer. Maybe the Great Burrow is open only to the dead.

Claustrophobia kicked in, and he lapsed into a digging panic to retreat from the Great Gopher and to reach fresh air. The shaft to the surface took forever, but finally Diggs broke into the open air and gasped for breath. His panic subsided until he saw a great plume of black towering to the sky.

What's that? The sight so disturbed him that he retreated down the shaft and dug in the direction of the B&B Mines – he hoped. I must see if the Emporium and Mine are okay.

***

Jeff McAlister raised himself to one elbow on the cot under the Crate's fly tent. The stoner's beach village remained quiet while most stuck close to their tents and shanties. Distant strains of reggae and rock wafted on the afternoon sea breeze, accompanied by the rhythmic sigh of the waves rolling out on the beach. His friend, Ricky Stone, napped on the adjacent cot. A mantle of restraint had settled on the village after yesterday's explosion and subsequent search for the victim. The band did not even set up, as no one felt like dancing. With no beer run, the taps ran dry. No one volunteered for the nightly ganja harvest. Some stoners had glimpsed their mortality for the first time and felt enough sobered and bummed out by this newly acquired wisdom to pack and leave. It's the beginning of the end, Rick mused.

Unable to sleep, Harpoon climbed on deck sometime after midnight, pulled a canvas chair from the wheelhouse, and let the cool salt air waft in his face. He looked at the clear sky speckled with blinking flecks. "Krank, you out there? I'm in big trouble here. I could really use some help." A wry smile indicated his chagrin. "I guess this is when most folks pray to God, not to a friend. Sorry, God, I meant no disrespect. I really can't come up with any good reasons for you to help me, but if there's any help available, I could sure use it."

The first ray of sun blasted over the horizon and hit Harpoon as he slept in his chair. He stirred, stretched, and felt completely refreshed, though somewhat stiff from the chair and the damp night air. Last night's dream about when he and Krank went mako shark fishing came to mind, he said aloud, "Yeah! That's a plan."

He knew the Warf Cat head boat would return at one o'clock with its boatload of day fishermen, all of whom needed their catch cleaned. He retrieved the plastic ice barrel from below deck and secured it to the back of the boat. Before going below, he stuck two deep-sea fishing rods in holders at the stern.

At one o'clock, he tied up at the fish cleaning and cold storage dock at Fisherman's Wharf. He set the plastic barrel on the dock. "Hey, Jimmy, I'd take a barrel of chum, if you could spare it."

The attendant took the barrel. "You'd be doin' us a favor, Harpoon. Goin' for sharks?"

"Yeah, I thought it'd take my mind off things."

"I know what you mean. Losing Krank has everyone upset. Listen, if you need any help shrimpin' let me know."

At about three o'clock, Harpoon again moored in the Blues berth. The plastic barrel, now about three-fourths full of fish guts and blood, rested securely tied to the stern of the boat. When he returned from using the head below deck, he was surprised to see the muzzle of Mako's and the Goon's Uzis pointed at him.

"We gave ourselves permission to come aboard." Mako motioned with the gun barrel for Harpoon to step away from the access hatch. "Now, to keep you from doin' something stupid, show us where the gun is."

"What makes you think I have a gun on board?"

"There's always a gun stashed, so hand it over, then we can get goin'."

"Look under the deck in the wheelhouse."

Mako motioned to the goon to go into the wheelhouse. "Is this the only one you've hidden?"

"It's the only one I own."

"Here, boss." The goon came out of the cabin brandishing the nickel-plated revolver.

"Put that thing away, you idiot. You want everyone in the harbor to see it?" Mako shook his head in disgust. "Ok, Captain, it's anchors away."

"Not really." Harpoon crossed his arms in defiance.

"Not really? You kiddin'?"

"I'm as serious as a dog shittin' peach seeds. Two things. First, we're not going anywhere until I talk to Lottie. Second, I need a fat envelope full of hundred dollar bills."

The goon stuck the revolver in Harpoon's ear, and cocked it. "You're not in a good bargaining position, asshole."

"Go ahead. Shoot, if you think you can make it out to the pickup point and back without me."

"He's got a point." Mako pointed to the goon. "Put it away." He took his cell phone out and dialed a number. After a pause he said, "Put the girl on" and handed the phone to Harpoon.

"Lottie, you there?"

"Yeah, I'm afraid I'm here. What the hell's happening?"

"Are you okay?"

"I'm okay except for being in this trash heap with this lunatic waving his gun around."

"Hang tight, and it'll all be over tomorrow."

Mako grabbed the phone from Harpoon, and she failed to hear his "I love you." Mako reached into his coat pocket and handed Harpoon an envelope.

Harpoon's countenance brightened. "You assholes cast off the lines, and we're outta here." He moved into the wheelhouse and immediately wrote the number he'd seen on Mako's cell phone screen before he forgot it.

The Blues roared into life and moved out of her berth toward the rendezvous point.

Cordon Blues, still in sight of land under a clear sky, ran in one-to-two-foot, crystal clear swells. The boat rocked gently as it quartered the waves. The goon looked in the chum barrel and recoiled in horror.

"What's that stuff?" he said has he held his nose.

Harpoon had lashed down the wheel and gone out on deck. "Chum for shark fishing. mako sharks are runnin'. Let's see if Mako has enough balls to catch one of his namesakes."

Mako stood up from the sorting table he leaned on. "Sharks? I hate fucking sharks, man."

"Like I say, I'm wonderin' if you have any balls."

Mako held up his arm cast. "How'm I gonna crank a fishing reel with this broken arm?"

"The Goon can crank in for you. Of course . . . if you got no balls."

"I ain't afraid a no sharks, man."

"Ok, it's a done deal. We'll do a little shark fishin' while we wait for your plane."

Harpoon returned to the wheelhouse where he remained for the rest of the trip. He ran faster than normal to assure there would be daylight when they reached the pickup point about sixty miles offshore. The trip's time would be reduced by at least forty-five minutes.

Mako and the goon took turns guarding Harpoon while the other went below and napped during the five-hour trip. They kept the Uzis at the ready even though Harpoon remained in the wheelhouse and showed no intentions of becoming a problem.

About five miles from the rendezvous, Harpoon lashed down the wheel and backed off the throttle. The wind had calmed, and the waves diminished into long low swells under a cloudless sky. The drift line of seaweed he had followed for miles held fish. Fish meant sharks.

He stepped out on deck, and the goon jerked the Uzi to the ready. "Easy cowboy, don't try anything funny."

"Exactly what sort of funny business would I try out here, asshole?" Harpoon continued to the chum barrel holding a coffee can. "Go wake your boss up. It's time to see if he's got any balls."

The goon walked to the quarters hatch. "Mako, come on up here."

Mako's Uzi preceded him out of the hatch. "What? What's the problem?"

Harpoon held up a coffee can of chum with blood dripping from it. "It's shark time." He emptied the can over the stern of the boat.

"I told you man. Fuck off"

"It's time for a little Mako-a-mako. How could a big bad guy like you pass up an opportunity like this?" Harpoon threw another can of chum overboard. Every few minutes he tossed out another can full and watched the surface behind the boat. He estimated they were about three miles from the pickup point when he saw the first fin break the surface over a quarter mile behind the boat.

The fin cut across the chum line then reversed direction and cut the line again before it turned ninety-degrees and headed for the Blues. Soon after, two more fins appeared, followed by another. Harpoon chummed more frequently as the fins moved closer. A mako leaped about three hundred yards back and plunged into the chum line. Harpoon chummed almost constantly now.

"Holy shit! I saw a fuckin' shark leap outta the water." Mako stood beside the sorting table. Almost transfixed, he and the goon moved toward the stern. "God, these bastards give me the creeps."

"I ain't never seen so many sharks, man." Goon shuddered at the scene before him. The outlaws focused so much on the sharks, they didn't see Harpoon return to the wheelhouse. He idled the engine and shifted the prop into neutral. Back out on deck, he stood by the chum barrel again. A shark breeched less than one hundred yards behind them. Harpoon untied the chum barrel and lifted it onto the stern gunnel. "We'll get the rods out in a minute, but first let's make sure we've got plenty of sharks." He dumped the remaining chum into the water, and a huge, blood-red ball bloomed in the water.

A shark in a feeding frenzy cut through the blood and guts, but before it cleared the crimson circle, a second shark caught the first by the tail and severed it completely. Blood shot from the injured shark like a fire hose. As more sharks moved into the frenzy, the water churned into bloody froth. A mako leaped from the gore, but a second caught it in mid arc and tore out a huge chunk of flesh.

The injured shark lay on the surface pitifully attempting escape. Mako and Goon stood at the stern spellbound. When Mako saw the incapacitated shark, he lifted his Uzi, let out a scream, and fired at the shark – almost cutting it in half.

Goon joined in and sprayed the feeding frenzy with his machine gun. "Take this you miserable bastards."

More blood boiled to the surface as bullet trails spewed into the water. Blood became so thick the smell was palpable onboard. An eviscerated shark floated to the surface with its guts hanging out only to be pulled under and gobbled by another. Mako and Goon hung precariously over the gunnel and intermittently fired bursts into the melee. Both laughed like crazy people.

Harpoon went back in the wheelhouse. He braced himself, looked once more at his adversaries, dropped the prop into forward, and crammed the throttle to the firewall, then killed the engine. The Blues leaped forward. The surge sent Mako's feet into a slow arc over his head. At the height of the backward summersault, he released the Uzi, which preceded him into the bloody gore. Goon had traced a similar acrobatic track, but now hung over the stern with both hands grasping the gunnel rail.

His Uzi hung inside the boat. He screamed and struggled to get back into the boat.

Harpoon ran to the stern, but the goon's eyes grew large before he arrived, and an agonized cry erupted. The goon clung to the rail for only a second more before he squeezed off one last shot and disappeared into the water. As the Uzi rattled to the deck, the discharged round ricocheted off the steel deck and hit Harpoon high in the fleshy outer part of his thigh. The shock of the bullet knocked him off balance. He saw Mako's head bob to the surface. The eyes bulged from their sockets, and the mouth was locked in a death grin, as a mako rolled and swallowed it whole. "That's for Krank."

Harpoon awoke in darkness and felt the back of his aching head. He had a knot the size of an egg, and a cut oozed moisture. I must have hit the deck when I fell. He sat up and saw the huge pool of blood under him. His thigh burned like someone held a blowtorch on it. When he ripped open his trousers, he saw the bleeding bullet hole, passing through the fleshy part of his leg. He made a tourniquet of his bandana and applied it over the wound. When he tried standing, pain seared through the wounded leg; it buckled under him, and he fell back on the deck. After resting a minute, he saw the Uzi a few feet away and crawled to it. He used the sorting table to pull up and the machine gun as an imperfect crutch. His good leg and the table held him while he waited for the pain to subside.

The distant hum of an approaching airplane drilled its way into his consciousness. I must not have drifted far from the pickup point. The airplane definitely headed in his direction. He moved around the table and faced its approach. These bastards might come looking for Mako. Not if I can help it. The plane had no night-lights, but Harpoon knew it was close. The sound increased in intensity with heart-pounding persistentence. Harpoon raised the Uzi as the plane burst out of the darkness only a few feet above the Blues. His machine gun opened fire on the plane's engine and cockpit, but it pulled up and circled the boat. He moved around the sorting table, tracking its course until it veered again and headed for the boat. Before he could fire, he saw machine gun muzzle flashes from the side of the plane. Bullets pelted the deck and kicked up splinters and clanged off of the steel around him. He felt something sting his ear and blood trickle down his face. A man hung out of the door of the plane with a blazing machine gun as the plane zoomed above the boat. Harpoon dropped to the deck, using the table for protection.

Ok, assholes, I'll be ready next time

The plane circled and bore in again. Harpoon fired where he thought it would approach. Its windshield was shattered when it passed. It flew erratically, and it never pulled up. The sound of the crash was loud even from half-mile away. "That's for Lottie."

He dragged himself into the wheelhouse and with the firewall and his good leg he pulled himself into his captain's chair. Dizzy from loss of blood, he held the wheel to steady himself. The motor roared into action and the Blues surged ahead. He set the course, lashed down the wheel, and pulled the cell phone from under the firewall deck. He scanned the screen - no bars. Damn! I've got to stay conscious until I reach a phone cell.

CHAPTER | 29

he swells rocking the boat soothed Harpoon until he broke into consciousness, felt the pain in his leg, and, dazed, thought where am I? I must have passed out. He shook his head to clear it and saw the wheel tied down. Both the compass and the GPS showed him on course and about four hours out of Port Aransas. The cell phone had three bars. I must be in the offshore oil platform cell. He found the number he'd remembered from Mako's cell phone screen and dialed it. The phone rang ten times with no answer. His brain spun out. "God, what if I wrote the wrong number?"

Lottie knew she must catch the goon asleep. She sat in a ratty old upholstered chair with the cotton batting blooming through holes worn in the arms. It smelled like a cat box. A telephone sat across the room on a table under a lamp with a torn shade. The goon had tied her hands behind her and taped her feet together. She had heeded his warning, "Be a good girl or I'll truss you up like a Christmas goose."

The goon yawned wider and more often as the night wore on. She spent her time straining against the tape on her ankles, loosening it. Finally his eyes closed up shop as the lids descended for good. Lottie waited until his snores rattled the window shades. She stood and hopped over to the table, backed up, and tried lifting the telephone receiver. With great dexterity she had just touched the phone when it rang. She let out a screech, and the goon bolted up upright.

"Operator, I have a phone number here, but I'm not sure it's the correct one. Could you look it up and give me the name, please?" Harpoon drummed his fingers on the firewall deck. "M. Ortega? Oh, could you give me the address also, please? One-nine-six-zero-zero Highway 44 West? Thanks."

The goon's head swiveled like a weathervane in a tornado "Wha, wha what the hell!" He saw Lottie hop toward the bathroom. By the time he pushed himself up from the broken- down couch, she hopped through the door and locked it.

The phone kept ringing as he pounded on the door. "Okay, bitch, I told you what would happen if you tried any funny business."

He pulled his Glock 9mm and fired three shots, the doorknob exploded, and the door swung open.

Lottie screamed as he shoved his way in and grabbed her arm and almost jerked it from its socket. "Get out here, bitch." Lottie screamed again.

The goon dragged her to a chrome dinette chair and shoved her down, then pulled her arms over the chair back. She let out a howl of pain, and he slapped her across the face. A trickle of blood ran from the corner of her mouth. The sound reverberated around the dingy room like a firecracker. "Shut up, you fuckin' bitch."

As he duct taped her to the chair, the phone rang again.

"Jesus Christ, is this telephone central?" He moved across the room and jerked up the phone. "WHAT? Is this you, boss?"

"I just fed your boss and your buddy to the sharks."

"Sharks! I hate fuckin' sharks."

"Mako and the other goon would agree with you right

now."

"Who's this? Why you talkin' about Mako and sharks?" The goon's voice rose with his confusion.

"I'm the man that's gonna cut you up into little pieces and feed you to the sharks if you don't listen closely and do exactly what I say. Understand?"

"Nobody's gonna do shit to me as long as I got the girl here, whoever you are."

"Stop talkin' and listen, asshole. You've got one chance to live through this. First, if you harm Lottie – you're a dead man. Got it? Second, you're probably too stupid to know kidnapping's a federal offense, and they kill you if you harm the victim. Forget about the sheriff, the police, even the Texas Rangers – unless you want to spend the rest of your life running from the FBI, do exactly as I say."

"Mako's dead?"

"Mako is shark shit even as we speak."

"Man, that's really cold."

"Not nearly as cold as what's gonna happen to you if you don't shut up and listen."

"Okay, okay. I'm listenin'."

"It's very simple. Deliver Lottie back home unharmed. Then hit the road and get as far as you can from Port Aransas and Corpus Christi. Do these two things and no one will be any wiser. You can live out your life undisturbed. At least until you do something else stupid. You with me?"

A long silence followed while Goon Two processed the information. "Take the girl back and hit the road. That's it?"

"You got it. The sheriff will kick in the door at 19600 West Highway 44 any minute, so get a move on."

"You know where I am? Wait a minute. What if you're lyin' about Mako?"

"Call his cell phone and see how good it works under water." Harpoon loosed a nasty chortle. "Now let me talk to Lottie."

After a pause Lottie said, "Harpoon, are you okay?"

"I was goin' to ask you that. Has this guy bothered you?

"Being around him bothers me, but I'm alright."

"Ask him if he's taking you home."

He could hear the question in the background. Back on the phone she said, "He's untying me and says he's taking me home"

"Good, now listen. Don't say a word about any of this to anybody. Lie low at home until I call you. Then come pick me up at the dock. I should be there in about four hours."

"You sure you'reokay? You sound different?"

"I'll make it. Wait for my call." Harpoon heard a horrible groan echo through the phone, followed by a gunshot and an appalling scream. "Lottie! LOTTIE! Are you okay?"

"Yeah, I'm okay."

"What was that?

"This idiot kept waving his gun around, so I kicked him in the nuts, and when he grabbed his crotch, he shot himself in the foot."

"Lottie! Leave this guy alone. I'm trying to get him to take you home."

"I've got his gun now, so I think he probably will."

"Let me talk to him."

"I'm not sure he can talk right now. He's rolling around on the floor in great pain and anguish."

"Lottie, have this guy drive you home and tell him to get out of town before the sharks get him. Whatever you do, don't talk to anybody about this."

"I'll wait for you."

Harpoon could hear her voice trembling and sense tears of relief at the news she soon would be home safe.

Time dragged like a sea anchor as *Cordon Blues* churned toward Port Aransas. The throbbing in Harpoon's leg increased until he shouted curses as he loosed the tourniquet and retied it. The bleeding had stopped, but the wound looked really ugly. The calm water was a Godsend since he could hold the leg still and not suffer from the gunshot being constantly massaged by a rocking boat.

A mist shrouded the boat, turning shore lights into paper lanterns hung low in the sky. His heart leaped when he saw a particularly bright light. "That's the Crystal Epistle Jumbotron." The mist blurred the message. He opened the windshield panel and strained to see the letters through his binoculars. About ten minutes later and a mile closer, after a fusillade of color and patterns, the background turned white and the black letters read "Memorial Service for Krank Saturday 11:00 am." Harpoon lowered his head at the finality of the announcement. Krank still lived in his heart, but holding the inevitable at bay was increasingly difficult.

Momentary relief from grief and pain came when Harpoon saw the ship channel jetty marker lights. He made a course correction, lining the Blues midway between the two jetties and watched as channel lights changed from halos with bright centers into crisp points of light, showing the way, to safe harbor. He dialed Lottie's home phone as he passed the jetty heads.

She answered on the first ring. "Harpoon?"

"I passed the jetty head, and I should be in the harbor in about fifteen minutes. I'll need help mooring the Blues and getting to your car."

"My God, Harpoon, what happened?" Her voice was laced with panic.

"The hole in my leg makes getting around very difficult. If you throw me the lines, I think I can tie off the boat. So you might head on over to the dock and wait for me."

"Should I bring help? An ambulance?"

"NO!! Don't bring anybody. Only yourself. I think we can do it."

"But why not bring help?"

"Lottie, listen! Nobody can know about this. You must

understand." His voice had a convincing firmness."

"Okay . . . alright. I'm heading out the door."

"Did the goon leave town?"

"He asked if he could have his gun back. I told him I would shoot him in the other foot if I ever saw him again. He agreed when I suggested he head for Mexico where he could get his foot fixed without any questions being asked."

When Harpoon swung the bow out and began backing into the dock slip, he saw Lottie and became emotional. So beautiful. So resourceful. So concerned. How lucky can a man get? He eased the stern against the dock end of the birth and moved to the cabin door. He hobbled to receive the stern lines Lottie threw onboard, but his leg gave way, and he collapsed to the deck.

"Harpoon?" Lottie clambered over the gunnel, quickly slipped the stern lines over the cleats and ran to Harpoon. "Are you okay?"

"A little trouble walking." He groaned as he tried to stand.

"Just lie there." She grabbed a boathook and pulled the bowlines aboard. Once tied off to the bow cleats, she went into the cabin and switched off the engine. Back at Harpoon's side, she looked at the bloody bandana around Harpoon's leg and almost swooned. "God, Harpoon, you're really hurt. How did this happen?"

"It's a long story, but right now we must get off this boat before anyone sees us. Drive my pickup onto the dock, and I'll try swinging over the side and into the truck bed."

She groaned louder than Harpoon when he lost his grip and fell into the truck. "Harpoon, I'm taking you to the hospital. You need medical attention."

"They have to report every gunshot wound."

"I don't give a damn. Here, put your arm around me and hang onto the side of the truck We're getting you into the cab, and then into Corpus and a hospital."

Once in the truck and into the twenty-mile trip into the

hospital, Lottie handed Harpoon a bottle of Vicodin. "Take a couple of these. You'll feel better."

Harpoon awoke as two male emergency nurses transferred him onto a gurney. The Vicodin did its job and his leg hurt less than he remembered as they wrestled with his wound. The attendants frowned a little when Lottie shouted, "Careful!" when they plopped him on the stretcher.

"We normally see the 'cut and shoot' stuff on the weekend." A nurse threw this old cliché over his shoulder at Lottie as he wheeled Harpoon inside.

Harpoon smiled up at the nurse. "It's not good to get smart with the lady tonight. She's a bit riled and most likely will kick you in the nuts." Harpoon chuckled a little at the prospect.

The admitting nurse's primary concern was his insurance information. Harpoon said, "I don't have insurance"

"How do you intend to pay for the treatment?"

"Do you take money?"

"Money?"

"Yeah, do you take cash?"

"Not very often." The nurse wore the look of someone who knew she was getting conned and felt determined not to allow it. "Do you have the ability to pay?"

Harpoon struggled getting his hand in his pocket and retrieved the fat envelope of hundred dollar bills. "How about this. Will it do?"

"Yes, that will do nicely, thank you."

He handed Lottie the envelope. "The lady will settle up when you're through patchin' me up."

Lottie's eyes grew large as she looked at the envelope, but she said nothing.

They wouldn't let Lottie remain with Harpoon. She paced and fretted for the hour they took cleaning up, suturing, and bandaging Harpoon. Finally the emergency room doctor came out to visit with Lottie. "It's a pretty routine gunshot wound in the outer flesh of his thigh. The arteries damaged were easily repaired and no bones were broken. The bullet passed all the way through the leg. He'll be very sore for days, but in time he'll recover completely.

"Oh, thank God." Lottie fought back tears of gratitude.

"He needs to be very careful about infection. So no baths for the first four days. Change the bandage daily, but let the sutures come off by themselves. Take these two prescriptions for an antibiotic and for pain."

"I'll make certain he follows your instructions and takes his medicine." Lottie nodded affirmation.

"We will keep him here overnight because his blood count is low, and he needs a couple of units of blood. He also has to fill out the police report and be interviewed by an officer. Both of which will happen tomorrow morning, but he should be ready to return home after that." The doctor halted for a moment. "How did the shooting happen by the way?"

"I don't know. He came in from shrimping and called me to come to the boat and help dock it." Lottie shrugged. "He went to sleep in the truck on the drive here, and I didn't get to talk to him about it. Musta been some kind of accident."

"We'll report an accident, but tomorrow morning he must tell the police exactly how it happened. Keep him still so the bleeding doesn't start again. Crutches would also help tomorrow."

A voice came over the intercom. "Code blue in the emergency room." The doctor turned on his heel and trotted back down the hall.

"Wait! What's a code blue? Is it Harpoon?" Lottie's voice echoed down the vacant corridor.

CHAPTER | 30

A weather system had moved onto the coast from the Gulf and the sky over Mustang Island roiled with plum colored clouds backlit with strobe-like flickers of lightening. When Lottie pulled into Roberts Point Park with an Island Joynt busboy in Harpoon's truck, a light drizzle flecked her windshield. Even the weather could not dampen her spirits.

"Ms. Lottie, you seem downright joyous this morning." The busboy cast a glance at Lottie.

"Rudy, I'm the luckiest girl in the world, so why wouldn't I be happy?"

"I don't know, but you've got a nasty bruise on your face. That'd take the edge off for me." He looked at her expecting an explanation.

She glanced at him. "Only a little run-in with a door. Nothing serious." She pulled Harpoons's truck beside her car and stopped. "If you'll drive my car back to the restaurant, I'd really appreciate it."

"You comin' back?'

"I've got to run an errand, but I'll see you guys this afternoon." She nodded her thanks to Rudy as he got out of the car.

She kept her window open a crack and breathed the clean air and fresh smell of rain as she hummed and sang along with the radio on the way to pick up Harpoon.

A part of her good cheer wore thin as the morning dragged on, filled with hospital paperwork, waiting for doctors to sign a release, cashing out, and finally the police interview. At noon, Harpoon made it from the hospital to his pickup under Lottie's watchful eye, with the help of a wheelchair, a nurse, and crutches. They had not cleared out of the parking lot before she asked, "Okay, what did you tell the policeman?"

"The truth – sort of." Harpoon did not look at Lottie.

"Sort of?"

"I thought it best."

"Okay, I'll ask again. What did you tell the policeman?"

"I told him it was an accident. A shark got tangled in the net, and I couldn't get it out by myself, so I got the pistol to shoot it. I slipped down on the slick deck and shot myself in the leg." He turned to get Lottie's reaction.

"He bought that?"

"He seemed kind of in a hurry, so, yeah, since this wasn't the 'Crime of the Year,' I guess he bought it. "

"Why do I feel like this might be the Crime of the Year? As in what happened to Mako and the Goon?"

"They had an accident also. They fell overboard and were eaten by sharks." Harpoon looked out the side window and waited for her response.

"Eaten by sharks? You're kidding me, right?"

"The evil bastards murdered Krank. This couldn't have happened to two more deserving assholes."

Lottie pulled over and skidded to a stop on the side of the road so she could look Harpoon in the eyes. "Right now you and I are the only two, besides the goon heading for Mexico, who know about my kidnapping and Mako and Goon being on the Blues."

"That's why I cautioned you not to talk about this thing. It's our secret."

"And you don't think I should know the details?" Lottie's brow knotted with concern.

"The less you know, the better. Well, actually, there's also the plane crash."

"The . . . drug plane . . .crash?" Lottie slumped under the weight of the revelation.

"Yes."

"Let me understand this. You single-handedly wiped out the drug trade in the Coastal Bend and survived with only a flesh wound plus a wad of money?"

" 'Wiped out' may be a little strong, but between the two of us, we dented them pretty good." Harpoon smiled for the first time. "I know one thing. After what you did to that Goon, I'll be careful of those feet of yours from now on."

Lottie could see the beach from where they parked. Rain pelted down and gusts of wind occasionally rocked the car. The waves pummeled the beach and rolled in to the dunes. The overcast sky looked dark and foreboding. Lottie sat and silently processed the information. Harpoon's attempt at humor escaped her, as all her joy drained from her face. Finally she said, "There's a memorial service for Krank at the Crystal Epistle on Saturday."

"I saw the announcement on the Jumbotron on the way in." Harpoon looked past the beach to the open sea, now battered by the wind. "It's hard to think about going out to sea without Krank."

"It's hard to imagine life without Krank." All of the excitement, stress, apprehension, fear, and sorrow caught up with Lottie, and tears trickled down her cheeks.

Lottie held an umbrella over Harpoon as he hobbled on his crutches toward her front porch. Once inside, they shook off the rain, and she helped him into her bedroom and onto the bed. "The doctor gave very specific orders. You cannot move around and start the bleeding again. So now you're here, it's bed rest and TV for you."

"Harpoon grabbed her around the waist and pulled her down into a kiss. "Maybe there's a little 'movin' around' we could try."

She kissed him again and pulled away. "See me in a couple of weeks."

After Rudy picked her up in her car and drove her to the Island Joynt, Cindy rushed up to her with a hug. "The prodigal has returned. God, we were worried about you. Where have you been?"

"I needed time to myself."

"I mean, Harpoon rushed in here Monday like a mad man looking for you, and that's the last we heard of you."

"Well, I'm back now, so I better see how things are going."

Cindy tried once again. "You're sure there's nothing wrong?"

"Positive, but thanks for asking." Lottie patted her in a consoling way.

"Oh! Reverend Jones came in this morning and almost emptied the 'All You Can Eat Breakfast Buffet $4.95.' God, that man can eat! He said he'd tried to call Harpoon, but with no success. He asked if you would have Harpoon call him."

The rain washed away the malaise shrouding the stoner beach colony since the explosion. Ricky and Jeff lay under their fly tent in front of the Crate and watched the stoners come out into the rain like bugs and leap and shout. Many had bars of soap and took much-needed baths. Ricky pointed at a group of four girls soaping up. "Ya, Mon, check it out: de young honeys naked as da day they's born. A lovely sight indeed."

"Yeah, who needs television?"

"Da ganja weed be drier than a popcorn fart out there in the field, Mon. Dis blessed rain gonna produce more buds for Jah's Holy Smoke. Life be sweet, Mon."

Jeff motioned out over the beach colony. "We need to

make sure the stoners know about the memorial service for Krank Saturday morning. I'm sure there'll be kickin' music on the Jumbotron."

"That Krank, Mon, he must a been somethin' special for da folks to get so worked up about him."

"He was a real hero here on the Island."

***

Tunnels everywhere flooded and collapsed as rainwater poured down the surface shafts. Diggs shouted orders to an unresponsive, stoned bunch of gophers. They seemed concerned only with the survival of the Stuff mines. Gophers too young to dig their way out of collapsed tunnels would drown, but no one seemed to care. Finally, Diggs gathered some lucid gophers to move the babies to higher ground in the hope they would survive. Digging vertical shafts with side tunnels was arduous work. After they relocated their young, safe from the tunnels flooding below them, Diggs and the others stretched out, exhausted.

As he lay there panting, the thoughts plaguing him since his close encounter with the Great Gopher in the Sky returned. He knew the discovery of Stuff had changed life in the gopher colony, but not for the better. Fun is fun, but without responsibility, the quality of life had slowly ground almost to a halt. The Stuff Mine and Emporiums made him wealthy, but at what expense? He must decide the best way to go forward.

***

Lottie's voice tinkled with laughter when she announced over the phone, "You'll be happy to know that Rev. Jones wants you to call him."

Harpoon had stalled for time while he wondered exactly what Rev. Hannibal Jones wanted. Krank's memorial topped the list of acceptable subjects, while the channel blockade demonstration to relight the Crystal Epistle's beacon hovered at the bottom. With great trepidation he looked up the church's number and dialed and hoped for no answer. No such luck! "Harpoon Conroy here, could I speak to Rev. Jones please?"

After a pause the reverend's voice thundered from the receiver. "Harpoon, thanks for calling. I've tried to reach you about a problem."

Harpoon cringed. "What problem, Reverend?"

"Our Minister of Music, Dick Walzem, left on urgent family business."

"Will he return in time for this weekend?"

"That's what I'm calling about. He has very serious problems, and I suspect we've seen the last of Brother Walzem. And we are without a minister of music for both Krank's memorial and the Sunday service."

"That's a problem. Can you call somebody in temporally? Maybe a member of the choir?"

"After much prayer and meditation, I feel you should fill the void for Krank's service." The reverend's voice assumed the quality of the "Invitation" at the end of a sermon.

"Me?" Harpoon choked.

"Absolutely. You knew Krank better than anybody. I'm sure you'll want to give a eulogy, and the music should be the blues music Krank loved. You and Slidin' Will can work out the music and practice with the choir early Saturday morning. Of course I'll say a few words also. There's no question it's God's will." The reverend's voice had a tone of finality.

"Reverend, I really don't feel I'm the one to lead a religious service of any kind."

"You're a good man, Harpoon, and that's all Jehovah God asks of anyone."

"Actually, I'm not in very good shape. I hurt my leg, and I can barely get around."

"Not a problem. We'll pray for a speedy recovery." After a pause he added, "So it's a done deal?"

Harpoon hung up. "Good God."

Thursday morning, the rain moved inland and left behind cobalt sky scattered with cotton ball cumulus. A fresh breeze brought moisture-free air and cooled the morning temperature below that expected for late July. Lottie fixed breakfast for Harpoon and decided against going to the Joynt. They agreed she should attend the Rotary Club meeting to maintain the appearance of normality. As she drove to Pelicans Landing Restaurant, Lottie saw that both islanders and tourists had a little more spring in their step after the rain. When she arrived, the parking lot indicated a well-attended meeting.

Small groups stood around and discussed everything from the weather, to the stoner beach colony, to the continued renaissance of good business, to the explosion that killed Krank. Each group greeted Lottie, and those who had not seen her since Krank's demise expressed their condolences.

Mayor Riley Glen and Chief Crump visited about something with Rotary President, Roly Odem and Coach Bull Bostich when Crump spied Lottie. He moved toward her. "Good morning, Lottie, how are you this beautiful day?"

Lottie smiled and replied, "Feeling much better thank you, Chief."

"Harpoon stopped by looking for you Monday and seemed really concerned. Was there a problem?"

"I only wanted a little time for myself. I should have told Harpoon and someone from the restaurant where I was. I guess I caused some folks to worry."

"Harpoon seemed really stressed out over a really big problem. Can I help with something?"

"Thank you, Chief, but it's business as usual from now on." Lottie smiled again and patted the chief on the arm for reassurance.

Roly Odem gaveled the meeting to order and asked Rev Jones to lead the invocation.

"Thank you, Brother Odem. But before the invocation I want everyone to know that the memorial service for Krank will be held Saturday at eleven o'clock at the Crystal Epistle. Krank was a very quiet man, but a solid keystone in the Island community. So those who wish to pay respects should do so on Saturday."

Odem lead the Pledge of Allegiance after the prayer, but old and new business went by almost without comment as a somber mood spread through the meeting.

Roly sensed the down mood and said, "Actually I have one piece of new business. Coach Bostich is bringing us a report on the upcoming football season."

The room erupted. "GO, YOU RIDLEYS!" and "FEAR THE TURTLE!"

Coach Bostich held up his hands. "Thank you, men, for your enthusiasm. We can always count on good ol' zealous Island fan support. We've got a good bunch of boys this year. Hard workers with no quit in them, so we will win some games. I'd say we might even win it all if we had a passer. I've tried out every kid on the team and not one of them can hit a bear in the butt with a bull fiddle. I picked the best three to work with myself. Hopefully, we can coach up a winner.

"Those who haven't got your season tickets should do so, 'cause I think this will be one of the most interesting seasons in many years. I've just got a feeling."

Wiley Coots said to his table, "The old bastard's got something up his sleeve. "

As Bostich sat down, the members stood and shouted in unison, "GO, YOU RIDLEYS!" and then sang the fight song.

CHAPTER | 31

The threatening bank of clouds in the south concerned Lottie as she drove Harpoon to the rehearsal for Krank's memorial service. Threatening weather always made islanders edgy. She turned to comment, but thought better of it as she could see the reflection and worry about the service knitted into Harpoon's brow. The clouds looked out of place in an otherwise beautiful day. The blue sky and bright sunshine brought out the bill caps and sunglasses, and people scurried to the beach. She grimaced as lightening stitched its way through the dark clouds ahead like gold threads sewn into black wool.

Her attention shifted from the weather to Harpoon as she pulled beside the handicap ramp in front of the Crystal Epistle. "I'll help you in and make sure they have a stool for you."

"No, I can get up the ramp with the crutches. I don't want folks gettin' too interested in my injury."

She jabbed him in the ribs. "Yeah, It's just not a macho thing, right?"

"Maybe, but I've gotta get goin' on my own sometime. Might as well be now."

She waited at the base of the ramp until he hobbled inside, and then headed back toward The Island Joynt and preparation for those close friends of Krank who would make a few toasts to him after the service.

About ten-thirty, Jeff and Ricky started the general trek down the beach toward the Crystal Epistle Jumbotron. Most of those who had watched the first Epistle service with the blues band joined in, plus many of the curious. They trudged along and looked like a modern day Moses march: people wore swim suits and carried towels, beach chairs, umbrellas, and styro coolers. The main difference was the sweet smell of ganja that hung in the sea breeze.

The appreciative stoner at the last Jumbotron outing staggered up to Jeff. "Hey, man, that's some really cool shit last time. This gonna be as frosty?"

"It's a memorial service for the guy that died in that explosion last Sunday, but I expect we can dig some cool tunes." Jeff reached out and caught the mobility- impaired stoner as he stumbled.

"Wow, man. You mean it's like a funeral or something?"

"Something like that."

"Wow, really far out, man!" The stoner paused as if in contemplation, then resumed his irregular tack down the beach.

Ricky pointed at the menacing cloudbank in the south. "Maybe we be in for rough weather, mon."

"Pretty ominous, but there's no rain. Looks a little weird."

Harpoon sat on a stool placed for his comfort, as he preferred not to climb the podium steps again. The sanctuary filled with those who came out of respect for Krank. Most wore church clothes and many of the women donned their mourning hats. Ted noodled a Hammond B3, bluesy version of "Flee as a Bird" under the murmur of greetings among the crowd. When the sanctuary filled about half, Ted moved into an up-tempo classical jazz rendition of "Didn't He Ramble" and had some of the audience fairly trucking down the aisles.

Slidin' Will's guitar and a saxophone sat at the ready. Krank's tom toms had survived the explosion in the bed of his truck and now sat on the offertory table where a casket or funeral urn might normally be.

Ted downshifted into a more formal version of "Flee as a Bird" as the choir filed in singing the lyrics to the funeral dirge. Harpoon, Slidin' Will, and the sax man joined in and backed up the choir as Reverend Jones moved onto the dais. When the choir sat, he walked to the pulpit and lifted his arms in a warm gesture. "Welcome, all of you. This packed sanctuary is a fitting tribute for Krank whom we all knew and loved. I understand there also are hundreds of folks down on the beach watching the service on God's Jumbotron.

"Krank chose to live a quiet, simple life here among us, rather than a life of fame and celebrity that he surely would have achieved with his athletic prowess. A life in which he never passed up an opportunity for helping others. A life devoid of the materialism with which we all are afflicted.

"Let's bow our heads in a prayer of thanksgiving for the blessing of having had Krank in our lives."

Reverend Jones lifted his hand to its full reach. "Lord God Almighty, Protector of Our Souls, and Giver of Eternal Life, we come before you today offering up our deep appreciation for allowing Krank to live among us. He set an example of what humanity can achieve when motivated by something other than our own egos. We ask now, Lord, take him unto your bosom so he might enjoy the fruits of a life well lived. Amen."

The reverend looked at Harpoon. "No one knew Krank better than Harpoon Conroy." He took the wireless microphone to Harpoon. "Harpoon had a little accident and he's not getting around too good, but he would like to say a few words about his friend, Krank."

Harpoon took the microphone and cleared his throat. "Krank's life meant many things to many people. You might remember him as a gifted athlete. Others remember him as a quiet man who went about town helping people. Those who knew him closely knew him as a mystic and soothsayer. But when I think of Krank, I remember him as a loyal friend. None of us ever knew anything about where he came from. And now with his death, we don't know where he went.

"We spent many days and nights together out shrimping. He really never said much, but I remember one thing he said that defined Krank. He said, 'Live in the world touching the outside of your skin, not the world inside your skin.' Krank lived for others, not for himself. That's why those who knew him loved him. And that's why we're here today."

After a pause to gather himself, Harpoon continued. "Slidin' Will and I wrote a song dedicated to Krank which we will play for you now."

As Harpoon looked at each of the musicians before counting off the introduction, the back doors of the sanctuary blew open with a report loud enough a few ladies screamed. A blustering wind blew down both aisles, and women's hats soared toward the sanctuary ceiling. The building shook slightly, and some of the faithful looked ready to bolt for the doors.

On the dais, Rev. Jones and the musicians stood transfixed as the two squall- winds roared down the aisles colliding in front of the pulpit, and a slow rotation built from the floor skyward until a whirling vortex formed. From the core of the vortex a figure gradually rose until the opaque blue lines of a hologram floated above the musicians. The figure wore a flat-brimmed hat, a poncho and soft knee-length boots. Its eyes burned like coals of fire, and the guitar that hung around its neck glistened. The rings on its fingers sparkled through the hologram mist. The figure looked around the room until its eyes came to rest on Krank's tom-toms, then raised its pick-hand high above its head.

Everyone on the podium stared at the vision like pillars of stone. Silence left a vacuum in the sanctuary. The choir and congregation sat, rigid in anticipation. The raised hand accelerated toward the guitar strings and on impact launched an ear splitting chord reverberating around the room and spiraling up the glass and aluminum Crystal Tower. The congregation gasped and held their ears.

Someone shouted from the back, "Jehovah God, save us. It's the Second Coming."

With only a slight pause, the vision's fingers flew over the strings and frets, starting softly and gaining in speed and volume. Chromatic scales, arpeggios, and glissandos rolled out of the guitar layer building upon layer. A haunting backdrop of Stevie Ray Vaughan's "Lookin' Out the Window" hung as an obbligato backdrop to the fusillade of musical notes that ricocheted in the sanctuary. The fret fingers sparked over the guitar neck now glowing the red of heated iron. The glow moved down the neck and crept over the guitar sound box until the whole instrument smoldered as if ready to explode.

Harpoon held his hand between the apparition and his eyes in a protective reflex as a mega electric arc shot from the end of the guitar neck. The apparition faded. The arc spiraled up the Crystal Tower, bounced off the aluminum frame, and climbed until it collided with the top of the mast, and God's Holy Lamp burst forth in a brilliant light. The beacon slowly rotated and built in speed until its whirling released a guttural siren howl that echoed the sorrows of the ages.

A feeling of dread seemed to blanket the congregation, and many knelt in fervent prayer. Harpoon felt more religious than at any previous time as he tried to find Lottie.

When the specter appeared on the Jumbotron, Jeff McAlister bolted upright from the beach towel on which he lounged. He looked around and saw most of the stoners equally attentive. Someone shouted, "Whoa, man. That looks like the ghost of Stevie Ray Vaughan." The crowd murmured a frightened agreement. The beacon's light and howl brought many to their feet.

The appreciative stoner staggered over to Jeff. "Man, this is seriously rad, man. How often do these people do this, man?"

Ricky looked up at the black cloud that now hung low over the Crystal Epistle. Deep inside the cloud, flashes of energy glowed and growled as if seeking escape. "No question, mon, this be the doin's of da Devil. This be some industrial strength evil, no doubt."

Many of those standing, collapsed while they held their ears as the siren howl of God's Own Beacon gained amplitude. The sound reached an unbearable magnitude, and a sonic blast exploded from the Crystal Tower and sent a bolt of electricity straight into the bowels of the cloud overhead. Instantly, the Jumbotron burst into millions of shards resembling snowflakes propelled outward and drifting toward the beach. The crowd ran screaming in every direction.

The cloud took the bolt of electricity like a boxer receiving a solar plexus punch. The flashes and gut rumbles from its interior increased in intensity. The growling accelerated until a mighty thunder clap erupted, and the cloud shot a giant lightning bolt careening toward the ganja patch on Ol' Walt Greely's property.

Their faith held the congregation in place until the electric show erupted. Harpoon saw Lottie swimming up stream, trying to reach the podium. People clambered over the back of pews, pushed and shoved in the aisles, and panicked as they fled the building. He shouted at Slidin' Will over the people's screams, "I've had enough Crystal Epistle for today." He limped down the steps to meet Lottie.

With Lottie for support, he made it to the handicap ramp. People ran shouting in a mindless mob as the volunteer firemen's personal alarms went off.

CHAPTER | 32

The Circle K manager stood in the parking lot and stared at the menacing black cloud that approached from the south. An unexplained sense of dread came over him. A bolt of lightening burst from the cloud and thundered toward him. He recoiled in terror. The hair on his arms stood erect as the electrical discharge surged. The lightning bolt struck several fence posts on Ol' Walt Greely's property. Each exploded and sent showers of burning shards high into the air. The flaming debris landed in the dry grass along the fence line and smoldered only a few seconds before they burst into flames that moved into the landward breeze and toward the dunes.

"My, God, it's headed for the marijuana," he shouted at no one in particular, then looked around to see if anyone might question his concern for ganja over his store building. He pushed 911 on his cell phone. "Hurry! There's a grass fire burning here at the Circle K on Highway 361."

"You mean Ol' Walt Greely's property? The one with the marijuana patch?" the dispatcher asked.

"That's the one!"

"The trucks are on their way!"

The Circle K manager waved frantically at the pump trucks as they careened toward him, sirens screaming and air horns blaring. He continued soaking the grass around his store with a garden hose, and then ran toward the fire truck when it pulled into the driveway. "Thank, God, you're here." He gestured wildly at the fire. "It's headin' this way."

The individual fires had linked up and roared into full bloom the width of the Greely property. Smoke billowed skyward, drifted over Highway 361, obscured vision, and created a traffic backup of tourists' cars and those who fled Krank's memorial service.

The stoners running from the Jumbotron explosion saw the smoke rise above the dunes at their village. "Evil be loosed all over the Island, Mon. The forces of darkness torched stonerville." Ricky wore his first concerned expression of the summer.

"No, I think the fire's behind the dunes."

"Be worse if da ganja patch be smokin' an nobody be home enjoyin' it. Most important, we gotta save da Crate, Mon, regardless." Jeff and Ricky picked up the pace. They ran through stoner village, past the Crate, and climbed to the top of the dunes. They panted from their run as they watched the conflagration roar toward the marijuana.

"It be the apocalypse, no doubt. A ganja inferno, and us upwind. Most regrettable."

Other stoners arrived and along with Jeff and Ricky watched the fire devour the marijuana. Their comments told their palpable sadness.

"Looks like it's over."

"The curtain rings down on one summer of happiness."

The cacophony of auto horns on the highway reached an unbearable level as motorists stalled by lack of visibility and dead-stop traffic voiced their displeasure. But Ricky, Jeff, and the stoners noticed the noise level subside as the fire consumed more ganja. Motorists got out of their cars and wandered around in the smoke while they laughed and slapped each other on the back in gestures of brotherly love. A few even hugged.

The stoners looked at each other, back at the fire, back at each other, back at the motorists, and shouted in unison "PARRTEEEE!"

En masse the group ran back down the dune around onto the beach access road and surged toward the highway. The Circle K manager, possessed by an unrecognizable sense of magnanimity, offered up free beer for those enmeshed in traffic and smoke. The stoners arrived and helped with the distribution. Music pumped from car stereos as the party gained steam. People jumped up and down in time to the music, shouting and laughing.

When Chief Crump returned from the memorial service, he had attempted untangling the traffic, but now leaned against his cruiser happily listening to the sounds and moving with the music.

After the firemen saved the Circle K, they knew the beach access road could contain the fire on one side and it would burn out at the dunes. So they worked their way through the smoke and horn-honking traffic jam toward the other side of the Greely property to control it from spreading down the island.

***

Rodolfo Rattler, stuffed with a surfeit of stoned gophers, slept under a ganja plant. He flinched slightly at what seemed the warmth of a beautiful rattler coiling up beside him. But the warmth grew more intense until he jerked awake and saw flames around him. *"Ahh, Chihuahua! Caramba! Madre de Dios!"* He shook his rattle in defiance but heard nothing. He looked at his singed tail and saw a black crisp where once was his proud rattle. *"Hijo! Chinga son!* A rattlesnake with no rattle, man. What will *mis amigos* think?" Humiliated, he slithered away toward an uncertain future.

***

Lottie and Harpoon finally got through the traffic jam and roadside revelers when the smoke cleared. At the Island Joynt parking lot Lottie said, "I think the crowd beat us."

Harpoon looked around the lot. "Looks like some folks need a drink after what they saw today."

"Include me in the group." She climbed from the pickup and moved toward the Joynt, then stopped. "Can you get inside okay? I should be in there helping." She didn't wait for an answer and hurried toward the bar.

When Harpoon finally wobbled through the Joynt's door on his crutches, he hesitated, somewhat surprised at the hushed tone of the bar patrons. The room was packed, but little was said, and the imbibers all looked at Harpoon with the raised eyebrows and shrugged shoulders of truth seekers. Finally, Wiley Coots asked in an unaccustomed, reticent manner, "Harpoon, can you tell us what the hell happened today?"

After a pause, Harpoon said, "Wiley, you know about as much as I do. All I can add is that for a couple of weeks, Slidin' Will, myself, and Krank saw and heard in different situations what we thought must be the ghost of Stevie Ray Vaughan. It's not something we'd ever talk about for want of bein' considered loonies. You all knew Krank as something of an Indian Shaman, and he kept saying 'the Powers were gathering on the Island.' I reckon he was right."

A murmur of incomprehension spread over the crowd, but their demeanor remained subdued.

Reverend Hannibal Jones enjoyed arriving early at the Crystal Epistle on Sunday mornings to study his sermon and to commune with God in preparation for its delivery at the eleven o'clock service. As he approached the Circle K and the blackened marijuana patch, a steady stream of old vehicles, camping equipment stuffed inside and strapped onto the roofs, pulled out from the Beach Access Road and headed out of town.

A broad grin covered his face as his basso profundo boomed out the ancient William Cowper hymn, "God moves in a mysterious way, His wonders to perform . . ." A catharsis of the previous day's events that surrounded Krank's memorial service flooded over him as he sang. The ghostly intrusion had not shaken his faith, but rather had strengthened it. He had spent much of the remainder of Saturday closeted in his office praying for understanding of what he and the congregation had witnessed. The result reinforced his belief in the power of God to accomplish things totally outside the comprehension of man.

At his first glimpse of the Crystal Tower with its beacon shining out a brilliant call to God, he shouted, "Praise be to God and His holy light. Let the Coast Guard put not asunder what God hath wrought. First Crustaceans 6:36." Closer to the Epistle Church he saw a solid line of cars headed opposite the outflow of stoner vehicles. These were later model cars for the most part, and they hesitated as if uncertain before they turned into the Crystal Epistle parking lot. When Reverend Jones pulled into the lot he didn't recognize any of the cars or their occupants. One car drove up beside him, the driver, a solid looking middle-aged man in a conservative suit, rolled down his window, and asked, "Is this the church where the miracle happened yesterday?"

"Miracle?"

"Yeah, the miracle we saw on You Tube yesterday. We drove for two hours to get here, hoping it would happen again."

Rev. Jones' eyes lit up at the stream of cars lined up at the entrance to the Epistle parking lot. "Brother, you're always welcome at The Crystal Epistle Church of Everlasting Enlightenment. Who knows what miracles God hath wrought? Come on in and be blessed."

***

After Diggs tunneled a shaft to the surface, he cautiously peered at the surroundings. He gasped in horror. He had no recollection of anything like the expanse of black, crusted soil. The shaded, green playground they had enjoyed while munching out on ganja was gone, along with all the plants upon whose roots the gophers relied. There certainly would be a famine in the colony. "But wait," he thought. "I have a huge warehouse of roots traded by gophers at the Stuff Mines & Emporiums – maybe enough for everybody." Other gophers too stoned or too lazy to dig a shaft themselves had pressed him for a look-see out of his shaft.

He crawled back down the shaft, hurried to D & D Stuff Mine & Emporium Number 1, and inventoried the stash of roots.

He continued his survey of roots at all five of the stuff mines. The cause of the apocalypse above ground bothered him while he traveled between each of the mines. This must be a warning from The Great Gopher in the Sky. A warning to mend our ways. What else could it be? We must return to the old ways and stop using Stuff. We have to do it. Don't mess with The Great Gopher.

***

Lottie observed the Joynt's full dining room and from a distance listened as the conversation roared around the Wisdom Table at breakfast and again at lunch on Monday. The pastors from the other denomination churches showed up at The Table, anxious to hear first-hand what had transpired at Krank's memorial service.

Wiley Coots said, "Fellows, it's not something that can be explained. I saw the thing floating there playing the guitar from hell, but I still don't totally believe it."

Mayor Riley Glen chimed in, "I've never seen the likes of it. Was it from the Devil or from God? I don't really don't know. All I know is the Crystal Epistle beacon is shining, and the marijuana patch is gone along with the stoners. So I guess the thing did some good."

The merchants looked at each other and wondered how that would be good for business. Before they could moan about their plight, a motel manager hurried up to the table. "I couldn't get away, 'cause the motel filled up last night."

One of the merchants asked, "Where did the business come from?"

"It seems someone videoed the vision on their cell phone and uploaded it on You Tube, and the town filled up with religious pilgrims coming to see the church where the miracle happened."

Wiley Coots laughed out loud. "No wonder Reverend Jones is not here. He's probably out at the Epistle selling tickets."

Somebody else piped in, "If he misses 'Wednesday Breakfast Buffet All You Can Eat For $4.95,' we'll know something then." The table erupted with laughter.

Lottie was concerned that morning when Harpoon said he had an appointment to keep, and hobbled out to his truck. In the afternoon she was about to call him, when he finally shuffled into the bar. She stopped wiping it long enough to roll a Shiner Bock in a napkin and slid the beer across to him. "So where you been, big boy?"

"Had a little business to attend to." He pulled on the beer and looked away, as if to avoid further inquiries.

"So . . . a man's gotta do what a man's gotta do? That it?"

"Something like that."

Harpoon left again early Tuesday morning without explanation. Lottie continued to wonder what could cause him to pogo around on his crutches rather than resting and rehabilitating.

Reverend Jones showed up early for the Wednesday Breakfast Buffet All You Can Eat $4.95. Lottie, who'd come in early expecting a big turnout both from islanders and from religious pilgrims, greeted him.

The Rev. broke into a big smile when he saw her. "Nothing adds more to the enjoyment of a good breakfast than the smile of a lovely woman."

"You seem especially joyous this morning, Reverend."

"God has seen fit to smile on all the good people on this island and to send us countless blessings. In the short space of four days, gifts have showered on us, so now the Epistle can order a brand new, bigger Jumbotron to replace the old one. Our congregation can now overflow onto the beach and enjoy the music and spoken words of God surrounded by nature's glory. Amen and sela."

"Sign us up for a Wednesday buffet advertisement when it's working again."

As she expected, the crowd followed closely behind Rev. Jones, and both the restaurant and the Wisdom Table filled quickly. All the Wisdom Table regulars directed their conversation at Rev. Jones about the vision in the Epistle. People still grappled with what they'd seen and tried to understand what had happened, but these mystical and spiritual considerations were trumped by a more important topic – football. Coach Bull Bostich entered the restaurant and strode toward the Wisdom Table with a smile plastered on his face like a slice of watermelon. The entire table stood and shouted in unison "GO, YOU RIDLEYS! FEAR THE TURTLE!"

"Gentlemen, this will be 'The Year of the Turtle'." Bostich could hardly contain himself.

The general clamor around the Table wanted more information about the Ridley's reversal of fortune.

"It's a pure miracle, men. A kid walked on the practice field Monday and asked if he could play ball. He's a well-built kid with lots of muscle, so I gave him some practice pads. Folks, nobody on the team can catch him when he runs. He can punt the ball into next year, and, best of all, he can hit a bushel basket from fifty yards when he passes. I tell you, gentlemen, the kid is a hands-down phenom."

The Wisdom Table rejoiced, "GO, YOU RIDLEYS! FEAR THE TURTLE!"

"Where'd he come from?" Echoed several of the wisdomers.

"He says he just arrived on the island and has no address yet. By God, he can sleep in my bed if he'll play for the Ridleys." Bostich shouted in his coach-speak voice, and the entire restaurant turned to see what the commotion was about.

"What's his name?" someone asked.

"He says it's Kawa. Only Kawa."

Harpoon remained in deep thought as he crossed the Aransas Pass Causeway headed back to Port Aransas. He had made a major lifestyle change and all the nagging negatives tugged at him. One thing he knew for certain, shrimping would not be the same without Krank. Most of the excitement of going to sea had drained from him. The incredible violence and mayhem he brought on himself and Lottie weighed on him like an anchor. The thought of killing Mako and his goon made him sag inwardly. Such terrible decisions he had made while he tried to make his lifestyle economically viable. And worst of all, there was Krank. How could he ever recover from the guilt? He knew now all he really wanted out of life was Lottie.

Lottie looked up from vacuuming when Harpoon arrived at her home mid-afternoon. In his excitement, he walked on his bad leg with little help from his crutch. "Come on. I've got something to show you." He grabbed her and danced around as best as a man on crutches could.

"Easy, big boy, I'm right in the middle of trying to get this place presentable again."

He grabbed her arm and towed her toward the door. "You can clean house anytime."

In his truck, he sang a blues riff:

Woke up this mornin'. Gotta make up my mind.

I said I woke up this mornin' I'd made up my mind.

Somethin' gotta change now. Gotta leave my old life behind.

When he turned onto his street, Lottie saw a vehicle parked in front of Harpoon's house. "You got company at your house?"

"Nope, a new life." He swung into his driveway, stopped abruptly, and slid out of the old pickup with something in his hand. When Lottie reached his side he said, "Check it out."

The Dodge Ram pickup sparkled in showroom Caribbean blue. A wire-caged trailer hitched behind glistened in the sunlight with an array of new lawn care equipment: riding mower, push mowers, string trimmers, blowers, hand tools – everything anyone might need for yard care. He took a sign from the sack in his hand and slid it into a frame on the side of the trailer. The sign read:

Cordon Blues

Landscape Service

361-749-6450

Lottie stood motionless and finally asked, "You're giving up shrimping? I never thought I'd see this. Amazing!"

"I've thought a lot since we lost Krank, and I can't see shrimping without him. With the new engine and net hoist plus the killer paint job Krank and I did on the Blues, Shrimp King bought her on the spot last Monday. So I've plowed all the money back into a new business."

"I know you like doing yard work around your house, but will you enjoy it every day?"

"With all these big fancy coast houses people are building, there's plenty of work. This plus the money from playing at the Crystal Epistle should make for a pretty good living. And besides, somebody must cut the grass for the Island widows, since Krank's gone, right?" He paused for a moment. "But can you put up with me hanging around all the time?"

"Your shrimping for weeks at a time all year long is the only thing I don't like about you. Constantly worrying about you. This is like the answer to prayer." She almost knocked him over when she hugged and kissed him.

When he regained his balance, he laughed. "Easy now. Don't go overboard." He pulled something from the pocket of his blue jeans and added, "I had enough money left for this." He held out his hand and opened a small, square velvet-covered ring box.

Islanders drifted into the football grandstands when the two-thirty bell announced the last physical education period of the high school day. Word had spread about the new phenom football player, and they wanted to see him in action. By the time the players suited up and ran onto the field for calisthenics, all of the Wisdom Table folks and many townspeople, including Harpoon and Lottie, sat in the stands anxiously waiting. Coach Bull Bostich pointed at Kawa and grinned up at the fans.

Bostich shortened calisthenics and went straight into scrimmaging. He set the ball on the twenty-yard line, put Kawa under center and called a hitch-and-go pass play. Kawa took a five-step drop and launched a bomb that hit the wide receiver fifty yards down field between the numbers. The stands erupted. "GO, YOU RIDLEYS! FEAR THE TURTLE!"

With each successive play, Kawa's exploits built a furor of excitement and the fans leaped and shouted. Bostich called a time out and came to the grandstand railing, where he was mobbed by fans. Harpoon looked at Lottie. "I'll be right back, I'm gonna ask coach something."

When Harpoon got Coach Bostich's attention he asked. "You think Kawa will need some extra money?"

"I suspect he'd appreciate the chance. Why? You have something for him?"

"I've got part-time during school and full-time summer work in my new landscaping business."

Bostich turned and bellowed, "Kawa, over here." When Kawa trotted up, Bostich pointed at Harpoon. "Harpoon here has part-time work during school and full-time work for you during the summer. You interested?"

Kawa looked up with the smile Harpoon remembered so well. "Yes sir, Mr. Harpoon, that would be good."

Beneath the grandstand at the far end where the discarded water hoses lay coiled like passionate snakes, and the detritus of past football games fluttered, wind-blown, against clumps of Johnson grass, a pair of slanted, smoldering yellow eyes peered out of the dimness between the seat risers. The eyes tracked back and forth and followed the movements of one particular football player. If you caught sight of those eyes, glowing like amber coals of fire, you would be terrified unless, through the gloom, you also saw Coyote smiling.

** END **

ACKNOWLEDGEMENTS

During the two decades that I owned a house on Mustang Island, I rose through the ranks of island culture from "Tourist," a pejorative epithet, finally to "Island Trash," a term of endearment among islanders. This required untold late nights, soaking up Island culture along with the required libations. I also joined in the commercial Island activity as a restaurant consultant and learned that playing on the Island is much more fun than working there. Some of the most enjoyable times of my life were spent in Port Aransas and with its wonderful denizens. Unfortunately, gentrification of Port Aransas has forced much of the Island Trash away from their roots. But this story is not about any of my Island experiences and is the product of my imagination.

My appreciation goes out to my friend, Alan Olson, a Mustang Island lifer, who told me, "You lack the experience to write about marijuana. Just stick to writing about wine." I obviously ignored his advice.

The members of Daedalus Writers Group: Cindy Leal-Massey, Ned Bailey, Linda Schuler, Florence Weinberg, Diana Lopez and Jim Peyton, all accomplished authors, and my wonderful freind Liz Mills, waded through chapter after chapter, applying the polish to the *Woke Up This Morning* manuscript. I'm fortunate to have friends willing to invest this much in helping me.

My long time friend John Mills, author and artist, and founder of Franklin Scribes Publishers, and David Mills contributed immeasurably with support, graphic design, and book design. To these and many others who helped along the way I offer my deepest appreciation.

APPRECIATION

A big hug of appreciation to you for purchasing *Woke Up this Morning*. If you enjoyed the book, you might check out *Vámonos!* and *Horizons Past.* Both are in Kindle and Trade Paperback format available through all major Internet booksellers.

Even more love if you write a Customer Review on Amazon or Barnes & Noble. Sharing *Horizons Past* on your Facebook page and on Twitter really helps also.

While you're at it, like www.facebook.com/authorbillstephens, and I really enjoy hearing from readers by email at stephens.billy @ att. net, so shout out.